STRAW IN THE WIND

STRAW IN THE WIND

Janet Woods

Severn House

This first world edition published 2010
in Great Britain and in the USA by
SEVERN HOUSE PUBLISHERS LTD of
9–15 High Street, Sutton, Surrey, England, SM1 1DF.
Trade paperback edition published
in Great Britain and the USA 2010 by
SEVERN HOUSE PUBLISHERS LTD

British Library Cataloguing in Publication Data

Woods, Janet, 1939–
  Straw in the Wind.
  1. Ship captains – Family relationships – Fiction.
  2. Abandoned children – Fiction. 3. Private investigators –
  Fiction. 4. Family secrets – Fiction. 5. England – Social
  conditions – 19th century – Fiction. 6. Love stories.
  I. Title
  823.9'2-dc22

ISBN-13: 978-0-7278-6893-0   (cased)
ISBN-13: 978-1-84751-235-2   (trade paper)

Except where actual historical events and characters are being
described for the storyline of this novel, all situations in this
publication are fictitious and any resemblance to living persons
is purely coincidental.

All Severn House titles are printed on acid-free paper.

Severn House Publishers support The Forest Stewardship Council [FSC],
the leading international forest certification organisation. All our titles that
are printed on Greenpeace-approved FSC-certified paper carry the FSC logo.

Mixed Sources
Product group from well-managed
forests and other controlled sources
www.fsc.org Cert no. SA-COC-1565
© 1996 Forest Stewardship Council

Typeset by Palimpsest Book Production Ltd.,
Grangemouth, Stirlingshire, Scotland.
Printed and bound in Great Britain by
MPG Books Ltd., Bodmin, Cornwall.

Dedicated to Kath Parkin,
a reader in Raywood, Victoria.
With many thanks.

Prologue

1835
Harbour House, Poole, Dorset.

*D*awn *was creeping over the horizon. The woman's tortured groans had ceased, her dying breath expelled in a long, defeated whimper. Her body had been washed and her long, dark hair brushed and spread about her on the pillow. Now dressed in a long nightgown, her hands were pressed together in prayer.*

Caroline Honeyman looked like an angel instead of an unfaithful wife.

The infant had her face turned towards the man. She was pale and limp, blue around the lips and wrapped loosely in a shawl. If she could have seen through those darkling, newborn eyes, she would understand why he didn't want her.

'I'm sorry,' the midwife said. 'The birth was too much for them.'

'You can go. I want to spend some time alone with my wife.'

The man crossed to the infant when the woman left the room. He gazed at her, his eyes maddened by grief and the impotent fury he felt. There was no mistaking the resemblance. She was Thornton's daughter! He lashed out, thumping the side of the cradle with his fist.

As if she'd suddenly decided to put up a fight for survival, the infant's chest expanded and she hauled in a breath of air. Her face screwed up, as though she'd smelled something unpleasant, and she gave a loud, demanding cry.

No! This couldn't be. He wouldn't allow it, not while he had the power to stop it! Taking a cushion from the chair he gazed down at the infant and whispered, 'I'll see you in hell first, you Thornton bastard,' and a tear rolled down his face as he slowly lowered it.

One

Sara Finn walked along a short carriageway that curved slightly upwards towards Leighton Manor. The evening sun came from behind, pushing her shadow tall along the ground. It was twice her length, which was five feet and four inches from head to heel.

Eighteen years old, and although Sara had suffered hardship in her short life, she was still young enough to enjoy the beauty nature had to offer and the optimism to hope that her lot would improve in time. Today she was taking her first step into the future, and what a blessing the day was.

The air was golden and warm, drenched with the drifting scent of roses carried on a faint breeze. When Sara rounded the bend her eyes widened because the overgrown grass in front of the house was a mass of dancing poppies, harebells and mayweed. To her right was a spreading oak, and to her left a cobbled yard with a small stable block. Behind the house a gentle downward incline of meadow was divided by a stream at the bottom, then it rose gently upwards towards a copse leaning against the skyline.

She stopped, and placing the bag she carried on the ground she shortened her gaze to Leighton Manor. It was a modestly sized manor built of stone, one easily managed by five servants – at least, that's how Mrs Pawley had described it. Sara absorbed the sight; the house was larger than she'd expected, about the size of the rectory she'd just left. It glowed a soft pinkish yellow in the late afternoon light. The windows were large, and designed to frame the views so they could be admired. The glass sent back gleams of orange. Three steps led up to frosted-glass panelled doors, which stood open for anyone to walk inside.

'My first position,' she said with some satisfaction, because she couldn't count her childhood on the farm in Gloucestershire as a position even though she'd worked there from dawn to dusk from the age of eight through to twelve. Nor could she count the time in the workhouse, where she'd packed pins and picked oakum until her fingertips were blistered and raw and callused. And neither could she count the three . . . no – it was almost four years since she turned fourteen. She'd spent them as a maid to Reverend Pawley, his eight children from his first marriage and their stepmother, Elizabeth, who'd once been the children's governess.

The reverend had never paid Sara a penny piece for her labours when he'd given her notice to leave, saying he'd taken her from the workhouse for her own good, that he'd fed, housed, clothed and educated her along with his own children. She should be grateful for that, and be happy that his wife had given her a reference after what had taken place.

'The cheek of him to accuse me of enticing his eldest son,' she muttered. 'I didn't invite Albert to corner me in the kitchen and try to kiss me, or to put his grubby hands where he wasn't welcome to. Hah!' she tossed indignantly into the air.

There was an ache in her feet and calves after her long walk.

'You'll be picked up at the station,' Elizabeth Pawley had promised her. But nobody had been there, though she'd waited over two hours.

'While the cat's away the mice will play,' the stationmaster had said mysteriously. 'Likely that the stable lad arranged to meet his sweetheart and has forgotten the time. Leighton Manor is about two miles away.'

'You mean I've got to drag this trunk for two miles, when I can hardly lift it?' Sara groaned. As well as her clothing the small trunk had several books inside, given to her as a parting gift by Elizabeth Pawley.

'I'll miss you,' Elizabeth had said. 'Keep up your reading and writing, Sara. You have a quick mind and a retentive memory that will hold you in good stead.'

'Leave the trunk if you like. I'll keep it safe in my office until the lad turns up,' the stationmaster had offered.

Sara hoped that her trunk would be safe as she closed her eyes for a few seconds. She had so very few possessions, but she was grown up, at last, and had paid employment thanks to Elizabeth Pawley, who'd had a friend who knew somebody who'd known somebody else who needed a housemaid. She intended to save every penny she earned, so she could buy her own house . . . oh, not as fine as this one perhaps, but a home of her own just the same.

She'd have a husband too, one who was pleasant as well as handsome and who wouldn't beat her . . . a tutor perhaps, because she liked learning new things and he could teach her when the dark winter cold pressed like a wolf against the door. In the summer they'd tend to their garden together. They'd have children too, so she'd have a family she could call her own. But that was only one of her dreams for the future – sometimes they changed.

The thought of being part of a family brought happiness surging up inside her. When she opened her eyes again she picked up her bag, hugged it against her chest and danced round in circles until she was out of breath, dizzy and laughing.

She'd better not use the front door, she thought, even though it was standing wide open in invitation. She hurried towards the stables and then went past them and around the corner to a door at the back. She knocked.

There was no answer. The door opened when she tried the handle and she stepped inside. She was in a kitchen; Sara's nose wrinkled at the state of it. There was a woman asleep in a chair with a tabby cat in her lap; her shoes were on the floor and her dirty bare feet were propped up on another chair. Her snores sounded like wood being sawn.

Sara supposed it was Mrs Cornwell, the housekeeper . . . though it could possibly be the cook. She'd been led to believe there was one. A bottle of port and a half-empty glass sat on the table in front of the woman.

When the cat jumped down and wove about her ankles Sara stroked its ear so it began to purr throatily. The figure in the chair snorted, then subsided into slumber again. Sara took her by the shoulder and gently shook her. 'Mrs Cornwell?'

A cough brought Sara's gaze to the inner door, where a neat, blue-eyed woman of about forty stood. 'I'm Mrs Cornwell. You must be my replacement.' She came forward, her gaze sweeping over her face. 'You're younger than Elizabeth Pawley's letter led me to believe, but it's a small house, so I dare say you'll manage if you stick to a routine.'

'I thought I was hired to be a housemaid, not the housekeeper.'

'You must have got mixed up then, because Mrs Pawley definitely said you'd been their housekeeper and had three years' experience. I can show you the reference letter if you wish.'

Sara had no intention of losing this position. Running a house wasn't all that difficult, and a maid's wage was much smaller than that of a housekeeper. 'Yes, I did. And there were eight children in the household, as well.'

'Well there are no children here, though Frederick Milson and his sister, Jane Milson, visit on occasion. They are kin to the late Mrs Leighton. You have to be careful when they're here, because they complain if things aren't to their liking.'

Sara took note of that. 'Why are you leaving the position, Mrs Cornwell?'

'I'm going to be wed. Mr Perkins is a widower, an estate manager up in Wiltshire, and he has three children who need a mother.' She gave a bit of a sigh as though it wasn't exactly a joyous event she was looking forward to. 'Perkins is a good, hard-working man.'

'I hope you'll be happy.'

'Thank you, dear. It's no good moping about your lot in life, is it? You've got to make the best of it you can, and seize any opportunity that comes your way to better yourself.'

Exactly Sara's own sentiment, except the thought of marrying into a family like the Reverend Pawley's wasn't really an enticing thought. She would much rather be in love, or better still, have a handsome young man return her love. A little thrill ran through her, because she was still young enough to believe in romance and hope it would come her way.

'The master will be home in a day or two, though I don't suppose the visit will last long. He gets bored easily when he's here. I've only stayed on to show you where everything is. Maggie,' she shouted at the cook, 'look lively. Miss Finn has arrived.'

Maggie's eyes opened and she gazed dubiously through them at her. 'She's a bit on the young side for the position isn't she, Mrs Cornwell?'

'That's what I thought, but the master won't see any difference, will he now? Besides, she has an excellent reference from her former employer. Where's Fanny? She was supposed to get the rooms ready.'

'Gone with Giles on the cart, I reckon. She said she wanted to visit her mum, and Giles was going to drop her off before he picked up the supplies I need, then get the new housekeeper from the station.'

'As you can see, I'm here. I walked. Giles will only have my trunk to pick up instead.'

'I can see that you're here, Miss. I'm not daft, nor am I the one who's blind round here . . . perhaps he went to see that girl of his, Jassy Bennett.'

A clock chimed in the depths of the house and the cook got heavily to her feet. 'Reckon I'd better get on with the stew.'

Mrs Cornwell frowned at the cook. 'Can't you cook anything but stew?'

'Of course, but I don't see the point. My stew is good enough for servants. I can never understand why Mr Leighton doesn't sell this place.'

'Because the master grew up here, and he likes it here, that's why. Count yourself lucky, you'd be out of a job if he did.'

'A lot you know. I've been here since Mr Leighton was a child, and you've only worked here for a handful of years. It's not as if you're a paragon of cleanliness yourself.'

There was evidence to back up that statement, Sara thought as she followed Mrs Cornwell along the corridor. She could only suppose that Mrs Cornwell didn't care about her position now she was leaving, but perhaps she never had. 'You can sleep in my sitting room for tonight.'

At least the housekeeper's quarters were clean.

The tour of the house revealed a well-furnished and comfortable abode, but even though the rooms were not large or numerous the housekeeping left much to be desired. The dust on the furniture was as thick as a blanket.

Mrs Cornwell saw her running her finger through it. 'Hardly anyone occupies the house and the staff have got into the habit of being lazy.' She sniffed. 'I never got on with cook.'

Probably because she'd allowed Maggie to take the upper hand, Sara thought. Most of her remembered childhood had been lived in squalor. While working for the reverend she had discovered that clean and tidy was better. Not only did it look better, it smelled better, tasted better and discouraged house pests such as rats, spiders and cockroaches. Ugh! She shuddered. She would put her foot down when she took over the house. She remembered the long grass at the front. 'Who does the garden?'

'Joseph Tunney. He and the stable lad tend to the outside maintenance and clean the windows between them. They also look after the horse.'

'I noticed that the grass needs cutting.'

'Mr Leighton likes it long so he can smell the flowers. Joseph and Giles don't like anyone interfering with their job, so you need to just concern yourself with the inside of the house.' She threw open a door and frowned as dust swirled in the shaft of sunshine coming through the window. 'This is the master's room, and he uses the sitting room at the front. He likes the afternoon sun on his face. I told Fanny to make the rooms ready today. I suppose I'll have to do it myself. Mr Leighton will bring his valet, so the room next door will need cleaning too.'

'I'll give you a hand, even though I'm not supposed to start until tomorrow.'

'I suppose you're thinking we're lazy here. Fanny is a bit simple. She's a good worker if you keep on her back. Cook is all right when the master's here, but she has a mouth on her sometimes. She's too old to get a position anywhere else though. The alternative is for her to go and live with her sister and her family, and they don't get on. Giles is willing, but so is his girlfriend and she leads him astray.'

Sara was not too young to know what the woman meant. To hide her blush she turned her mind to the job at hand. Thank goodness someone had put dustsheets over the beds because at least the feather mattresses wouldn't need beating. They made the beds with clean sheets and covers, shook dust from the rugs out the windows, polished the furniture with beeswax and washed the floors.

When they'd finished Sara said, 'You won't mind if I have a word or two with the staff, will you? I intend to start in the same way as I mean to carry on.'

Mrs Cornwell had shrugged then, and smiled. 'I just hope they'll listen.'

When they'd finished cleaning they found that Fanny had returned. She was a strong-looking girl and she smiled widely when she saw Sara. 'You're pretty.'

Sara remembered Mrs Cornwell saying she was a bit simple. 'Thank you, Fanny. Where have you been?'

'To see my ma.'

'From now on you cannot visit your mother until you've finished your work, and you must ask me first, so I don't have to worry about where you are. Do you understand, Fanny?'

'Yes, Miss.'

'Now you're back you may go and clean the stairs and the hall.'

'Yes, Miss.'

Maggie snorted.

'Is there something you need to say, Maggie?'

The cook whirled around. 'Who do you think you are marching in here giving us orders?'

'I'm the new housekeeper. If you don't like it, say so.'

Maggie's arms went to her hips and her chin thrust forward. 'I don't like it.'

'Thank you for being honest; I shall be likewise. I don't like doing the work other people are being paid to do. This kitchen is dirty, and that will attract vermin. Please clean this kitchen up and get on with your job. If you'd rather not work under me then I know somebody who would be happy to step into your shoes.'

Maggie gasped, and her voice took on a whine. 'We'll see what the master has to say about this.'

'I doubt if Mr Leighton will appreciate the fact that he's paying his staff a wage to sleep all day,' Sara said drily. She could almost see Maggie's mind working, and wondered which way she'd jump. To her relief, eventually the woman came to the conclusion that she was better-off doing as she was told.

Maggie shrugged. 'I was just having a nap, that's all, Miss. I'm sorry, it won't happen again, I'm sure.'

'So am I, Maggie . . . neither will drinking your employer's port happen again, I hope, since I think it was that which caused the need for a nap.'

'Yes, Miss . . . I mean . . . no, Miss.'

Sara exchanged a glance with Mrs Cornwell, who smiled encouragingly at her. She noticed a young man at the door. About her own age, he was muscular, had hair the colour of ripe wheat, pale-blue eyes and a ready smile. 'You must be Giles.'

'Aye, I am, that.'

'I'm Miss Finn, the new housekeeper. Did you pick my trunk up from the railway station? The stationmaster was keeping it safe in his office.'

'He wasn't there. I'll pick it up tomorrow when I take Mrs Cornwell to catch the train.'

'Why weren't you there to meet me, Giles? I was told to expect someone.'

He flushed. 'Sorry, Miss Finn, I had something else to do first, and when I got there you'd left.'

'Where's Joseph Tunney?'

'It's his day off, Miss.'

She nodded. 'I see.' And she saw only too well because it accounted for the stationmaster's remark about the mice playing when the cat was away. She'd already formed the impression that most of this household took advantage of the absence of the owner, and the house lacked an efficient manager. That would come to an end. 'Try not to let it happen again, Giles, else I'll have to talk to Mr Tunney about it. You can all go about your business now.'

After dinner, and she had to admit that the lamb stew was excellent, Mrs Cornwell showed her how to do the menus for the week, then they went through the stores list and the linen inventory. 'The house provides skirts, blouses and aprons. Two outfits a year apiece. They're in the linen cupboard. No doubt you can find something to fit, though the hems might need taking up. If you pin them up, Fanny will do them. I've taught her to sew, and she enjoys it and is good at it.'

'That's nice to know. I can sew, but it's something I dislike doing.'

'I've ordered the stores a month ahead, so it will give you time to get used to what is where. There's a market in Taunton, and Joseph keeps a vegetable garden. Giles fetches fresh milk from the farm every morning. There's no mistress in the house. Finch

Leighton is a widower and he relies very much on the house-keeper to keep everything up to date.'

'What's Mr Leighton like?'

'Easy-going, but he gets restless and bored easily. Don't move any of the furniture around. He likes everything to be in its proper place.'

After that there was very little to be said. In the dying light the air took on a misty purple hue and was filled with insects and perfume. They walked around the garden together, visiting the stable with its one horse, named Curruthers. It snickered softly at them.

Later on, and lacking her nightgown, which was in her trunk, Sara stripped down to her chemise, wrapped herself in a blanket and stretched out on the couch. This little domain would be hers tomorrow, was her last thought before she fell asleep.

Fanny woke her, bringing an offering of a neatly hemmed skirt, a blue striped bodice and a white starched apron, all of which had been ironed.

'Thank you, Fanny. Your stitching is so neat. Well done.'

Her words brought a wide smile to the girl's face.

Sara dressed, tidily braided her long hair then headed for the kitchen. She had to set the employees a good example.

She found she didn't have to. Maggie was already up and cooking breakfast. The kitchen looked cleaner, and the woman gave her a wary look until she smiled and said, 'That smells delicious.'

Maggie beamed at her. 'Fresh eggs, smoked bacon and sausages, and some fried tomatoes if you like. And there's some toasted bread, or you can have it fried. Giles likes it fried, but Mr Tunney prefers toast.'

'Toast sounds wonderful. If you pass me the toasting fork and bread I'll make my own.'

An hour later, Mrs Cornwell had been sent on her way with Giles in the cart. Sara was touched to see that they'd bought her a farewell gift to remember them by, a pair of kid gloves with pearl buttons for best.

'More than she deserved,' Maggie said. 'She's only worked here for five years – not that she dirtied her hands, mind, she made poor Fanny do it all.'

When they'd finished waving they all went back inside and Sara told them. 'I understand the master is to arrive tomorrow. We need to get this house looking much brighter. The silver needs polishing, Maggie. Fanny, you can put a shine on all the mirrors.'

'It's ironing day.'

'You can do the ironing afterwards. I'm going to clean my rooms, then the study, in case the master wants to use it.'

'There's no reason why he should,' Maggie said.

'Which doesn't mean to say that it should be left to collect dirt, and neither should the rest of the house come to that. It will make a bad impression on visitors, who will think Mr Leighton keeps a slovenly household,' Sara said.

Maggie's hands went to her hips. 'Here, you watch what you're saying. I'm not slovenly, and the state of the house is none of my business. It was Mrs Cornwell's, and now it's yours. Besides, the master doesn't often have visitors.'

'I know the state of the house is my business, Maggie, and I'll be keeping an eye on the kitchen as part of it. Where's Mr Tunney, has anyone seen him?'

'Joseph had his breakfast early, and is spreading compost. After that he's got the border to weed. You'll get to meet him at dinner. Did you want him for something?'

'No, it's just that I haven't met him yet.'

'Joseph is a bit bashful. Chances are that he'll make himself known sooner or later,' she said, and Sara had to be contented with that.

It was a busy morning, but the house was beginning to take on a soft glow.

The study was filled with books that had wonderful leather bindings with gold letters. There was a picture of the late Mrs Leighton on the wall. She was beautiful, with light-brown hair, gleaming blue eyes and a mischievous pursed smile that made her appear to be about to burst into laughter.

The dress she'd worn for the portrait was hanging over the back of the chair in her room upstairs. The rich, dark-red satin was faded, the fabric ripped and stained. Her personal items were still on the dressing table. Perfume bottles, a dressing-table set, and a pair of silk gloves. A diamond ring and bracelet and a string of pearls with a locket clasp were where they'd been left.

'The master knows where everything is, so don't move anything,' Mrs Cornwell had said, and she'd turned back the blue satin spread to show her the stains. 'Diana, her name was,' and she'd lowered her voice to a whisper. 'The room is kept locked. I'm showing it to you so you know. When the master's down here, sometimes he comes in here and sometimes he don't. It's morbid keeping things like this, if you ask me.'

'How did she die?'

'There was an accident in the rig, a deer came out of the hedge, the horse reared and Mrs Leighton was thrown. She banged her head on a log. Mr Leighton had the reins. He blamed himself, even though he was badly injured himself. I don't like coming in here. It makes me shudder just thinking about it. She died on that bed, her skull cracked open like an egg. It was a blessing really because the fall addled her wits. When she was conscious she didn't know anyone. She just lay there dribbling and couldn't do anything for herself. That was several years ago.'

A sad tale, Sara thought, but it was in the past and self-pity was not a trait to be either encouraged or admired, Reverend Pawley had often told her. There were plenty of jobs to be done that would keep her busy, like the unoccupied rooms. Once the house was clean it would be easier to keep it clean.

She went into the garden to pick a bunch of roses. Rounding a corner she came across a weathered-looking man sitting on a log. He touched his cap. 'Miss Finn, is it then?'

'It is. You must be Joseph, or would you prefer Mr Tunney?'

'Joseph will do. You're making the dust fly, I hear. I can't say it's not about time.'

'It certainly is. I've never seen such a dirty house, but I like to keep busy.'

'It's a sad place that needs to feel cared for again. If those roses are for the house they needs their thorns clipping off. Give them over here.' Taking a knife from his pocket he nipped the thorns off. 'There, now they can't be the cause of an accident. You've got to be careful with roses, sometimes a scratch can cause a body a lot of damage.'

'Thank you. Where's Giles?'

'Can't rightly say, Miss. Gone out on the cart, I reckon.'

She hoped Giles would remember to collect her trunk.

Back in the house she arranged the roses in a glowing copper bowl, set them on a table in the small sitting room then went into the study with her dusters and a bucket of water. It was going to take her longer than she expected. All the books were covered in dust and the ashes from the last fire were still in the grate. She was soon busy, and an hour later everything was to her liking.

The clock struck midday and she made her way to the kitchen. Maggie gazed at her. 'Mrs Cornwell used to have her meals served in her rooms. She kept herself to herself, she did.'

'I'd rather eat in the kitchen with the rest of the staff, if you don't mind.'

'It's a bit more friendly-like, so I don't mind, seeing as you ask. Mrs Cornwell thought she was a cut above us, especially when she got herself engaged.' Maggie sniffed. 'She answered a notice in the newspaper from a man wanting a mother for his brats.'

There was some chicken soup and freshly made bread to revive them. Sara was relieved to see Giles come in, and asked him, 'Did you remember to fetch my trunk, Giles?'

'Yes, Miss.'

'Good.' She supposed he'd put it in her rooms. 'Have you finished the ironing, Fanny?'

'Yes, Miss.'

'Then you can help me with the drawing room after we've had a break. That was a delicious soup, Maggie.'

'There's nothing more tasty than a nice bit of chicken,' the woman said, 'except a nice bit of beef or pork, of course. Then there's lamb. The master is partial to it. He likes it roasted with potatoes and parsnips. And he likes apple pie. He's very easy to please, really.'

The drawing room caught the morning sun. Like the rest of the house it was dirty. She pulled the dustsheet off the piano and smiled. Elizabeth Pawley had made piano lessons part of her education, and although she wasn't an expert, she had picked it up easily. She ran her fingers up and down the scales to warm her fingers and make them more flexible, as she'd been taught. The piano needed tuning, but it wasn't too bad, and she played a couple of short Bach pieces before moving on to a lively Chopin waltz.

A crash interrupted her short concert. Her heart thumped against her chest when somebody uttered a solid curse, followed by, 'What in hell's name is this I've tripped over, Oscar?'

Two

'It appears to be a travelling trunk, Mr Leighton.'
Her employer!

What a stupid place to leave a trunk. Help me up please, Oscar.'

Sara flew through the drawing-room door, across the hall and to the porch, where a man was being helped up by another. 'I'm so sorry . . . it's my trunk . . . are you all right, sir?'

'Apart from a bruise or two, though I dare say I'll survive it. Where's Mrs Cornwell? Go and fetch her.'

'Mrs Cornwell has left.'

'Damn it to hell, I was hoping to get here before she departed.' He turned her way, the brim of his hat shading his eyes. 'Has the new housekeeper arrived?'

'I'm the new housekeeper, Sara Finn.' When she held out a hand he ignored it, so she brought it down to her side. Perhaps employers didn't lower themselves to shake hands with servants.

'You sound too young to be a housekeeper.'

'As you see, sir . . . but I'm competent.'

'Not if you leave travelling trunks in my path.'

Finch Leighton was younger than she'd expected him to be, in his early thirties. 'Actually, I didn't leave it there. I didn't *know* it was there.'

His mouth twitched. 'Ah . . . that explains everything satisfactorily, Miss Finn. It's your trunk, but you didn't leave it there and didn't know it was there.'

'That's right, sir.'

'Am I to think it grew legs and trotted there all by itself?'

She wanted to laugh at the scene that conjured up, but didn't dare. 'It's not up to me to tell you what to think, sir, but that action would be highly improbable unless the leather it's made from is still attached to the animal it came from.'

Mr Leighton looked disgruntled. 'Do you have an answer for everything? No . . . for God's sake don't answer that.'

She shrugged, and didn't, just murmured, 'Sorry.'

Oscar picked up Mr Leighton's walking stick and put it in his employer's hand with a cheerful, 'Here you are, sir.'

'Thank you, Oscar. Take the luggage and unpack then make sure my room is ready for occupancy. I'll be in the sitting room.'

Fanny had come into the hall and was gazing at them with her mouth open.

'Can I get you anything, sir?' Sara asked him.

'I dare say you could, but I'm not satisfied with the explanation you've given me with regards to the trunk being left for people to trip over, and I'm not going to allow you to wriggle out of it that easily. Also, I need to know more about you if I'm to trust you with my family home.'

She smiled at Fanny. 'Fanny, go and tell Maggie that Mr Leighton has arrived. Perhaps you'd like some refreshment, sir?'

'Hello, Fanny,' he said without looking at the maid. 'Tell cook I'm ravenous and we want tea, and whatever she has handy in the way of cake. After you, Miss Finn.'

Fanny smiled and scurried off as Sara headed for the sitting room. There was something odd about her employer. Apart from the slight limp, there was the way his fingers trailed lightly along the furniture. Well, he wouldn't find any dust left from *her* cleaning that was certain. In her last position she'd been kept at it from dawn to dusk, and work had become an ingrained habit. Closing the door she watched him head for the couch. He removed his hat, set it beside him then turned towards the bowl of roses. Gently he cupped his hands around them and inhaled their perfume.

'Lovely,' he murmured and turned to gaze at the chair on the other side of the table. He was a handsome man with a fine-boned, but taut-looking face. His eyes were a soft brown. 'Where are you, Miss Finn?'

She became aware with a sudden, pitying jolt of shock. 'I'm here, near the door. I didn't realize you couldn't see.'

His head moved her way. 'Nobody told you?'

'No.' And she hadn't picked up the clues. No wonder he'd cursed. 'I'm sorry the trunk was left there. I walked from the station and couldn't carry it by myself, so I left it with the station-master to be picked up.'

'And it was picked up by Giles and left on the doorstep while he unhitched the cart, then stabled the horse. No doubt he was lured into the kitchen by the smell of Maggie's cooking and forgot about it. It's Thursday . . . chicken broth, yes?'

She nodded, and then remembering he couldn't see her, she cleared her throat. 'Yes.'

'The house smells different, of polish and fresh air. The trouble with not having anyone living here is that the staff don't bother. Except for my room, it usually smells of dust. Come and sit opposite me.'

When she'd settled herself, she told him, 'Be assured, I will bother and so will the rest of your house staff from now on.'

'You are how old?'

'Eighteen.'

'Good Lord, am I employing babies now? Was that you I heard playing the piano?'

'Yes, sir.'

'How do you look . . . no don't tell me. You have a quick, light step so will be fairly small. Your voice is low, but you have laughter in it, so at least you won't screech.'

When she laughed, he smiled. 'You don't giggle, you chuckle. Musically, you're competent, but the piano is not. It hasn't been played since . . . well, for quite some time, really. I must get it tuned so you can provide me with entertainment occasionally. Can you sing?'

'Like a crow at Christmas.'

He laughed.

'Do you play the piano yourself, sir?'

'Sometimes.'

'You should practise.'

'You think so? Perhaps I will. Ah, here comes Maggie.'

A few seconds later a knock came at the door and Maggie entered carrying the tea tray. She had a beaming smile on her face. 'You'll never guess, sir.'

He sniffed the air. 'Almond cake.'

'No, sir . . . it's apple and cinnamon. You never could tell the difference.'

'Leave the tray please, Maggie. Sara will see to me. I can see I'm going to have to train her into doing things my way.'

'If you say so, sir.' Maggie offered her a smug look.

After Maggie had left, she said, 'How did you lose your sight, Mr Leighton?'

'It happened five years ago, when I killed my wife in an accident . . . it was a blow to the head. I survived, but my sight did not.'

She refused to give in to the shock she felt at his words. 'How do you like your tea?'

'Is that all you've got to say?'

'What do you want me to say? I can't argue with you because I wasn't there. You were lucky.'

'You were twelve then, and probably still in your nursery.'

'No, sir . . . I was in the workhouse then. We slept three to a bed. How did you say you wanted your tea?'

'I didn't.' He gave a small huff of annoyance. 'Milk in first, and the liquid one inch from the top. There's a small groove on the surface of the table. Place the cup and saucer there with the handle facing towards the door. The plate with the cake goes to the left of it.'

She did as she was asked and watched as he reached for the cup then lifted it to his lips. 'Stop watching me and tell me what you look like, Sara. What colour are your eyes?'

She chuckled. 'Almost the same colour as yours.'

'What are mine like? I forget.'

She doubted it as she gazed at them. They were lighter than hers and they looked like normal eyes, though the dark centre didn't seem to react. 'They're the colour of toffee . . . or dark amber.'

'Ah, you're a poet. I would call them brown.'

'Are you sure you can't see?'

'Quite sure, though sometimes I think I can see light. The doctor tells me I might be imagining it, and I probably am. My father had brown eyes too. Which parent did you inherit your eye colour from?'

'I couldn't say . . . I never knew either of them.'

He sucked in a breath. 'I'm sorry, that was insensitive of me.'

'Oh, I don't think about it much. Besides, it's best to ask if you want to know something.'

'You're pragmatic for one so young.' When she didn't answer he said, 'You do know what that means, don't you?'

She smiled. 'I've always had to take a practical approach. I learned to read and write and I have a good memory.'

'So you're educated and can play the piano, despite being in a workhouse? Why did you say I was lucky?'

'Because you could see before the accident and know about colours, shapes and objects. If you'd been born without sight it would have been much harder.'

'I haven't thought about the accident from that angle.'

'Then perhaps you should. It will encourage you to appreciate what you have.'

He laughed. 'You're disconcerting, and I don't know whether I like you, Sara Finn. I'm sorry I cursed. I hope I didn't shock you.'

'I've heard worse curses . . . or should that be better curses? And may I make one thing clear, Mr Leighton? I find you disconcerting too, and haven't decided whether I like you, either.'

'Then we'll get on famously, I'm sure. You're not going to allow me to feel sorry for myself, are you? I warn you, I do on occasion.'

She grinned. He was an unusual man and she was warming to him. 'I shouldn't think so. Will you mind if I go now? I was about to clean the drawing room when the piano practice interrupted.'

'Yes, I will mind. Eat your cake, drink your tea and make polite conversation . . . if you can. You're my housekeeper, and we have things to discuss, since I don't want any more unpleasant surprises, like obstacles left in my path.'

The gentle reprimand reminded her that this man was her employer, and her straightforwardness could be mistaken for familiarity. Her face heated. Thank goodness he couldn't see her embarrassment. 'I'm sorry. I didn't mean to be rude. I've never run a household before and thought I'd been hired as a maid, not the housekeeper.'

'You came with an excellent reference, I understand.'

'Yes. From Mrs Pawley. I worked in the Pawley household for four years.'

'And left there because . . . ?'

Her face reddened even more and she mumbled. 'There was a disagreement with one of Reverend Pawley's children. I slapped him and Reverend Pawley dismissed me.'

'You slapped your employer's infant? Are you usually violent towards children?'

'You don't understand,' she said desperately. 'Albert isn't an infant . . . he's about my age.' She unleashed a dash of fierceness. 'I'd slap him again if I had to, only harder.'

The stately tick of the carriage clock that stood on the mantelpiece marked the sudden silence. It was a pretty clock enamelled with flowers and it had a melodious chime on the hour and also struck the quarter. She'd wound it only that morning.

His voice was a bit of a sigh when he said, 'Ah . . . now I understand. The Reverend Pawley dispensed with your services for your own protection.'

She snorted.

'Come, come, Sara,' he said softly. 'The man couldn't have kept you in his employ under the circumstances.'

'I agree, but neither did he have the right to blame the incident on me. He owed me over three years' wages when I left. He said he'd educated, fed me and housed me for several years as well as giving me a shilling to spend now and again, and that would have to do.'

'Did he educate you?'

'I could read and write before I got there, we were taught in the workhouse, but I could do both before that. I was allowed to sit in the children's lessons with Mrs Pawley. She was the governess then. In return I used to help teach the younger ones. I needed that money, I wanted it to put towards my house.'

His brow furrowed. 'Your house . . . you have your own house?'

'Not yet, sir. It's the house I'm going to buy when I've saved enough money. It needn't be big, but it must have two bedrooms at least. It's for my old age, you see, in case I don't marry and have children, but become an old spinster. The spare room is so I can take in a respectable, paying lady boarder. I wouldn't want to end up back in the workhouse. I'm going to be called by my proper name then, too.'

'Which is?'

'Serafina.'

He gave a faint smile. 'After a famous Italian abbess. You're surprisingly sensible for one so young, you know.'

'You have to be when you're poor.' She ate a second piece of cake. It was delicious, and she sighed. 'Maggie's a good cook.'

'She is that. Might there be any of that cake left?'

She placed it on his plate, then said, 'Another cup of tea, sir?'

'Yes please, Serafina Finn. So tell me, where did you get that unusual name from?'

'It was on a piece of paper that said who I was. I was named after an aunt, though people usually called me Sara because they couldn't spell Serafina. I'm used to Sara.'

'Then that's what I'll call you, and we'll use Serafina for special occasions. Do you still have the paper?'

'No, sir. I think it was burned.'

'Then you can't prove who you are. Can you remember your aunt?'

She poised for a moment with the teapot held in mid-air, then poured the liquid into the cup. 'Sometimes I can remember an elderly woman with wrinkles around her mouth and eyes, and with a loud voice. I think that might have been her.' She thought for a moment then said, 'I have a feeling that she was kind.'

'In what way?'

'I don't know, because when I remember her I don't have any bad thoughts, and I missed her when she left, I recall.'

'You forgot to put the milk in first.'

'Sorry . . . how did you know?'

'My hearing is acute, as is my sense of smell.'

'Does it make any difference to the taste?'

'Damned if I know. I'm a creature of habit, and that's the way I've always done it.'

Adding the milk in she stirred it with a silver spoon, hoping that Maggie had washed it after she'd polished it. It seemed to be satisfactory to his taste.

There was a knock at the door and her employer's valet came in. He winked at her. 'Sir?'

'What is it, Oscar?'

'I've checked the house and all is satisfactory.'

'Good, then I'll go up to my room and change. Thank you for your company, Sara. I'll leave you to get on with your tasks.'

She didn't know whether to be relieved or not after he left, unaided, except for his stick. He must have counted the steps, she thought, because as he neared the stair he extended the stick he carried to locate the first one.

Carrying the tray back to the kitchen she complimented Maggie on her cake then called to Fanny to bring a bucket of warm water.

Later, she went past the small sitting room. The door was open and she saw Finch Leighton sitting in his chair, his face turned towards the sun coming in the window. How boring to be without sight, she thought. She must try and think of something that would keep him occupied.

There was very little left to do in the house now, just the day-to-day upkeep to keep it clean. When she knocked at the door he turned his head her way and smiled. 'Sara?'

'Yes . . . would you like me to read to you, sir?'

'Not at the moment, I'm quite happy with my thoughts. But thank you.'

She wondered what those thoughts were as she backed away.

Finch was thinking about Sara.

His new housekeeper was certainly efficient, if a little pert. Still, she was youthful and had answered his questions with honesty, but sometimes with an air of defensiveness. She would not be a subservient member of staff but she would get things done − already had in the short time she'd been here.

Oscar had gleaned enough from the staff to discover that she'd already put Maggie in her place. Fanny liked her and thought she was pretty, Giles had a healthy respect for her and Joseph said she was a sprightly piece of goods, like his wife had been. Oscar had told him she had a face with delicate bones, with a small nose, fair skin, a big smile and long dark hair that reached to the small of her back.

She also smelled good as she moved past him in a stir of fragrant air. She was a mixture of polish, to which lavender oil had been added unless he was mistaken, of scrubbing soap and roses. In fact, her smell blended with the house.

He rose and moved around his sitting room. Once it had been his parents' house, but his mother had married and had gone to live in America after the death of his father. She had died there. Diana had taken it over, refurnishing it to her own taste. Now and again she'd entertained her friends here and the room had resonated with laughter as they'd gossiped together.

Picking up an ornament from a table his fingers ran over it. It was the shepherdess in her blue frilly dress. A hand's width away was the shepherd. The ball of Finch's thumb sought out a small imperfection in the glaze. He'd won them at a shooting contest at the local fete the year after he'd married Diana.

He worked his way around the room. Here on the lounge were four embroidered cushions his wife had fashioned, depicting Leighton Manor in the various seasons. Summer had been left unfinished, and Mrs Cornwell had completed it. If he was careful he could feel the change in the embroidery stitches. Diana's stitching had been so fine when compared to Mrs Cornwell's, which was slightly clumsier . . . though that could be in his imagination.

He voiced his thoughts, reminding himself. 'Because I loved Diana I now think of her as perfection.' She'd been far from it.

He moved to the mantelpiece, using the map in his mind. Lightly he touched the clock. Apart from the noise, it felt alive, the tiny vibrations clicking off time against his palms. He jumped when it chimed, and grinned. A quarter past four! The clock had been a wedding gift, but Finch couldn't remember from whom. Diana would have.

Everything was in its place. The face screens had been embroidered by his mother. The fender, fire-dogs and sparks screen were in place around the empty grate. He'd wished that he and Diana had had children together; it would have settled her down, and he'd like to have had a daughter to remember her by.

You're not too old to marry again and produce children.

'But who would want a blind man,' he murmured.

Diana had been young when they'd married . . . like Sara Finn. He'd been seven years older, too old for her in his mind. She hadn't wanted children, and as a result their personal relationship had been unsatisfactory.

He had worked his way round the room. Now he had nothing to do but sit in his chair again, enjoying the sun's warmth against his skin as he inhaled the scents coming from the profusion of wild flowers growing in the overgrown garden outside the house – once neatly trimmed grass and flower beds.

'At least my efficient new housekeeper hasn't changed that,' he murmured, wishing that she were older, and therefore more sensible. He didn't like change, and she was bound to forget he was blind and put obstacles in his path. Her youth alone would rearrange the quietness of his home. Already her scrubbing brush had intruded into it, scrubbing away last week's dirt, or was it last month's . . . or even last year's? Boredom would eventually move her on to remove the memories from someone else's past. He should get rid of her now, before she settled in – send her packing.

He remembered the house she yearned for with its two bedrooms. What a pathetic ambition for a girl with a splendid name like Serafina. But it was everything to the girl, and she was prepared to work and save for it. What right had he to prevent that by dismissing her, and just because she was young?

There was a breathy, snoring sound near his feet. He patted his knee and the cat sprang up to settle in his lap. 'Hello, Fingal. It didn't take you long to find me.' His fingers went under the cat's chin with a gentle caress and Fingal's purr increased in volume.

There came a clatter of feet from the depths of the house, and Maggie's shrill voice. 'Here puss . . . where the devil has that dratted cat got to? He should be wearing his collar.'

Sara whispering. 'I'll find him, Maggie.'

'Hear that, Fingal? You should be wearing your bells,' Finch whispered.

The cat offered him a dubious meow.

He heard Sara's footsteps lightly pattering over the tiled floor of the hallway. She was making kissing sounds in a quiet way to entice the cat to her.

'Fingal's in here,' he said.

'Sorry, I didn't mean to disturb you . . . he escaped from the kitchen before Maggie got his collar on.'

He held out a hand. 'Give it to me, I'll do it.'

He misjudged, and took her hand with it. He noticed that her fingers were callused, and as she tried to withdraw her fingers he tightened his around them and said, 'Stop wriggling.' He turned her hand palm up then ran a fingertip over them. 'Did you get these at the workhouse?'

'Mostly. It was picking the tar from the oakum that did the damage.'

He gave a faint smile. 'You bite your nails.'

The tension in her hand increased. He remembered that she'd slapped the reverend's son for taking liberties. He released the pressure in his fingers in case she read more into the gesture than he'd intended. Her hand recoiled instantly in a sudden jingle of cat bells.

Fingal sprang from his lap in the direction of the open window, remembering no doubt that the cat bells warned the birds and mice of his presence.

'Damned sneaky cat!' she said with some exasperation. 'I'll have to go after him. In the meantime you'll have to keep a look out for him, sir.'

'I will,' he said, and he chuckled. 'Off you go then, Sara.'

Instead of going towards the door her feet pattered towards the window. Her skirt brushed his knee and she momentarily blocked off the sun's warmth on his face before she followed the cat over the sill. She must have realized what she'd said because when she was outside the window she whispered to herself, 'You fool, Sara, what will he think?'

Finch thought that the word fool didn't come into the equation. He thought Sara was a hard-working girl who deserved something better than life had given her, and he could do something about her withheld wages to start with. At least that would contribute towards housing her in her old age. He chuckled at the thought of a young girl planning for her future as an ageing spinster, then laughed out loud that she'd leaped out of the window after the cat. It appealed to his sense of humour.

Mindful that Fingal was on the loose and would sneak back in and attack his ankles on the slightest whim, Finch climbed the stairs cautiously. 'Oscar. I need you to write a letter for me. Take it down in pencil first, so I can attend to your spelling.'

There was a rustle of paper and the sound of a pencil being sharpened.

'To whom shall I address it, sir?'

'The right reverend, the Lord Bishop of—'

'You're writing to the Bishop?'

'Don't sound so surprised. He is a relative, after all.'

'No, sir. I mean, yes, sir. It's just that we don't often write to him.'

'That's because my secretary usually does it for me. Do get on with it, Oscar, else we'll be here all day.'

Finch waited until the scratch of Oscar's pencil paused, then said, 'My Lord, esteemed uncle, there is a matter I wish to pursue which concerns one of my house staff, Sara Finn . . .'

Oscar said, 'How do you spell pursue, sir? Is it an *e* or a *u*?'

Finch sighed. The letter was going to take a long time.

Three

The premises were situated not far from the precincts of the Temple.

Adam Chapman. Private Detection Agency. The gold lettering stood out against its dark-green background of fresh paint over the door. It announced Adam's profession with authority as well as discretion.

On one side of the agency stood a jeweller's establishment. The premises on the other side provided accessories for gentlemen, such as hats and gloves, cigar cases, snuff boxes, and the like. Both were well patronized.

Positioned across the road, Adam gave the woman beside him a faintly self-conscious smile. 'What do you think, Celia?'

His sister smiled. 'I think it's perfect, exactly what you deserve. I'm so pleased you left the esquire off, despite mother's insistence. She's invited Edgar Wyvern over to dinner again on Saturday. They get on remarkably well, I think.'

'I've noticed. Would you mind if something came of it?'

'Not if it makes mother happy. You know how much she loves entertaining. Edgar has asked her to act as his hostess next month. I believe he intends to introduce her to his colleagues and their wives.'

'I think Edgar is just what our mother needs, but that aside,' and Adam smiled at his sister as he brought her back to the matter at hand. 'You know, there will be much more accounting than you're used to doing now we are an agency. I'm going to hire a clerk to work under your direction.'

'Dearest Adam, you can have no idea how much I'm looking forward to getting out of the house, being useful and having the opportunity to earn my own salary. Now mamma has made her own circle of friends at Chiswick and is in demand, she no longer needs me. And thank goodness she's stopped trying to find a husband for me. Having a spinster daughter on her hands is an embarrassment to her, I think.'

He took her hand in his and squeezed it in silent sympathy. 'Marriage for the sake of convenience would never work for either of us. You're only a couple of years older than me, Celia, and I'm certain you'll meet the perfect man before too long.'

'Is there such a thing as a perfect man? I would be quite contented with an imperfect one if he was the right one. What about you, Adam?'

'I haven't met her yet, but if I had—'

'She would be a mixture of the sisters, Charlotte Hardy and Marianne Thornton.'

'Two clever and lively women who adore their husbands and children.' He smiled at the thought. 'What more could a man want?'

'Beauty perhaps,' she said a little wistfully.

His sister was of average height and slightly angular. Her hair fell midway between light and dark brown and was straight, whereas he'd inherited curls. Eyes as grey as his own shone with intelligence, her fair skin was without blemish, and her mouth and nose were well shaped.

Celia had her own quiet elegance, but her shy manner tended to make her fade into the background. She'd be a wonderful wife for any man who'd take the trouble to win her heart.

'The Honeyman sisters certainly have that,' and he said it with so much enthusiasm that Celia laughed.

'Oh dear, Adam. I do hope you're not smitten with either of them.'

'Only in an openly admiring way. It wouldn't do me much good if I were seriously smitten, since they're happily married to men who adore them. By the way, we've been invited to the official opening of Nick Thornton's new emporium, followed by supper, next week.'

'Will we attend? I've heard so much about them from you that I've been longing to meet them.'

'Then we'll go. We've been invited to stay overnight so will be comfortable. I want you to buy yourself a new gown for the occasion.'

'What about the agency?'

'We won't be open for business until next week, when my investigators arrive. I'm about to put a notice in the window to that effect, but I already have enough work lined up to keep them busy.' He handed her the key. 'After you, Celia.'

When they crossed the road and let themselves in, Celia said, 'I know you won't have lace curtains, but I still think your clients would appreciate some privacy. Could we have some half curtains at the downstairs office windows? At least that would shield them from prying eyes. Gold would be pleasant; it would go with the lettering and with the fittings. You could always draw them back if you need more light.'

'Hmmm . . . I might compromise on dark green.'

'Then we'd look like a funeral parlour. Light green,' she said firmly, knowing that she'd already won the argument.

He laughed as he fixed the notice to the door. 'You'll be wanting a plant in a pot next.' She'd already given it consideration if her expression was anything to go by.

She said, 'The sisters were involved in that child stealing case you had, weren't they?'

'That was Seth Hardy, Charlotte's husband. It turned out to be all above board, though the boy's grandfather took some convincing. Unfortunately, he died a year or so after the case was settled and the custody was sorted out. Edgar Wyvern is one of the trustees to the boy's estate.'

Poole

Thornton's Emporium was in the main shopping street and covered the sites of what were once several small shops. Inside the main door was a small, crowded foyer. Behind, a staircase leading to the upper floor served to accommodate a brass band.

Refreshments were set out. Bunting had been hung. Savouries, sweetmeats, punch and lemonade were being served by waiters bustling about with trays.

Celia could see why her brother admired the sisters, especially the younger one. Marianne Thornton, blue-eyed and petite, her face framed by dark hair, kissed Adam's cheek. When they were introduced, Celia found herself being embraced too. Marianne linked arms with her. 'What a lovely gown; that lavender shade is so soft and pretty. Adam has told us so much about you. You must come and meet my husband . . . you won't mind if we abandon you for a short time, will you, Adam?'

Nicholas Thornton was tall, black-eyed and handsome, and had recently retired from being a sea captain after being shipwrecked.

'Nicky, my darling man, this is Adam's sister, Celia.'

His arm went around his wife's waist. Gently he pulled her against his side and grumbled in her ear, 'Aria, my love, haven't I told you that it's undignified to call me Nicky in public?'

Marianne giggled. 'You wretched creature, that tickles, and you are totally undignified, that's one of the reasons I adore you.'

A roguish grin came her way. 'Hello, Celia. I'm pleased Adam brought you. It's about time. I was beginning to wonder if he considered us worth meeting.'

Her eyes widened. 'I assure you, Mr Thornton, Adam has great respect for you.'

'Stop being such a wicked tease, Nick,' Marianne scolded him. 'You thought no such thing.'

Nick chuckled, took Celia's hand in his and bore it to his lips. 'Has Aria taken you round the emporium yet?'

'Lor, Nick, Celia has only just stepped over the threshold. Besides, it's not open until the mayor has done the speeches, the sandwiches and cake have been eaten, and everyone is prepared to spend their money. I'm going to buy that little box with the mother-of-pearl inlay.'

'You're not supposed to spend the profits before we make any.'

'You can give it to me for a birthday present instead, then it won't cost me a penny.'

Amusement filled his eyes. 'There's something wrong with your logic.'

'I'm sure that *you're sure* that you're right, but one way or another that box is going to be mine. I want to introduce Celia to my sister. Can you see Charlotte anywhere?'

Nick's height gave him an advantage. 'Charlotte is over by the fountain looking bored. Miss Stanhope has cornered her and is yapping like a fox terrier.'

'Oh, good, then we'll rescue her.' She kissed his cheek. 'I'll be checking up on you from time to time so behave yourself. Follow me, Celia.'

He chuckled, and called after them as they sauntered away, 'Don't forget to let Celia get a word in edgeways.'

'Nick is such a dear,' Marianne said, as they threaded through the crowd. 'We have a son who looks just like him. It must be wonderful having Adam for a brother; he's so sweet, and agreeable and he never looks bored when I chatter at him, though he probably is.'

'I hold a great deal of affection and respect for my brother. He stepped in to support my mother and myself when our father died.'

'I understand that you help him by keeping the books for his business. How clever of you. I wouldn't know where to start.'

'Now his business is expanding I'm to have an office and a clerk to help out. It's the least I can do, and I'm really looking forward to working outside the home.'

'Ah, there you are, Charlotte.'

At the sound of Marianne's voice Charlotte Hardy looked up. Celia's first impression was that the woman had a guarded expression. Then she smiled, and her face puckered with mischief. 'Marianne . . . you remember Miss Stanhope, don't you?'

'Only too well,' she said under her breath, then, 'How could I forget her? How do you do, Miss Stanhope.'

'I was just saying how pleased I was to get an invitation as a special guest to the opening, Mrs Thornton. So kind, and unexpected,' she gushed. 'We've been panting to see the goods you have for sale. My sister said a ship came in and the entire cargo was for Thornton's Emporium.'

'Yes. It's been such an exciting time. My husband arranged the shipment of rare and exotic oriental artefacts. Aunt Daisy has her eyes on a sweet little silver and lapis lazuli card case. It's awfully expensive and I meant to put it to one side, but we've had so much to do that I completely forgot until just now. Anyway, I thought I might buy it for Aunt Daisy's birthday. I do hope it doesn't sell before I can get there.'

When Miss Stanhope's eyes began to gleam Charlotte smothered a laugh behind her hand.

'Oh, isn't that your sister Lucy by the door? I do believe she's looking for you. She said to tell you she'd learned something important when I last saw her. Oh, and before you race off,

Miss Stanhope, may I introduce Miss Chapman from London. She works for a detecting agency.'

Miss Stanhope's eyes rounded. 'My goodness how terribly exciting, and such unusual employment for a woman. You must tell me all about it. Are you working on a case now?'

'Really, Miss Stanhope, you don't expect Miss Chapman to discuss her cases. Just imagine . . . she might be investigating a skeleton in your very own closet.'

Alarm chased across Miss Stanhope's face, and she was gone before Celia could assure her that she was doing no such thing.

Charlotte, who had lighter hair and similar features, but who lacked the fine bones of her sister, laughed. 'That was really too bad of you, Marianne. I could hardly keep a straight face. She'll rush to buy that case to prevent Mrs Phipps from having it.'

'Oh, I'm counting on it. Nick ordered several of them. Miss Stanhope always gets into an absolute froth when we run into each other. It's something to do with the fact that she was revealed as the gossiping creature she is after Nick returned home and she was proved wrong over some rumour she started.'

Charlotte's face reflected some private inner anguish as she reminded Marianne, 'Nick put me in my place too, but at least he let me off lightly.'

'That's different. You're my sister and I expect you to jump to the wrong conclusion because you practically brought me up, and you always have. We've spent half of our lives quarrelling and making up again. Char, you know I love you dearly.'

Celia was aware of the earlier love triangle with Nick Thornton, the one that had caused a serious rift between the sisters. But it was all over now.

Marianne's quick smile came. 'Lor, I'm so bad mannered. This is Celia, Adam's sister; aren't they alike? I wish I was a little taller like you, Celia; height is so elegant, don't you think so, Charlotte?'

'Yes, indeed. I'm so happy to meet you at long last, Miss Chapman. Adam has spoken of you often. May I call you Celia?'

'Of course you may. I'm led to believe that you don't stand on ceremony, so I shall use your first names in return if you don't mind.'

'We were very grateful for Adam's help in finding our dear stepson last year, you know.'

'Adam doesn't usually become personally involved, but in your stepson's case he felt partly responsible for the worry he caused you, and for John's disappearance. It was a pity that the boy's grandfather died before he could get to know him well, but at least he got to meet him.'

'He did, indeed.'

'Oh, there's Aunt Daisy and the Reverend Phipps.' Marianne waved to them. 'They look so happy now they've finally wed, and they didn't tell anyone; they just got a special licence from his bishop, and said the words in front of the altar.'

'Hurried marriages must be a Thornton family trait,' Charlotte said darkly, but with laughter in her voice.

'Hah! What about you and Seth? You proposed to him about an hour after you met and you didn't even tell me what you had in mind, you hussy.'

Charlotte gazed to where a man with an upright bearing was talking to Adam. When he caught her eye and smiled, her face as well as her voice softened. 'Seth was the best idea I've ever had.'

Although Celia smiled, envy stabbed at her. To have a man look at her in such a warm and tender manner would be wonderful. Being with these two beautiful sisters made her feel all the more ordinary, and they didn't seem to be in the least aware of their fortunate looks. But then, neither did they seem to be aware of her indifferent ones.

Her mother had formed a close friendship with the lawyer, Edgar Wyvern, and it now seemed inevitable that their relationship would develop into something more. If Adam married, which he probably would one day, she would come second to his wife and children. She didn't think there would be much call for female clerks. So who would support her then?

'The mayor is shaking hands with the people outside,' Charlotte said to Marianne. 'You'd better go and join Nick. He's already got the beginnings of a frown on his face and is looking around for you. I'll take care of Celia.'

'I'm sure I'll think of something to put him back in a good humour. Do I look presentable, Charlotte?'

'When do you look anything less than perfect? I should hate you for that reason alone . . . not to mention all the other qualities you have.'

Indeed, Marianne looked exquisite in a dark-blue brocade gown with a lace collar. Her lace cap had blue ribbons. Blue ribbons and flowers decorated her hair, which was drawn into a bun. Dark, slender ringlets coiled down her jaw line to her collar and her eyes were a sparkling blue. No wonder Adam admired her and Nick adored her. She had a happy nature that attracted people.

Marianne skirted the back of the crowd, bestowing smiles on those who sought to catch her eye. She joined her husband from behind, whispering something in his ear before slipping her hand into his. His frown disappeared like magic when Marianne smiled at him, and he raised her hand to his lips then held her gaze for an intimate moment, looking as though he wanted to devour her.

Charlotte turned Celia's way, and murmured, 'Take a lesson from my sister if you marry a difficult man . . . feed him honey.'

'Is Mr Thornton difficult then?'

'Not since he married Marianne,' Charlotte said with a smile. 'Do you have a gentleman in your life, Celia?'

'Nobody has ever showed the slightest interest in me so far, since I have no looks to speak of, or fortune. I doubt if I'll ever marry.'

Charlotte gave her a frank look. 'I don't see why not. Daisy Phipps has recently married and she must be nearly twice your age. Also, she resembles a plucked chicken and you don't.'

Celia's quick burst of laughter at Charlotte's outrageous state-ment attracted Adam's attention, and he grinned at them both.

The sisters were lucky in their marriages, Celia thought, but she was lucky in having Adam for a brother.

The crowd parted to let someone through.

Charlotte's breath hissed through her teeth when a man patted Nick Thornton's shoulder and kissed Marianne's cheek.

Curiosity prompted Celia to ask, 'Someone you know?'

'Nick's uncle. Captain Erasmus Thornton.'

It would have been rude to ask a reason for the animosity in evidence, but Charlotte furnished her with one anyway. 'We don't get on. If I don't tell you why, I imagine someone else will, but I warn you, it's a sore point with me. Marianne seems to live comfortably with it though. However, she's a nicer person than

I'll ever be. Years ago Erasmus fell in love with my mother. She died giving birth to his child.'

Celia didn't allow her shock to show. 'Oh . . . I'm so sorry. That must have been hard for you and Marianne . . . and the infant, of course.'

'The child died too.' Astute eyes came her way. 'I'm surprised Adam hasn't told you.'

'He discusses his cases with me sometimes and asks for my opinion, but he rarely makes comment on the lives of those concerned.'

Charlotte quickly changed the subject. 'Oh, look, here comes the mayor . . . let's go and join the men before the speeches start. I just hope they're not too pompous and long-winded.'

Erasmus Thornton was hoping the same. He'd come straight from his ship, *Daisy Jane*, and had left his first mate in charge of unloading the cargo.

Despite his previous opposition to Nick opening a shop, however grand, Erasmus was proud that his nephew had stuck to his plan and had achieved what he had. Nick had the right wife behind him too. Marianne was a little restless sometimes. Like her mother before her, she resembled a little wild pony.

Nick understood that she needed to be kept occupied. He was teaching her to sail the small sloop he'd bought, and when she sat at the window with her face turned towards the heath and she wore a wistful expression, Nick understood that, too, and he'd take her there where she could be at one with nature, leaving Alexander at Harbour House with his cousins.

She'd go out on the heath, taking Seth's stepson John with her if he was home, or so Nick had told him. She'd come back with armfuls of heather, pine needles in her hair, bare feet and a wide smile on her face.

Marianne adored Nick and she adored her son, and seeing them all together made Erasmus realize what he'd missed out on by not marrying. Nick had been right when he'd stopped earning his living from sailing the oceans.

Erasmus would have done the same for a woman he'd loved. But when Caroline Honeyman had died he'd lost his mind for a short time. He'd pushed himself, his crew and his ship almost beyond capacity in the mad turmoil of his grief until something brought him back to his senses . . . the fact that he had a nephew who needed his care and his guidance.

Uneasily, he remembered that he'd promised Marianne that he'd try and find out the truth. If the girl born to Caroline Honeyman was alive – as Marianne suspected – and if she proved to be his daughter, then he would have done her a great injustice by not providing for her. But it wouldn't be too late to redress that.

What if she proved to be George Honeyman's daughter?

Erasmus remembered George's voice as if he was standing next to him. The man had swallowed a skinful of brandy and had been swaying back and forth.

'You took the woman who belonged to me, and you killed her. The infant was a Thornton, there was no doubt about it. She couldn't be allowed to live, so I waited until the midwife was gone then smothered her with a pillow.'

Closing his eyes on the anguish he felt, Erasmus thought: I must have fathered the child. George wouldn't have taken the life of his *own* child, and neither would he have taken her to the orphanage. George *must* have killed the infant. It had struck him then. Had George killed Caroline, too?

The burden of that knowledge had been hard to bear – too hard for George, who'd spent the next few years drinking himself to death. Erasmus had to live with his remorse as well as his suspicion, that his love for another man's wife had been the death of her, as well as their baby daughter.

Even now he found it hard to think of George Honeyman committing such a hideous act, and he couldn't bring himself to tell the sisters that their own father had confessed to killing the child. He doubted if Charlotte would believe it anyway.

It had been a long time since he'd come to terms with it, and longer still before he'd allowed himself to be persuaded that the infant might be alive, and that George had left her at the orphanage – not only to keep them apart but to punish him as well. Erasmus had never repeated what George had said to anyone.

When he opened his eyes it was to find that Adam Chapman had moved into his line of vision. There was the answer. The young man was a detective, and a very good one from what he'd heard. He'd try and get him alone and ask his advice.

A burst of clapping brought Erasmus out of his reverie. The ribbons were cut and the band began to play. After the ceremony, the band struck up a lively march and his foot was trampled on by Miss Stanhope who nearly pushed him out of the way as the surge of shoppers headed into the various departments, where salesmen and women were on hand to relieve them of their cash.

He cornered Adam Chapman and held out his hand. 'My name is Erasmus Thornton. I'd like a private word if you've a moment, though it will have to be now because I need to get back to my ship.'

'My pleasure, Captain Thornton. I'll walk back to the quay with you and we can talk on the way, then we won't be interrupted. I'll join you outside, after I've informed my sister of my whereabouts.'

He didn't keep Erasmus waiting long, saying when he returned, 'Celia is just about to be taken on a conducted tour of the emporium by Marianne so there is no need to hurry.'

The young man listened without interruption as Erasmus briefly outlined the problem. It was hard to find the right words. When he did, stating them left a raw, aching void in his stomach, as if he'd ripped flesh from flesh.

'So you want me to find out if the girl is alive or dead?'

He shrugged. 'Aye, that's about it.'

'After all these years, why do you want this?'

'Marianne wants it. She's convinced that her sister is alive.'

There was a sceptical look in Adam's grey eyes. 'So, you're doing it for Marianne. Trying to prove her wrong, perhaps?'

'Hell, no! I'm hoping she'll be proved right and that George Honeyman . . . well, never mind.'

Chapman didn't seem to notice his slip. 'Why then?'

'Damn it man, why do you bloody well think? I loved her mother. If the infant was my daughter and she's still alive I might be able to do something for her.'

They strolled down High Street, Adam apparently deep in thought. Then he said, 'You mentioned George Honeyman?'

'Did I?'

'You know you did. If there's anything further I need to know tell me, otherwise we're both wasting our time.'

Erasmus hesitated. 'George was drunk at the time, and it would split the family apart if they found out.'

'You've trusted me with this story so far, and I must know that I have your absolute honesty before I decide whether or not to involve myself in this. I'm discreet, and your secret will be safe in my hands.'

'George told me that the infant had looked like a Thornton, and he'd smothered her with a pillow.'

Breath hissed between Adam's teeth.

'After he told me that I began to wonder, and I couldn't get the thought out of my head . . . did he kill his wife, as well?'

'And you didn't relate your suspicions to anyone in authority?'

'I'd already done George enough damage, and I'm not in the habit of kicking a dog when it's down. I could have broken him entirely, but it wouldn't have made me feel better about myself or bring Caroline back. Then, there were the girls. Who would have looked after them? George was a bully and an indifferent father, but he was better than nothing. I kept a roof over their heads for all those years when he was drinking himself to death.'

'You owned their house?'

'And the business. I won the deeds in a poker game. George was reckless and going downhill fast. Better me than someone who would have sold the place from under them.'

'If George told you he killed the infant, why do you believe differently now?'

'I have no strong belief that she is alive, but if she is then my fears will prove to be unfounded. George wouldn't have killed Caroline and left the baby alive.'

'Therefore your reasoning is that if the child is still alive, Caroline Honeyman is more likely to have died a natural death giving birth to it.'

'That's my drift.'

Chapman frowned as his direct gaze engaged the brown eyes of Erasmus, and Erasmus found it hard to look away. His voice was quiet, but just as direct. 'There's something you're not telling me.'

Erasmus gave a faintly, self-mocking smile, yet the hairs on the nape of his neck raised when he admitted, 'Only because I'm superstitious and because it would be of no use to you, Mr Chapman.'

'Allow me to decide that.'

He hesitated for just a moment then he sighed. 'Marianne heard a whisper in the wind coming off the heath, and it told her the girl's name.'

'And you don't believe it was a figment of her imagination.'

'I believe Marianne when she said she heard what she did. She has strong . . . *instincts*.'

Chapman didn't as much as turn a hair. 'A straw in the wind?'

'I expected you to laugh and call it a nonsense.'

'I discount nothing. You never know where seemingly non-sensical or unimportant details can lead. You're a surprising man, Captain Thornton.'

He shrugged. 'You get to believe in instinct and signs when you spend your life at sea.'

'I imagine you do. I might as well tell you that I don't want to jeopardize my relationship with either of the two families, or cause a further rift between you and them. This infant could prove to be a catalyst to cause further unrest within your family. If she still exists, as well as being a half-sister to Charlotte and Marianne she is possibly your daughter, a niece to your sister, a cousin to Nick and an aunt to the children of the family.'

'You pick things up quickly, young man.'

Adam nodded. 'Moreover, she will also be an adult now and may be perfectly happy with her lot in life. She might be married. She might be a whore. She might not want to know you or she might welcome you with open arms. Her situation, needs and wants will have to be taken into account, and you might end up disappointed. But as long as you realize that, if the other adults agree I'll take an extra day here and see what I can find out before I decide.'

Dismay closed wolf teeth around Erasmus's tough seaman's heart. He had not thought that far ahead. Perhaps it was a foolish idea and he should forget it. But he didn't want to disappoint Marianne. Then he realized he wouldn't have to, since her sister would do it for him. 'Charlotte Hardy will never agree anyway.'

'She will if it's put to her the right way. Better leave that to me. What did you say the name was that Marianne heard?'

'I didn't, but it was Serafina,' he said.

Four

'Very well, Adam, since the others have agreed, I have little choice, unless I'm to suffer Marianne's reproachful looks and sighs for the rest of my life. And if Erasmus Thornton doesn't get your help, he'll simply hire someone else. Why didn't he ask me himself?'

'Because he knew there would be an argument and you'd turn him down.'

Charlotte sighed. 'I imagine I've given him enough reason to think that. At least I know you'll be discreet, Adam. Just don't ask me any questions.'

Adam didn't let his dismay show. 'I was hoping to start off with you and Marianne. You must have memories of the night your mother died.'

'Yes, I do.' She sighed again, the pain in her eyes there for him to see. 'My mother was in agony, her screams went on and on until she was too tired to do anything but groan.'

'Where was Marianne?'

'She couldn't stand it. She went out on the heath, and just as I was getting worried about her she came back. It was almost dark and I reprimanded her. She said she'd visited the gypsies, and one had told her that the baby would be a girl. But she was trembling and scared and I think she instinctively knew that our mother wouldn't survive the birth.

'The baby was born during the night. It was a full moon. I remember looking out of my bedroom window, because the water and heath look so pretty in the moonlight. Marianne woke and crawled into my bed. She was scared and so was I, but we didn't know why. I told her a story and we cuddled each other until she fell asleep. I stayed awake, and I went to see my mother. She was lying still. There was blood on her nightgown, and the baby was there too.' Charlotte closed her eyes. 'She was on the bed . . . so little and naked and quiet . . . then . . . Marianne called out in her sleep and I went to her.'

Tears trickled from under her lids. 'That's all I remember until morning. Our father woke us at dawn, to tell us that our mother and the baby had died. He was beside himself, weeping and wailing and banging his head against the wall. He scared Marianne. She ran downstairs and hid in the hall cupboard.'

'Your sister said she heard the baby cry.'

Charlotte shrugged. 'Marianne has always had a vivid imagination . . . she could have dreamed it, or heard an owl taking its prey on the heath.'

Charlotte was keeping something back from him – something she wanted to forget herself, perhaps. He held the glance she threw at him.

'Is that what you believe, or what you want to believe?'

Her eyes slid away. 'I don't know, Adam. I don't want to remember what happened in my childhood. Growing up without a mother, and with a father who was drunk for most of the time, was unpleasant. Marianne liked her freedom, and I had to try and keep her under control. I was always on edge, trying to appease our father, whose temper was uncertain at the best of times. Marianne seemed to go out of her way to vex him. I tried not to bully her, but I know she resented my authority. I was only two years older than her, after all. I seemed to live in perpetual fear that one of us would do the wrong thing and upset him.'

'Marianne appreciates what you went through.'

'She does now. I was often wrong about her and I know I was unfair to her when I didn't credit her with any sense. She has plenty of good sense, otherwise she wouldn't have gone on to the heath that day. I feared for her sometimes.'

'Feared for her?'

'Pa used to turn against her in a way he never did with me. It was as though he saw our mother in her, and remembered she'd been unfaithful to him. Sometimes when he was drunk, he called her by our mother's name. He took a riding crop to her for answering him back, once, and I thought he was going to kill her. She was covered in welts and bruises.' Charlotte faltered, and her face paled. 'I pray that she doesn't remember those times. I begged him to stop hitting her but he wouldn't, so one day I picked up his gun and threatened to shoot him with it.'

Adam hadn't expected that. As his eyes widened in surprise he thought that Charlotte had been incredibly brave to defend her sister against a man. Even so he didn't disturb the thread of her thoughts.

'Pa laughed, and although he'd taught me to shoot he told me to go ahead and pull the trigger, and put him out of his misery. So I did. Marianne hit my arm to divert the shot. It went wide, and the ball creased the top of his ear and buried itself into the panelling in the hall, thank God. It's still there.'

She suddenly paled and a fine sheen of perspiration covered her brow. When he noticed she was trembling he crossed to the sideboard with her coffee and added a measure of brandy from the decanter. He placed it in her hands. 'My dear, I've upset you, and I'm sorry. Here, drink this down.'

'No, it's not you, Adam.' She swallowed the remains of the coffee as he'd urged, grimaced, then shuddered and pushed the cup away from her.

'Shall I fetch Seth?'

Before his eyes she pulled herself together and gained her strength. 'No, it was just a faint and I'm beginning to feel better. The worst thing was, I didn't try to wound pa. I wanted to kill him. Marianne was so small and helpless – too small to fight back. Her eyes were so wounded and bewildered. I told him that if he hurt her again I'd wait until he was asleep, and I wouldn't miss the second time. He broke down and cried then. It worries me to think I've inherited his temper. I don't let go of grudges easily.'

He lightened her mood with, 'Rest assured, if you ever point a gun at me I'll run in the opposite direction like a hare with the wind under its tail.'

Her eyes lit up with amusement. 'Adam Chapman racing a bullet might be a sight to behold.'

He laughed. 'Marianne has a good head on her shoulders; no wonder she loves you so dearly.'

'I know that now, Adam. For the first time in my life I'm happy and contented, thanks to Seth. I don't want things to change. So yes, I want to believe that Marianne imagined that cry. If she didn't, it means that the baby lived, and . . .'

'Have you an opinion on what might have been the fate of the infant?'

Her face closed up and she murmured, 'Not one I want to

think or talk about. I've already said more than I meant to.' Her lovely mouth twisted in a wry smile. 'You have a sneaky way with you, Adam. You asked me two questions and despite my resolve not to, I answered all the questions you didn't ask, as well.'

'Perhaps it's because I'm a good listener and you needed to answer them. If there's anything else you might have forgotten—'

'No, there isn't!'

It was said too emphatically, but he let it go, giving a faint smile. 'You've been helpful. You know, Charlotte, you have more goodness in you than you give yourself credit for. Will you mind very much if your sister is found?'

'I don't know. If she exists, and if you happen to find her, ask me then. It's hard to be civil to someone you've despised all your life.'

'I'm sure you'll manage if the time comes.' He stood, picking up his hat and gloves. 'Be sure that I'll keep you informed through Marianne, who has been appointed by Erasmus Thornton to act on his behalf.'

She shook her head. 'I never imagined he'd have a conscience.'

Gently he kissed her cheek. 'Most people do. Captain Thornton is no exception and he's in an awkward situation. It could be that Marianne has given him the incentive to act that he needed. People are often surprising.'

Seth came from the study when they went into the hall. His glance went immediately to Charlotte's face, and he relaxed, as if reassured by what he saw there. He moved to her side, and said, 'You're leaving already, Adam?'

'Yes, I have some enquiries to make, and my cab is waiting. Thank you, Charlotte, you were very helpful, and I hope it wasn't too painful.'

After they watched the cab leave, Seth smiled at her. 'Well?'

'I wished you'd been in there with me.'

'I thought my presence would have been intimidating.'

'You never intimidate me, but you do make me aware of being cautious.'

'Adam is a family friend now. He is totally discreet, and there's no need for caution.'

Her eyes met his and she smiled. 'I want to tell you something, Seth.'

'Is it that you love me?'

'Of course not.' Her eyes mirrored her consternation in case he misconstrued her words. 'I do love you though, didn't you realize?'

'Yes, but say it again in cold blood.'

An expression of shyness appeared in her eyes and she offered him a breathless little chuckle that charmed him. 'I love you, Seth Hardy. There, will that do?'

'Perfectly. You've never told me that before, you know.' Cradling her face in his hands Seth bowed his head and kissed her before smiling. 'You taste of brandy. Can this account for your tongue being loosened?'

She laughed. 'Adam gave me the brandy because I nearly fainted, and he thought his questioning was the cause. However, the fault lies with you, since we're expecting an infant in the spring. That's what I had to tell you.'

A smile spread across his face. 'I'll accept both blame and responsibility in equal proportions, but we mustn't forget your willing participation in the creation of this infant, especially when it makes for such pleasant reverie.'

'I hope you have other things you can think about during the day.'

'Yes . . . but they're not half as pleasant.'

Colour touched Charlotte's cheeks and she buried her face against his shoulder. She'd never expected to love a man so completely. 'Stop teasing me, Seth Hardy.'

Marianne had told Adam that the funeral parlour had gone. However, death had not travelled far from the place, for the premises now sold the weapons that caused the final end product. *Henry Palk and Son. Sporting guns. Duelling pistols. Sword sticks. Weapons of defence.* Bars guarded the window and the glass panels in the door, which also had a stout metal lock to secure it. The shop front resembled a prison cell, but perhaps it was designed to deter aspiring robbers by showing them what to expect.

Henry Palk was in residence behind the counter, looking like a fixture. 'I haven't had a sale all week,' he said gloomily, when Adam introduced himself and stated his business.

'I wondered if there were any funerary records left behind.'

Henry looked doubtful, then he brightened. 'As I recall there are some papers down in the cellar. I'll get my son to take you down and you can have a look when he comes back. It's a gloomy hole though and it smells a bit. Sometimes we store bits and pieces down there. Not that we keep much on the premises, and we always take the bolts home with us.'

He gazed doubtfully at Adam's immaculate appearance. 'It's easy enough to go down but it's as black as a coal bunker. A tall man like you will have to stay bent over lest you thump your head on the beam. Best you leave your hat and jacket up here with me so they'll stay clean. At least your trousers are dark.'

'That's kind of you, Mr Palk.'

The door opened as he spoke and a man who appeared to be in his forties entered. He was of a short, stocky stature.

'This is my son, Thomas Palk. Thomas, Mr Chapman is a detecting agent making enquiries about a deceased person. I said he could look through that old trunk in the cellar and go through the funeral parlour records. Take him down if you would.'

'Right then, I'll fetch a candle. Come through behind the counter, sir; the trapdoor is in the back room.'

'They used to prepare the bodies for burial in that back room,' Henry offered with a shudder.

Thomas rolled his eyes. 'Someone has to do it, and at least it's a profession where you don't run out of clients. You can help me lift the trapdoor if you would, sir.'

Henry took Adam's coat and hat from him. 'Keep a look out for ghosts,' he said, as Adam followed Thomas down.

Henry had been right. The cellar was small and low, and smelled of damp, mould and mice. It was also filled with cobwebs and scuttling creatures and Adam thought he might have welcomed a couple of ghosts to scare them off. He found a trunk full of yellowed papers that seemed to be in a state of decomposition, and which were filed in a manner that offended his tidy mind. He had to squat on his haunches to go through them.

Thomas said, 'You won't mind if I go back up again, will you, sir? I can't abide the feeling of being closed in down here.'

By the time Adam was halfway through the papers his back

ached from bending almost double and his hands were black with dirt. But he'd found what he was looking for, the record of the interment of Caroline Honeyman some eighteen years before.

Henry had some soap and water waiting for him. 'Best you wash those hands before you touch anything.' He gently brushed cobwebs, dust and a couple of spindly long-legged spiders from Adam's trousers before handing him his coat. 'I'm going over to the inn to take a bite of something to eat. They do a tasty steak and kidney pie there, if you happen to be hungry.'

'Indeed, I am. I'd like to thank you for your trouble, so perhaps you'd be my guest.'

A smile spread across Henry's face. 'That's right generous of you, Mr Chapman. I won't say no to that.'

Henry had a small circle of friends he lunched with, businessmen like himself. Adam learned more at the inn where they took their repast. A couple of rounds of ale loosened their tongues.

'Mr Chapman is making enquiries about Mrs Caroline Honeyman.'

'She's long dead.'

'He knows that, don't he?'

'Then why is he making enquiries?'

Three pairs of eyes gazed at him.

'I'm making them on behalf of the relatives. They're interested in what happened to the infant.'

Henry said, 'That will be Nicholas Thornton's young woman, I reckon. She came in looking for information when she was little more than a girl. I didn't let her down in the cellar though. It's not a place for a young woman.'

Another of the young men grinned. 'Now there's a nesh piece for a man to have in his bed. No wonder Thornton the younger didn't bother going back to sea.'

Laughter cackled. 'An old codger like you wouldn't know what to do with a woman like that.'

'I remember her aunt, Constance Serafina Jarvis. She used to live over Dorchester way.'

Adam's ears pricked up. Serafina again . . . the name Marianne had heard in the wind. Had it been a quirk of nature that had captured that name and placed it in Marianne's head at that moment? Had it been more – a connection between the spirit and the living perhaps, or was it a straw in the wind? He'd solved cases on a slimmer premise.

He threw her name into the ring. 'Constance Serafina, a pretty name. I can't say I've heard her mentioned before.'

They hastened to enlighten him.

'No wonder, since her name was the only pretty thing about her, as I recall. They reckon the family had gypsy blood in them from way back, and Serafina was the name of some gypsy queen who married outside the tribe way back.'

'Constance was a spinster lady who had a fortune she'd inherited from an uncle. She left a small legacy to her Honeyman nieces, and the rest of it to the orphanage she started over Dorchester way. George Honeyman was furious. He'd run up a debt and was counting on it, you see.'

'He got nothing, and serve him right,' Henry said. 'He was a bad bastard and a rotten drunk, handy with his fists.'

Adam allowed the conversation to run its course and hearing nothing more of use he took his leave and went over to the church. The burial register revealed nothing, and Caroline Honeyman's memorial tablet told him nothing more than he already knew.

He stood, the afternoon sunshine warming his back, gazing at her grave. George was buried next to her, having claimed his wife in death. Instinct was telling Adam that the youngest Honeyman daughter was still alive, though the evidence he had was only of the slimmest kind.

'Only you know whether my search will be fruitless, and you can't tell me,' he said to the slab.

He held his breath when a song thrush came down and perched on the tablet. It cocked its head to survey him with a beady eye.

'I'll believe it if you sing,' he whispered.

The bird flew to the branch of the nearest tree, opened its throat and sang its exquisite song.

Adam smiled as the creature flew off. He wasn't superstitious. He didn't believe in signs . . . at least, not until now. He'd never wanted to before.

From necessity he packed a lot into his day. His next destination was the orphanage at Dorchester. It was still there, and functioning. He explained his quest to the matron in charge.

'Constance Serafina Jarvis was before my time. But we do have records in the basement. I can't allow you to take any away, of course.'

Hopefully, it was not as cramped and dirty as Henry Palk's cellar had been.

They passed rooms full of neatly dressed girls who were busy at needlework or lessons. 'We bring them up to be practical as well as educated to a certain level, so they can be gainfully employed.'

The records were filed in batches of ten years. 'Who are you looking for?'

'Her surname would have been Honeyman and she would have been newly born.' He told her the date. 'She'd be eighteen now.'

The matron went through the files. 'Only one child was brought in on that day, and she was five years old. She was accepted by one of the volunteers on duty. That's not usual, but Miss Jarvis suddenly remembered some urgent business on that day, and apparently had to rush off.' Matron handed him the file with a smile. 'Here, it's all on the file and if you want to take notes, you can. We rely heavily on women who volunteer their services. They don't do any of the hard work, but they teach the children to sew or do beadwork, and read the bible. It makes them feel useful, especially if they haven't got children of their own. Sometimes they'll sponsor a child if they show promise.'

It was not what Adam wanted, but he read through it anyway. One of the names seemed familiar. He stored it in his memory until he got back to Poole, then asked Marianne. 'Who is Miss Stanhope?'

Baby Alexander was walking from one piece of furniture to the other, well aware of the admiration of his mother, because he kept stopping to look at her and collect a smile of encouragement. Alex giggled when Marianne groaned and said, 'There are two, Agnes and Lucy. They're the most prolific gossips in town. Why do you ask?'

'A Miss Stanhope was on duty at your aunt's orphanage on the day your mother died. I thought I could stay another day if it didn't put anyone out, and we could call on them.'

'Lor, Adam, they keep their mouths as tight as oysters when

they're round me, in case I bite their tongues off. You're certainly welcome to stay longer. I'm sure Erasmus is just as comfortable sleeping on his ship.'

Celia smiled from one to the other. 'I met Miss Stanhope at the opening of the emporium. She invited me to visit them for afternoon tea. Marianne told her I was a detective.'

'We'll see how good a detective you are when you discover what you can about that day.'

Adam laughed when Celia's smile faded and she asked, 'How do I do that?'

'Lead Miss Stanhope gently round to it and let her talk.'

'But what do you want to know?'

'I want to know if a newborn baby was taken into the orphanage that day. If so, try and get Miss Stanhope to expand on it with some details. Who took the baby there? What happened to the child?'

'But you said you looked at the records and the baby wasn't on them.'

'Sometimes records are not what they seem. The question arises; under such circumstances would Constance Jarvis have put a relative's child on record?'

The smile left Marianne's face. Picking Alex up she hugged him tight. 'If the baby went to the orphanage that means someone took her there.'

'Yes, of course.'

When Alex began to protest at being restrained so tightly, she said, 'Sorry, my darling lamb.' Kissing the soft fold of his neck until he began to laugh, she placed him back on the floor. There, he began to thump her knee with his palm for her attention. Adam allowed Marianne to reach her own conclusion.

'It must have been my father. He was the only one there, except for the midwife.'

'Who is no longer alive.'

'My God! He *did* give my baby sister away. How could he have carried out such an awful act?'

'Marianne, my dear. I did warn you that opening this particular Pandora's Box could prove to be painful to all concerned. I understand that your father thought that Erasmus had fathered the infant. Does that make the action more understandable?'

The generous curve of her mouth tightened a little. 'I'm glad my father didn't keep her, for he would have made her life miserable. But if he thought Erasmus Thornton was the father he should have handed the child over to them. Erasmus brought Nick up as if he was his own son. The baby could have lived in a decent home with Erasmus and Daisy. It's not right that she was punished for something that wasn't her fault. All this time Erasmus believed her to be dead.'

'Perhaps she *is* dead, my dear.'

Clear blue eyes assessed him, and the assessment was followed by a grin. 'Adam, your nose is twitching because you instinctively sense that she's alive even while you question why you're being irrational. You're going to follow that instinct because you've discovered that you actually have one, and that alone intrigues you.'

Celia gave a small hum of laughter. 'Well said, Marianne.'

Adam's smile came in a slightly shamefaced manner. People didn't usually see through him that easily. 'Yes, I'm intrigued, and I want so much for her to be alive. But we must not lose sight of the fact that even if she survived her birth she may not have survived infancy or childhood.'

'But you'll look for her, regardless?'

He smiled. 'I'll do my best to find out what happened to her. Shall we give her a name?'

'Serafina, after my aunt who ran the orphanage,' Marianne instantly said, and Adam didn't bother wondering why the name came as no surprise to him.

Five

Sara hummed as she went about her work. She'd been here for a month, and had never felt so happy. Her efforts had brought about change. The house shone, and everything proceeded as it should – except for the locked room of the late Mrs Leighton. To her way of thinking, even a shrine to the dead should be kept clean and tidy.

'You take so much pride in this house that anyone would think you were the mistress,' Maggie had said to her once, and indeed she sometimes did feel like it was hers. She'd love a home like this with a sweeping staircase, a library, and a garden that smelled of apples and roses, and her own staff of servants. She'd treat her servants better than she'd ever been treated herself – excluding Mr Leighton, of course – and they would respectfully call her ma'am.

Holding her apron up like a ballgown she tripped daintily down the stairs, the hand holding the duster polishing the banister rail at the same time, because she didn't believe in taking a wasted journey, and it was a job she needn't do next time.

Oscar had taken Mr Leighton into Taunton, where he had business to conduct. She'd discovered that he'd been a barrister before his accident.

'Not that he ever needed to work, since he'd inherited handsomely, but some of his cases were for people who couldn't afford to pay,' Maggie told her knowledgeably one day. 'Mr Leighton was always willing to help the underdog if he thought they deserved it. Not like his wife.'

'What was Mrs Leighton like?' she'd asked her.

Maggie went to the door and gazed out into the corridor before closing it and coming back. 'Diana Milson was nothing fancy, but she was beautiful. Her parents had a small printing shop. Nothing would please her though, and she treated anyone she thought was under her like dirt. I don't know what he saw in her, really I don't. She had the looks, but she was too flighty for the likes of a nice gentleman like Mr Leighton if you ask me.'

'Did he love her?'

'He was besotted with her at first; he fell for her looks, I reckon. But she began to show her true nature after they'd been married a year or so. All he'd wanted was a quiet family life with a couple of children. Mrs Leighton wanted to entertain and be admired all the time. He wasn't lively enough for her. She often invited her friends down. They drank too much, and they shot guns at everything that moved. The countryside bored her to tears, she told him when he complained about them. He put up with it, but they argued, and sometimes she'd storm off back to London without telling him. On the day she died—'

Giles had come in the back door then, and the conversation had stopped.

Sara gazed at the portrait of Mrs Leighton, at the blue twinkling eyes and the red gown. For the first time she noticed that the twist to Diana Leighton's mouth had a hint of discontent to it.

'I'd be discontented if I was dead at that age,' she whispered.

She did some piano practice while Mr Leighton was out, but she couldn't get Diana Leighton out of her mind. Closing the piano, she fetched the room key from its hook and her feet carried her up the stairs to the room that his wife had used. She told herself that the door hinges needed oiling when it creaked.

The red gown had dark patches where the blood had dried, and it had faded into its folds. She opened the door to the dressing room where gowns were laid out on their trays. A rack held a row of dusty shoes. There were various accessories, reticules, scarves, hoops, stockings and petticoats. They smelled of stale perfume and perspiration – of dust and death. Pearls spilled out of a turquoise box on the dressing table. Several rings were scattered, a ruby pendant dangled from a mirror and a gold bangle set with diamonds circled a pair of cream silk gloves.

She picked a ring up and wiped the dust from the stone. Catching a beam of sunlight it sent an array of intense rainbow colours across the walls. She placed the ring back in exactly the same spot, marvelling that such a small clear stone could twinkle so fiercely in the sun.

'You like everything to be neat and clean, so I suppose this room annoys you,' Finch Leighton said from the doorway, and she jumped.

He was perceptive.

'I'm sorry . . . I didn't hear you arrive.'

'You were playing the piano. What are you doing in here?'

Thank goodness he couldn't see her guilty blush. 'I was curious.'

He gave a faint smile. 'I can understand that. When you stop being curious you can go back downstairs. Lock the door behind you; my late wife had a habit of leaving her jewellery everywhere.'

'Would you like me to pick it up so you can put it in your safe?'

'No, Sara. Just leave the room as it is, please.'

'There are cobwebs in the corners and dust—'

'I know exactly what's in here, and where it is. Resist your need to scrub and polish this particular portion of my life. Some of us find comfort in the cobwebs and don't need to be constantly dusted off. Can you do that, Sara?' This time his voice was curt enough to cut her.

She followed him out. Closing the door she locked it and then placed the key in his hand. Hoping he couldn't hear the injury in her voice, she said, 'Here's the key, sir. Best you keep it in case my curiosity gets the better of me again. I'll be in my rooms if you need me. I have time on my hands and have some mending to do.'

He almost growled, 'When you've recovered from your sulk I'd like you to join me in the sitting room . . . and don't keep me waiting for too long.'

Sara opened her mouth, thought better of it then shut it again and stalked off.

She kept him waiting for ten minutes – ten minutes in which she came to the conclusion that she'd been at fault and owed him an apology. Fetching a tray of tea she took it through to the sitting room.

His head turned towards her when he heard her footsteps.

'I'm sorry,' they both said together.

He smothered a laugh. 'I was too snappy.'

'No, it was me. I was too intrusive and inquisitive. I wouldn't have stolen anything.'

'Good gracious, I didn't imagine you would.'

'But you said . . . and there is a lot of jewellery lying about.' She felt guilty and confessed, 'I dusted a ring. I've never seen a real diamond before and it twinkled so in the sun.'

Pouring his tea, she placed the cup and saucer in its usual place, the plate next to it, and a snowy-white napkin across his lap. 'There are two small apple tarts on the plate.'

'Thank you, Sara. There's a purse on the table. Inside is an envelope with your name on it. Keep the purse. I bought it in Taunton.'

'Someone has written to me? But I don't know anyone.'

'It contains your wages from Reverend Pawley.'

She was astonished. 'But . . .'

'I wrote to someone I know who looked into the matter for me. Your former employer said he'd intended to pay you all along.'

'Hah!'

'Exactly my sentiments.'

'How much money is it?'

'Just under fifteen pounds.' Drily, he told her, 'Reverend Pawley deducted your keep and your train fare, and his own train fare as well. It's fully itemised on the receipt. By the way, he said you have no respect for your betters.'

'What makes him think he's better than I am? He's a man, not a saint.'

Her employer chuckled at that.

Sara collected the purse. It had a peacock embroidered on it. She couldn't imagine having such a sum as fifteen pounds all at once, and she gasped out, 'It's a fortune. Thank you so much. It's a very pretty purse.'

'Oscar said you'd like it.'

'I'll have to find somewhere to keep the purse safe.'

'It won't take up much room, I'm sure. There's a box in the library that's disguised as a book. I'll send Oscar to your quarters with it then you can hide it within plain sight of everyone. Nobody will think of looking for it there.'

She gave a short laugh. 'Thank you, Mr Leighton. I like you much better than Reverend Pawley.'

'I like me much better than the reverend, too. I'm pleased to have been of use. The key to my former wife's room is also on the table. I'd prefer it if you kept it safely with you, since I've mislaid mine.'

'I'll keep the key in the box as well . . . and I'll keep a lookout for your key, sir.'

'You won't find it here, it's somewhere in my London home. I'm not usually careless, but I suppose it will turn up before too long. I'll be going back to London in two weeks' time.'

'Oh, I'm sorry to hear that.'

'Are you? Why?'

'It's been nice having you here. It made me feel as though I'm earning my keep.'

'I'm quite sure you *have* earned it. But I'll be back in time for Christmas.'

'Do you ever invite your friends to stay?'

He chuckled at that. 'I have plenty of opportunities to socialize with them in London. I enjoy the peace and quiet here.'

'May I ask you something?'

'Oh dear, the caution in your voice tells me I might not like the question.' Laughter came into his voice. 'You're not going to propose marriage to me, are you?'

'*Mr Leighton!* That would be most unseemly, besides, I don't like you *that* much.'

'In consideration of your planned spinsterhood it would be a contradiction on your part, too. I'd also have to decline, since I have no inclination to take a wife at the moment, especially one young enough to be my daughter. State what's on your mind then, Sara. I can always tell you to mind your own business.'

'You said it was your fault that your wife died.'

'I said I'd killed her.'

'Yes.'

'And you want to know what happened, I suppose?'

'I know there was an accident. How was that your fault?'

He drew in a breath. 'We entertained guests that weekend. One was her *admirer*, and they were closer than they should have been. Diana liked going to the theatre and balls. She insisted on going back to London with them. I was angry, but I drove her to the station — too fast. There was the sound of a shot, someone game shooting, I suppose. They didn't succeed since a deer sprang out of the hedge in front of us, the horse panicked and I couldn't hold it. We went over a stump, the wheel sprung and we were tossed out. We both hit our heads on the same log. You know the result. If I hadn't been driving so fast she'd still be alive.

'Thank God Freddie turned up when he did . . . he'd left something at the house,' he said.

Sara curbed her instinct to place her hand over his. 'How long ago was it?'

'Nearly five years.'

'Isn't it about time you forgave yourself?'

'That's easier said than done. Enough of your prodding now, Sara.'

'May I say something else?'

'No, you may not. I will now exert my authority to tell you that this conversation is at an end. Go and do something housekeeperly.' His hand jerked as he picked up the plate. The apple pies slid off the plate and into the napkin on his lap.

'Damn and blast it!' she said, before he could.

'You're a plague, Sara Finn.' He burst out laughing.

When she got back to her quarters she placed the key back on its hook, and Mr Leighton didn't ask her for it in the time remaining before he left for London.

'The master stayed longer than he usually does,' Maggie said as they watched the cart head off for the station.

'Mr Leighton said he's going to spend Christmas here.'

'He was in a good mood with himself this time. Perhaps he's beginning to get over her.'

'He told me he had an argument with her on the day she died.'

'Aye, the poor man. She wouldn't settle to marriage. She married him for his money, and a generous man he was too. He gave her everything she wanted, and got nothing in return.'

'I expect he'll meet someone else to love eventually. He's a handsome man.'

'But he's blind, so he can't do much.'

'That wouldn't matter to a woman who truly loves him.'

'It'll matter to him, you mark my words. I'm surprised that Mr Frederick and Miss Milson didn't visit while he was down here.'

'Perhaps they didn't know he was here.'

'Likely he didn't tell them, since he finds their chatter tedious. I can't say I like the pair of them much, so I won't miss them.'

'Why don't you like them?'

'I don't know, it's a feeling I have about them. You'd best keep an eye on them if they do come. I don't trust them, and neither did Mrs Cornwell.'

Sara and Fanny stripped the beds. They cleaned the rooms, aired them, then scattered lavender bags about the room before covering over the mattresses and chairs with the dustsheets.

Outside, autumn had set in with a fiery display. Leaves twisted and fluttered through the air in shades of orange, red and brown. Baskets of fruit were brought in from the orchard. Some were stored and some became conserves. The bottles lined the larder shelves like soldiers standing to attention, ready for use in the lean months.

There was very little to do in the house, but Sara had a plan. She went to see Joseph Tunney. 'I have an idea, Joseph.'

'Have you now, Miss Finn?'

'You know how Mr Leighton sits and looks out the window, and never goes out until Oscar takes him?'

'That I do.'

'What if we made him a path where he could safely walk by himself?'

'I don't understand, Miss Finn. How can he walk by himself if he can't see where he's going?'

'Easy. We could put in some posts with a guide rope going from one to another. All he'll have to do is keep his hand on the rope. It could go around the front meadow to the oak tree, visit all the flower beds, then take him around the side and the back of the house to the walled gardens, where he can sit and listen to the birds in summer if he wants.'

'Or he can go in the other direction to where the loop ends, and go straight to the back,' Joseph said, looking thoughtful.

'Mr Leighton could even have his own garden patch to keep him occupied. Something that smells or tastes nice. Herbs, perhaps, or flowers.'

'Or both,' he suggested. 'He used to take an interest in the garden when he had his sight.'

Unrolling a piece of paper she handed it to him. 'See, I've worked out this plan. What do you think of it?'

Joseph smiled as he looked at it. 'That's a good plan, right enough.'

'Can we get the walk done in time for Christmas?'

He nodded. 'I'll measure it and work out how many posts and how much rope we'll need. Giles will take the list in and buy the materials on the account. You can dig the holes for the posts, seeing as you've got it all planned and know where they're going to go.'

She experienced doubt. 'I've never dug any holes before, and I'm not very good at measuring, but I'll try.'

The gardener cackled with laughter. 'I was only teasing, Miss. Digging holes is no job for a sweet little lady like you. The good Lord blessed Giles with strength for this very purpose.'

Within a fortnight the garden had grown a series of posts rooted in cement. Metal rings were screwed to them and a rope threaded through. Tying a scarf around her eyes Sara closed them for good measure and carefully made her way around the rope loop holding on with one hand. After five minutes she stumbled and let the rope go. It jerked away from her, and, although she groped around she couldn't find it again.

She began to realize the difficulties Mr Leighton had to face and was nearly in tears when she pulled off the scarf and said to Joseph, 'I don't think this will work as well as I thought.'

'Aye, it will, Miss. It's a good idea and I don't know why we didn't think of it before. Remember, Mr Leighton is used to being in the darkness now and is careful of his step. You're not.' He began to undo the knots holding the lengths of rope in place.

'I hope I never will be. Why are you taking the rope down?'

'It will rot quicker if it's left out in the weather when it's not in use. We'll put it back up when he comes. It will be a nice surprise for him. Giles thought it might be a good idea if he made some little signs with pointing arrows to hang on the posts, too, so Mr Leighton will know where he is, didn't you, Giles?'

The lad smiled. 'We'll put "front door" on the one here. Then one at the gate.'

'But how will he read it?'

'Easy. We'll write it on the wood and Giles will carve round the marks. The master can trace around them with his fingers and spell them out.'

'What a wonderful idea, Giles.'

'Aye, I reckon he can be proud of himself for thinking that one up. Mayhap you could help him with the letters. He hasn't got much learning. He came from a big family, see, and his ma and pa didn't get around to sending him to school.'

Giles blushed. 'Pa reckoned I was too big and soft in the head to get any learning inside me.'

'You're not daft, Giles. You just haven't been taught. We've got plenty of time on our hands when Mr Leighton is absent. I could teach you to read and write if you'd like. Could you spare him for two hours a day, Mr Tunney?'

'Reckon he could get up an hour or so early to see to the horse and clean the stable. Teaching him to write would be kind of you, Miss.'

'Very well. Starting from Monday I'll have a school in my sitting room from ten a.m. until noon during the week. We'll see how you get on.'

Sara was pleased when Maggie approached her on behalf of Fanny, who also couldn't read or write. 'She's too shy to ask, and she'll work ever so hard, won't you Fanny, love?'

Fanny nodded.

Despite the hardship in her life, perhaps she'd been lucky to have received some education, else she would have ended up like Fanny and Giles, Sara thought. She found Mr Leighton's library to be a treasure trove. He'd gone in there sometimes and he'd run his fingers gently over the spines of the books, tracing the gold leaf as if he was trying to read them with his fingers.

The pair was eager to learn, and Giles soon managed to write out the alphabet in a discernible hand. His eyes gleamed, as if he thought that his pa's dismissal of his abilities might be wrong. By the end of the first month Giles could write his name reasonably well. He could recite the alphabet too, and he knew his vowel sounds.

'Good. Now Giles, let's see if you can write down some words.'

He gazed expectantly at her, chalk poised over the slate like a dog eager for a run.

She laughed. 'It's not going to be that easy. I want you to go into the garden for ten minutes and write down the things you see.'

'What things, Miss?'

'Anything . . . grass, sky, earth, leaf . . .'

'But how will I know which letters to use?'

'You'll know when you sound them out. Try it.'

She turned to Fanny after he'd gone. The girl's tongue circled her mouth as she laboriously struggled with her letters. She sat oddly with her left arm held behind her back. Fanny gazed up at her, smiling, as though happy with the thought that she was learning something. She didn't retain information as easily as Giles.

'You know, Fanny. You might find it easier to write if you held your chalk in a different way and put your other arm on the desk.'

'I'm not allowed to use my other hand else you'll cane me, Miss.'

Puzzled, Sara gazed at her, realizing what was wrong. A painful memory came to her of the workhouse schoolroom, and of children with their hands tied behind their backs! 'Do you find it easier to use your other hand?'

'Yes, Miss.' She hung her head.

'There's nothing shameful about writing with your left hand. I want you to put the chalk in your other hand so I can see how well you write your name with it.'

It wasn't a perfect solution because the side of her hand rubbed across the letters she'd written and smudged them, and it also looked awkward. But Fanny wrote faster, and the letters had more form to them, and once she graduated to a pencil it wouldn't smudge.

'That looks good, Fanny, well done. You're making good progress.'

Fanny smiled proudly at the praise.

A week later, Giles's sweetheart joined them. Jassy Bennett was a buxom lass with round rosy cheeks covered in freckles, hazel eyes and a ready smile. 'Pa said I can come to school as long as he doesn't have to pay anything.'

The glory that was September and October passed into a still, grey November with misty mornings that smelled of bonfires.

A message arrived from Oscar saying that he'd be bringing the master down halfway through November, and they'd stay until after Christmas. Fanny put an extra shine on the furniture, Sara went through menus with Maggie and placed bowls of the fragrant pot-pourri she'd made in the summer around the house. The guide rope was threaded through the new walk and Sara went into Taunton to order the extra provisions they'd need, and to arrange for their delivery and the winter supply of coal for the fires. She also bought some small Christmas gifts.

Giles left Sara at the crossroads since he was visiting the farmer to pick up a flitch of bacon, and to take the opportunity to visit Jassy at the same time.

'Tell the farmer that we'll need an extra jug of milk every day, and tell Jassy there will be no more lessons until Mr Leighton has returned to London. Tell her she should keep practising with the chalk on her slate,' she called out, as he headed towards the farm.

Her basket over her arm, and wrapped warmly in her grey, hooded cloak Sara enjoyed the walk. She enjoyed even more the sight of the house through the bare branches of the trees, and the smoke trickling from the chimneys. She didn't think much about family because sometimes it hurt inside to remember things that she didn't want to, like never feeling as though anyone had ever loved her . . . like the pain of the physical beatings and the hunger.

But there was a feeling inside her sometimes, of something different waiting for her . . . something better in the future, an adventure perhaps, and it was like a voice blowing on the wind. She held her hand against the flow of the air and felt the tingle of it in her palm and the excitement in her belly. But when she slowly closed her fingers over it she felt it all trickle away out of her reach.

Deep in thought, she didn't notice the trouble waiting for her as she rounded the bend in the drive – until a menacing growl brought her back to the present.

In her path stood a rough-coated brindle lurcher, its teeth bared in a snarl, its neck fur hackled up into spikes as if it was wearing a collar of hedgehogs.

She stopped, holding her basket in front of her in defence, and said nervously, 'Good dog.' Not taking her eyes from the dog she edged round it and backed up the drive. The dog followed her, keeping its distance. When she got to the open space she ducked under the rope, intending to cut across the lawn.

A series of rattling growls and her nerve broke. She began to run. In the corner of her eye a second dog appeared from the shadow of the porch and joined in the hunt. The oak tree! She veered right and picked up speed. As she was about to leap on to the seat, teeth sank into her boot and brought her down. When its teeth penetrated the leather, she screamed and lashed out with her basket. The dog abandoned her foot and joined the other one in worrying the hem of her cloak between them.

There was a yelp as she connected with one of the dogs. Loosening the strings on her cloak she let it fall then scrambled on to the seat and pulled herself up into the safety of the lower limbs of the oak. The two dogs leaped up at her from the seat, their snarls ferocious. When they realized they couldn't reach her, they lost interest, took her cloak between them and dragged it around the garden, snarling and tearing it to shreds on the thorns of the rose bushes in the process.

'Freddie. Call them off,' a woman shouted.

There came a shrill whistle from the side of the house and the dogs' ears pricked up. They disappeared off towards the copse, dragging the cloak between them. Keeping a cautious eye out, Sara scrambled down from the tree, picked up her scattered things and limped over towards the door as fast as she could.

The woman who'd called out was in the porch. She was a year or so older than herself, taller, and with pale-blue eyes and light-brown hair. She stepped out of the shadows to bar her way. 'Who are you?'

'I'm Sara Finn, the housekeeper, and you are . . . ?' Sara already had a good idea who the female was, and her words confirmed it.

'I'm Miss Milson, Mr Leighton's niece.' Sara was subjected to a hard stare. 'My uncle must be out of his mind to hire somebody as young as you.'

'I expect Mr Leighton knows his own business best, don't you? Excuse me, Miss Milson, I need to tidy myself up. Do you know who those dogs belong to?' Of course she did.

Miss Milson gave a light laugh. 'They're Freddie's dogs. He's my brother.'

'They've ripped my cloak to shreds.'

'Oh, don't be so stuffy. We were just having fun; we thought you were Fanny.'

When Sara went to walk round her Jane Milson moved in front of her.

'Excuse me,' Sara said, 'I need to go indoors.'

A hand came down on her arm, fingers hooked like claws. 'There *is* a servants' entrance, Miss Finn, so I suggest you use it.'

Tight-lipped, Sara shrugged the arm away, turned and hurried round the side of the house. She nearly bumped into a man coming in the opposite direction. The dogs sprang at her and he spoke gruffly to them. They sat instantly, but though they were leashed and couldn't reach her she gave a strangled scream.

She didn't have to wait for the man to introduce himself. He was too much like Miss Milson to be anyone else but her brother. He had the remains of Sara's cloak over his arm. 'Is this yours?'

'Yes it is mine, and it's ruined.'

He shrugged. 'It's only a cheap rag.'

'It wasn't a rag before your dogs got hold of it. It was those dogs who attacked me, and from now on I'd be obliged if you kept them under control.'

'You're a saucy little madam for a servant.' His smile was a well-honed sneer. 'Do you know who I am? I'm Frederick Milson.'

He was chubbier in the face than his sister. His eyes had a slightly bulbous look, like a frog. 'Yes, I do know. I'm Sara Finn, the new housekeeper.'

He scrutinized her for a few moments then grazed his finger gently down her cheek. 'My uncle always appreciated a pretty female; it's a pity he can't see you.'

Taking a step back she glared at him.

'Oh dear, so you're keeping yourself for marriage, are you?'

She blushed. 'I don't know what you mean.'

'I'm sure you do.' He huffed out a breath. 'You don't know what you're missing. If you change your mind let me know, I'll make it worth your while.'

'Get out of my way, you . . . *creature!*'

He stepped aside, laughing. 'Sorry that the dogs gave you a

fright. They'll be all right when they get to know you.' He took her by the wrist and, although she resisted, he didn't loosen his grip. 'Oh, do behave, girl. I'm not going to hurt you. I'm going to introduce you to my dogs.'

When she relaxed he said, 'Bunch your fist . . . good . . . now allow them to smell your hand . . . pat them.' He let go of her hand.

She was tempted to swing her arm round and give him a good slap. As if he sensed it, he said, 'Don't be aggressive towards me, as they can smell it. And they can also smell fear.'

She saw the sense in being on friendly terms with the dogs. As for their master, he could go and eat mud! After a moment or two of caution the dogs wagged their tails and vied with each other for more pats.

He handed her the remains of her cloak. 'Don't worry, girl, I'll make sure your cloak is replaced.'

'Thank you. Excuse me now. I need to tidy myself up.'

Stepping aside he bowed slightly, his eyes glittering when he allowed his gaze to linger on her breasts. He smiled when she clutched her tattered cape against her bodice. 'My pleasure, my dear.'

It was a relief to get away from him. When she entered the kitchen, Maggie's lips tightened. 'I imagine you've just met Mr Frederick Milson and his sister? They came bowling up in the station cab about an hour ago. What did you think of them?'

She managed a wry smile.

'Well, all I can say is, thank goodness the master will be arriving tomorrow.'

Six

> *Dear Mr Chapman,*
> *We met recently at the opening of the Thornton emporium. I'm acquainted with your delightful sister, Miss Chapman, who was a gracious guest at an afternoon tea hosted by my sister and me.*
>
> *Yesterday, I came across a small notice in the local paper requesting information about a certain infant who was left at a certain orphanage on a certain day, and mentioning a certain reward. I would be grateful if you would keep the following information confidential.*

Adam winced. Did Lucy Stanhope need to dramatize her prose by the use of verbal dittos?

Celia smiled at him and raised an eyebrow.

'Lucy Stanhope is being a bloodhound,' he told her, and dabbed his mouth with a napkin.

'Ah, one of the dreaded gossip sisters,' Celia said with a grimace.

'Hush, Celia. How can you be so mean about them when they inform me that you're a gracious and delightful creature.'

Celia grinned at him. 'That was a state that was unbelievably difficult to achieve and maintain at the time, believe me. Does Miss Lucy have any information? As I told you, her sister was reluctant to say anything, though they were as nervous as hens and you could see they were dying to lay their eggs and cluck loudly.' She sighed. 'Failing to get them to talk proved to me that my detecting abilities are without merit at present.'

'Marianne was of the opinion that it was because her husband had put Agnes and Lucy Stanhope firmly in their place, and had been rather forceful about it.'

'What does the woman have to say for herself?'

Adam quickly read the rest of the letter, then his eyes sharpened. 'Apart from what we already know, she says that when Constance Jarvis was taken ill and it became apparent that she wouldn't survive, her coachman and his wife moved to a farm in Gloucester. She writes: *They already had two children of their own, a girl and a boy. But a former maid who visited her there told Lucy that she saw two girls living with them, and they were of a similar age.'* Taking his eyes from the words he gazed up at her, smiling. 'This is progress, something you paved the way for since your presence at their tea party gave them the means to approach me.'

'Perhaps the person who told Lucy Stanhope made a mistake.'

'You mean the maid might have been cross-eyed and saw the same girl twice?' He laughed. 'That's possible, but not many people are unable to count past two. The maid also told her that the girl looked like Constance Jarvis's young ward. The couple denied it though, saying she was their niece.'

'Isn't it possible that she *was* their niece?' Celia laughed when she saw the gleam in her brother's eyes. 'I can see that the letter has piqued your interest, since your nose is twitching, as Marianne once pointed out. Out with it then, Adam.'

'It was rumoured that the farm was bought with a legacy from Miss Jarvis. She believes the place was called Tumblesham, and it was situated in the Forest of Dean area.'

'Are you going there?'

'I most certainly am. You can handle the office for a short while, and if you can't, you have plenty of competent help at hand. I shouldn't be more than three days.'

'What was the name of the coachman; did Miss Lucy say?'

'Christopher Fenn. His wife was called Emmy.'

'Don't forget Edgar Wyvern wants to talk to you. He's coming over for dinner tonight.'

'I haven't forgotten. I won't be leaving until the morning, anyway.'

They exchanged a smile, both of them with the same thought, that it was slightly strange that their mother's swain should seek the blessing of her son, who was less than half his age.

But Adam's interview with Edgar Wyvern turned out to be more illuminating than that.

After dinner the older man, who was a distinguished barrister of fifty years, retired to the front room with Adam. Sipping at his brandy he said, 'You know that I hold your mother in great affection and esteem, Adam.'

'Indeed I do.'

'Then you wouldn't put any objection forward if we married?'

'Of course not, Edgar. And I speak for my sister, as well. We both want our mother to be happy.'

'I'm sure I can support your mother in a manner that she'd enjoy and appreciate. Your sister as well, if she'd care to come and live with us. She would socialise with many more people, which would give her a chance to meet a suitor, if that's her wish.'

Adam offered him a faint smile. 'That will be for Celia to decide, since she is of age. But my sister enjoys a quiet life, and I think she's reconciled herself to spinsterhood, and being useful by working and earning a living for herself.'

'I'm not advocating that we marry her off to the first man who takes an interest in her, nor abandon her need to be usefully employed. But rather, that she moves in an environment where she can meet people in a more social atmosphere. I entertain often, as you will discover.'

Adam remembered Celia's laugh ringing out when she'd been with Marianne Thornton. Perhaps his sister did need friends of her own age. It was not up to him to say what she did and didn't need. It was entirely possible that she'd enjoy having a home and family to look after. He brought his mind back to what Edgar was saying.

'That would leave you free to conduct your own life in the manner a young man should, without the added responsibility of providing both moral and financial support for your sister.'

'I enjoy Celia's company. Have you talked to my mother about this?'

'Your mother agrees with me. Much as she loves and trusts you, she would prefer to have her daughter living under her own roof. I believe she intends to talk to your sister while we're absent.'

'I see.' How quickly the course of a life could change through the intervention of another. The thought of going back home to an empty house every evening was suddenly uninviting. 'Celia will do as our mother asks, of course. I'll miss her if she leaves though; my sister is a good companion.'

'Because I've sprung this on you rather suddenly I do have a solution to offer you.'

'You usually do, Edgar,' Adam said with a chuckle. 'I've never met anyone so thorough, or so well prepared for a discussion. I envy you.'

'Your own skills of reasoning are to be admired.'

'Let me hear your solution then.'

'Lease your property here in Chiswick to a suitable family, and take up gentlemen's rooms in central London, which will be more convenient for you since they'll be serviced.'

'I suppose you already have one in mind.'

Edgar chuckled.

'If you take up my offer, I'll then be able to introduce you to my club. As my principal heir it wouldn't hurt you to make the right sort of contacts, and a gentleman of your age has his own needs and liaisons to consider.'

Adam's liaisons in the past had been few and far between, due to the fact that his available funds were used for necessities rather than pleasure. There was also a lack of privacy to consider. Something suddenly registered on Adam's brain and his jaw nearly dropped open. What had Edgar said? Had he heard it correctly? 'I think I misunderstood you, Edgar.'

Edgar grinned. 'About the liaisons or the fact that I intend to make you my heir?'

'Since I'm quite able to handle any of the former which may come my way . . . that leaves only the latter.'

'You didn't misunderstand. I have no kin of my own except for an elderly uncle, who at the age of ninety-two has already outlived his two offspring. As my stepson you'll be named as my heir. I also intend to provide for Celia, and should she marry or not, there will be a trust fund she can draw an income from so she has some degree of independence where finances are concerned.'

'Did my mother—?'

'I haven't discussed my finances or plans with Florence or Celia, so neither has been informed as yet. I'd rather it was kept confidential between us for the time being, Adam. Rest assured, if anything happens to me your mother will be well taken care of.'

Adam took a sip of his brandy then shook his head, which was in a state of turmoil. 'I don't know what to say, Edgar. You've been exceedingly generous and I thank you.'

'You're a fine young man, Adam; your father would have been proud of you.' Edgar downed his brandy, rose to his feet then held out his hand. 'Let's shake on it, then go and join the ladies.'

Adam's mother was out of her mourning dress now, and was gowned in a sweeping silver-grey watered taffeta, the delicate lace collar secured by a gold brooch, its central garnet seated in small pearls. Just turned forty-five, Florence Chapman had a fine complexion. Her blue eyes were clear, her hair mid-brown. She was a handsome woman, but there was an anxious look in her eyes.

Did she really imagine he'd object to her marrying Edgar? Tenderness filled his heart and he crossed to where she sat, kissing her on both cheeks when he got there. 'Congratulations, mother dear.'

'Oh dear, I thought you would mind, Adam.'

'Why should I mind when your happiness is so dear to me? Celia, are you happy with the arrangement? I'm quite happy to continue to provide for you.'

Celia smiled and nodded. 'Perfectly. It's about time you had a life of your own, dear brother, and I'll see you at the office on most days. Besides, if you're more central, mother and I will be able to see you any time we wish.'

Odd, the rapport he had with his sister, something that had been there since he could remember. They'd always understood each other and today was no exception.

'When is the wedding to be?' he asked.

'On Saturday the twenty-eighth January,' Edgar said calmly. 'That should give us time to make the necessary adjustments in our lives.'

The following day Adam found himself in Gloucester. The countryside itself was overwhelmingly majestic, the hills dressed in various shades of rich green. The forest had a misty, mysterious appearance, reminding him of an illustration from one of his childhood books. He wouldn't have been surprised if knights in shining armour and dragons with fiery breath emerged from the dark interior to challenge him.

Instead, there were sheep grazing everywhere, watched over by shepherds and their dogs. Dredging through his mind for trivial information, Adam recalled that people born within the hundred of St Braivels had the right to graze their pigs and sheep in the Forest of Dean – a hundred being a geographic division. The term was a little cloudy though, since it was also applied to the ability to supply one hundred men at arms, or that the land was able to sustain one hundred families.

The day was cold, the air heavy with mist and the foliage dripped with water that clung to his coat and hat. The afternoon would darken early and the country with its craggy hills, twisting lanes and the broad sweep of the Severn and its tributaries would easily have swallowed him, had he not hired someone with local knowledge.

'How did you get the name of Ham?' he asked his guide.

'Short for handsome, it be,' the man said with a throaty laugh, and Adam smiled, for Ham Thomas was far from handsome. He was almost colourless, stocky, with thin yellow hair, a wide nose and thick, fleshy lips. Lushly broad of vowel, he'd seemed eager to earn himself a shilling or two.

'The rig is only used for funerals and weddings, and we haven't got none of them today, though Annie Parkins has got a loaf in the oven if you asks me, so she'll be taking that man of hers up the aisle before long. Tumblesham Farm, be it, sir?' He scratched his head. 'What would you be wanting with that sour old bugger, Tyler Fenn, then?'

Adam's ears pricked up. At least one of the Fenn family still lived there. 'You know him, do you?'

'Since he first come here, when I was a lad. Let me warn you, sir, he'd sell his own daughter for a shilling if he had one.'

Adam took note of that and employed a little subterfuge. 'I understood Mr Fenn had two daughters and a son.'

'No, that were Christopher Fenn and his family before him. Hard-working enough, but they never could make a go of that place. They didn't know farming, see. Cholera took them all off not long after the present owner come to stay.'

It sounded to Adam as if his quest was over before it had started, but he knew better than to take such statements at face value.

Ham kept on gossiping as they plodded up a steep hill. 'Place is run-down now . . . you won't mind if I stay outside will you, the place fair creeps me out . . .'

Tumblesham Farm certainly was run-down, but it could be brought up to scratch with a little work. The farm consisted of a two-storey building built of local stone, with a slate roof. A barn and a couple of outbuildings stood to one side. It looked abandoned, cold and grey. The stone was damp with mildew near to the ground. Small, dirty windows gazed blindly over the long clumped grass, and a mud patch barred their way.

Adam shivered. He was just beginning to wonder if he was wasting his time when he saw a scribble of smoke issuing from one of the chimneys.

'I'll turn the horse round in case we need to make a quick retreat, then I'll join you, sir. I doubt if you'll be long unless you have something in your pocket for Fenn to profit from. And if you have, keep your hand on it.'

Ham was right. Fenn, a powerfully built man, opened the door to his knock and gazed at him, his face surly. 'What is it you want?'

Adam didn't bother with any niceties. 'I'm looking for a girl who used to live here with Christopher and Emmy Fenn.'

The man stared at him, his eyes all at once wary. 'What's that to do with you?'

'They were your relatives, were they not?'

'Doesn't mean to say I knew them.'

'I've been told that you moved in with them.'

'If it's any of your business I came to help with the farm at my cousin's request. They died not long after, and they was taken away and buried. Cost me a pretty penny, it did, but I inherited the farm, all clear and above board, me being the only relative.'

'Did all three of the children die?'

His eyes shifted sideways and he shrugged. 'I reckon there was only two kids in the family, mister. One of them were a lad, the other were a female. They were skinny, sickly brats.'

'I didn't suggest there were more kin, but rather that there was an orphan child in their care. Think carefully, Mr Fenn . . . the second girl was about twelve years of age.'

A thin woman of about thirty with stringy hair stuck her head round the door and said, 'Who is it, Tyler?'

'Mind your own bleddy business and get inside,' he snarled.

Fenn turned, and was about to follow her when Adam said, 'I'm acting on behalf of relatives . . . there's a reward for information leading to her whereabouts.'

The man chewed the inside of his cheek as he contemplated him, then he said, 'How much is the reward?'

Adam lowered his initial figure to a quarter of the amount, simply because he didn't like the man. 'A pound.'

Fenn nodded. 'Come to think on it there was another girl here, a dirty, ragged little brat . . . a servant, she were.'

When Fenn paused, Adam asked him, 'What happened to her?'

The man cupped his ear. 'How much did you say that reward was?'

'It depends if the information I'm given has enough truth in it for me to regard it as plausible.'

Fenn's voice rose, and Adam was relieved when he saw Ham edge into his side vision. 'Calling me a liar, are you?'

'No . . . are you one?'

When the man's attitude became pugnacious Adam knew he risked getting his nose flattened. He'd be sorry if he did because it was a rather handsome nose, or so his mother had told him. He was not a coward, but he was not the type of man who employed brute strength to settle an argument either, unless his back was to the wall. He'd rather use his wits.

'Just for that I want double what you're offering. And I'll want it up front before you get anything out of me, mister. Take it or leave it.'

Adam was quite happy to take it, though he didn't show it. He took the money out, kept a firm grip on it and sent the man a look of enquiry. 'Well?'

The aggrieved Fenn said, 'That girl weren't my responsibility, and I didn't want the brat hanging around here calling the place home and pretending she was my relative when she wasn't. But I made sure she was all right. I took her over to Wiltshire and left her on the doorstep of Northfield workhouse at Yatesbury.'

Adam placed the reward money in the man's hand and it disappeared into his pocket. When Fenn spat on his hands Ham loudly cleared his throat and Fenn's sour glance went to the younger man. Ham, who was of similar size but considerably younger and fitter, was now slapping a stout stick against his palm.

Fenn's nostrils flared as he sucked in a breath. 'And that's all you're getting out of me, so bugger off the pair of you, and don't come back unless you want an arse full of buckshot!' The door slammed in Adam's face and the bolt was shot.

Far from being annoyed, Adam smiled as he navigated the mud puddle back to the road with Ham in tow. Fenn had delivered a useful mouthful for his money, and now there was an unexpected and interesting twist to the puzzle. Which of the two females had survived, the Fenn girl or the unfortunate daughter of Erasmus Thornton?

'I thought Fenn were going to hit you, sir,' Ham said.

'So did I. Thank you for standing at my side.'

'Oh, I wasn't willing to fetch mesself a clout on the beak from Fenn. I just reckoned you might need someone to carry you out of there.'

Adam grinned when Ham cackled with laughter. 'Do you know where the Northfield workhouse is in Wiltshire?'

'Reckon I do.' He gazed at the lowering sky in a calculating manner. ''Tis best for the nag if we go in the morning, sir. It's quite a step, and this mist will only get thicker. Fancy's willing, but her old bones do ache in this weather unless she's tucked in her stall early . . . isn't that right, my sweetheart?'

The horse turned her head, tossed her head and flapped her whiskery lips at him.

'There, didn't I tell you, sir. I reckon my mam can give you a meal and a bed for the night. She'd be right happy to have a visitor, though she doesn't say much.'

Just to make sure that the Fenn in residence had been telling him the truth, they stopped to visit the grave of the former Fenn family on the way home. They lay in the same grave. Christopher. Emily. Jeffrey and Mary, aged eleven and twelve. The grave saddened him.

Ham's mam greeted him with a toothy grin, and her pleasure at the unusual event was evident in the tuneless song she sang as she hurried around him, laying out her best bits of china and lace for his use.

A small girl was tucked up on the day bed, her cheeks flushed. 'My mam's looking after her for my sister. It's nothing much. The doctor said she's got a rash, but it isn't much of one and she'll be better in a day or two. My niece's name be Annie, ain't it my darlin'?'

She had fair curls. 'Hello, Annie,' he said giving her a smile.

The child gazed shyly at him and whispered, 'Hello.' The rash she had was barely discernable.

Mother Thomas's hospitality was boundless. In her spotlessly clean and aromatic cottage, Adam's stomach was filled with lamb stew and dumplings, followed by a huge slice of pie brimming with apples and covered in creamy blobs of custard.

He went to bed in the whitewashed upstairs room, where apples on the windowsill were lined up in an orderly row. He had to bend his head if he wanted to stand upright, lest he crack his head on a beam.

He tried to imagine his own mother being so hospitable with so few conveniences, and couldn't. His mother would consider this tiny cottage little more than a hovel . . . and Ham's mother, who was prematurely aged from a life of hard work, her social opposite. Which of course, she was. But Ham's mother was a sweet, generous woman all the same, and Adam felt comfortable in her home, and glad that the world was filled with people like her and her son. Groaning with food he fell asleep instantly.

They left at dawn the next day. The morning was crisp with frost, and the high roof of the sky gradually brightened into pink and gold stripes before fading into blue and white stipples. They took with them a basket containing a breakfast of ham, boiled eggs, cheese and a hunk of newly baked bread.

Ham and his mother had been agreeable hosts who found pleasure in the simple things of life. Adam was sorry to part with Ham, though he compensated him handsomely for both his and his mother's services. He bought a rag doll for Ham to take home for Annie, before he watched horse and cart plod off back towards home.

At the workhouse he learned that a girl called Sara Finn had been left on the doorstep. They had kept her for two years. Then Reverend Pawley, who'd been responsible for the spiritual welfare of the inmates, had been offered a parish and needed a new governess and a maid of all work.

Elizabeth Agar, who worked in the schoolroom, had applied for the job. Elizabeth suggested that Sara Finn go with them, because she was a clever child who could help tutor the reverend's younger children in their letters.

'Are you sure Sara's surname was Finn, and not Fenn?' he asked the matron.

'It could have been Fenn, I suppose. Sometimes we have to take their word for it that they give us the right name, and we don't always spell them right. I've heard that Sara has moved on from there and has got a good position somewhere else. You should visit Elizabeth Agar, she'd know . . . though she's Mrs Pawley now. She married the reverend. He probably married her to save paying her wages after his wife passed on. He was always a mean old sod.'

Adam experienced relief that the young woman he sought had found a decent situation. He couldn't imagine what it was like being an orphaned child who was suddenly without friends or family.

Hiring a chestnut gelding he presented himself at the small manor house where the Reverend Pawley resided, and gave his card to the maid who opened the door.

Was this pale-faced little waif Serafina? No, she bore no resemblance to the Honeyman girls. Moreover, Serafina would be a young woman of eighteen by now, he reminded himself. This one was several years younger.

He was invited into the drawing room where a woman waited. 'My husband is not at home. I'm Elizabeth Pawley. Can I help you?'

So this was the woman who'd befriended Serafina in the workhouse. She was plainly dressed, and fair of face without being pretty. He smiled at her. 'I'm looking for a young woman called Sara Finn.'

Brown eyes engaged his. Her voice was low and cultured. 'Why are you looking for Sara?'

'I'm being hired to by a man who thinks he might be her father.'

She sucked in a breath. 'Only thinks . . . doesn't he know?'

'He's not sure.'

'He waited a long time to look for her.'

'Because he thought she was dead. The situation is too complicated to explain.'

'I would hate to see Sara hurt. What if it turns out that she
isn't his daughter?'

'I can't shield her from that sort of disappointment. She's
eighteen years old and will have to come to terms with it.' When
a doubtful look crossed Elizabeth Pawley's face, he said, 'What if
Sara *is* his daughter? Doesn't the very fact that I'm looking for
her suggest that there might be some truth in it?'

'Yes . . . of course.' She sighed. 'Sara left here after a disagreement with my husband. I gave her a good reference and she's
now working for a friend of an acquaintance of mine. It's a good
position as a housekeeper.' Crossing to a desk she took a piece
of paper, wrote down a name and address and handed it to him.

'She lives in Somerset. Leighton Manor is about two miles
past the railway station in Taunton, I understand.'

'Thank you, Mrs Pawley. If it will stop you worrying, at the
moment I'm just trying to establish the fact of who she is. I have
no intention of barging in on her. It might be several months
until contact can be made, because the man seeking her is away
at sea. There are other family members to consider too, so I'd be
obliged if you would keep this to yourself.'

She nodded.

'Oh, by the way, did you ever hear Miss Finn refer to herself
as Serafina?'

Elizabeth Pawley's only reaction was genuine puzzlement. 'No,
never.' She shrugged then said hesitantly, 'What are they like . . .
her family?'

'Why do you ask?'

'Sara was different to most girls who were in the workhouse.
Although she was poorly dressed, she'd had an early education
which had formed her manner of speaking, and which had given
her a thirst for knowledge. She had a good mind, one that retained
everything she read.'

'Sara remembered being educated early in life?'

'She didn't have to. You can always tell when somebody has
absorbed the basic learning skills. They are a joy to teach since
they tend to be more curious about things. They're also more confident with letters and numbers, and able to think for themselves.

There was nothing missish about Sara Finn. She was a hard worker, straightforward and practical.' Elizabeth Pawley smiled. 'Sara had a fine intellect though, one that led her into debate inappropriately on occasion, since she often spoke without thinking.'

Charlotte and Marianne came to mind and Adam wanted to laugh. It sounded like a family trait. 'The families involved are in trade . . . her prospective father is in shipping.' Adam picked up his hat. 'I must go now. Would you like me to keep you informed of my progress?'

She gave a faint smile. 'That's kind of you, Mr Chapman, but there's really no need, and my husband wouldn't approve.'

'Oh . . . why is that?'

Mrs Pawley managed an amused chuckle. 'He doesn't think Sara is suitably grateful for his earlier patronage.'

'And is she?'

She smiled gently at him. 'I'm sure Sara will find a way to inform me should something out of the ordinary happen in her life. You don't have to worry that I'll repeat this conversation to her, either. I'd not like to see her hopes elevated, then come to nothing.'

Sara Finn must be a very special girl to have made a good friend like Elizabeth Pawley, Adam thought as he left.

He hesitated, because he'd woken up that morning with a slight dryness to his throat. Still, it was mild, and another day wouldn't make much difference. He must try and get a look at the girl while he was here. Taunton was not too far away, and another day or two could see his curiosity satisfied.

Seven

There was an atmosphere of tension in his house. Finch could smell it in the air, like smoke from a fire that barely smouldered but had not yet ignited.

He stood in the hall, listening. For what, he didn't know . . . the sound of a breath in a corner perhaps, a footfall on the stair or a creak of someone rising from a chair.

He was just about to relax when there came a crash from upstairs and a scream of anger. 'Take it away, you stupid fool! I asked for tea, not coffee. Now clean that mess up.'

Fanny's voice brayed with fright. 'There was no need to do that, Miss. You've broken it. I'll get into trouble.'

'It serves you right, and don't answer me back.' The sound of a vicious slap was followed by a yelp.

Someone was expelled in a rush from the door to the kitchen. Sara Finn, he thought, something confirmed when she whispered something that sounded suspiciously like '*nasty little witch!*' under her breath as she propelled herself past him, clad in a cloud of lavender polish. She was travelling fast and her footsteps changed to a whisper on the thick stair carpet.

Finch was about to wonder why she hadn't noticed him, when he realized that the clock had chimed a quarter past the hour just after he let himself in, and the hall would be in darkness.

Oscar was still outside fetching the luggage from the cab that had delivered them from the station, for they'd caught the afternoon train instead of the morning one. This time, at least, there had been no obstacle in the porch.

Finch followed after Sara up the stairs and towards the guest rooms.

Fanny's voice was thick with tears. 'I didn't throw it, Miss.'

Sara soothed the distressed maid. 'I know you didn't, Fanny. You go down and help Maggie in the kitchen. I'll clear up the mess.'

'I don't know what Mr Leighton will say . . . that was part of his best tea service.'

'I'll tell him that it wasn't your fault.'

There was a light laugh, followed by Frederick's voice. 'Are you suggesting that my sister threw it, that it's her fault?'

'I know what I heard, Mr Milson. There was no need to hit Fanny.'

'I'll slap you as well if you don't keep your place.'

Sara Finn said, and with a dramatic menace that made Finch smile involuntarily despite his annoyance, 'I'm not Fanny. Slap me and I'll slap you back.'

'Then you'll be dismissed without a reference.'

'Not when Mr Leighton learns the truth. He's a fair man.'

'Try and convince my uncle that Jane did anything wrong. He's not going to take a servant's word over ours.'

'Luckily I don't have to make that choice since I heard exactly what went on,' Finch said from the doorway. 'Thank you, Fanny . . . Sara. Both of you may go downstairs.'

'But the mess—'

'Will be picked up by the person who caused it in the first place. Jane, when you've done that, I expect to see you in my study. You too, Frederick.'

Fanny scuttled off and Sara followed her reluctantly, giving a faint, exasperated sigh. Finch gave a faint grin. She was bristling to do battle, and it must have been Sara he'd smelled burning. She would just have to smoulder while she waited her turn.

'Must I, Uncle?' Frederick drawled. 'Jane didn't mean anything by it.'

'I have no intention of discussing the matter further now. Five o'clock in my study, understood? It will give everyone time to cool down.'

'Oh God! We're much too old to suffer an official reprimand.'

'It's a pity you don't act it then.' He hardened his voice. 'Five o'clock in my study.'

Another smell wafted to his nostrils. 'Do you have those dogs up here? You know they're to be kept in the stables when you're not out walking with them. The last time you brought them I tripped over one and I nearly fell down the stairs.'

'We weren't expecting you until tomorrow, and they like company. You don't need to worry about tripping over them; they're not wandering free, they're in my room,' Freddie said.

'Stop arguing and take those dogs to the stables.'

Jane sighed. 'Goodness, such a fuss, Uncle. They'll only howl, and Aunt Diana would have allowed Freddie to keep them in the house.'

'Tunney will look after them. As for your aunt . . . she is dead, and has no say in the matter now. Get on and clean up that mess, please.'

'Sorry I spoke, I'm sure.' Her injured voice contained a sullen note. 'We're only passing through and I thought it would be nice to stop and visit our favourite uncle. Now I'm beginning to wonder whether it was worth it.' Jane began to pick up the shards of china. The pieces were dropped on the table with a clatter. 'There, it's done.'

'And the liquid?'

'Most of it went in the fire.' She heaved a sigh. 'Pass that piece of cloth, would you, Freddie?'

There came the sound of the tiles in the fireplace being wiped, then a hiss of steam as the wet cloth was thrown on top of the coals. The smell of singed coffee filled his nostrils as he left them and made his way to his own room.

The mess wouldn't have been cleaned up properly because Jane would have taken advantage of his lack of sight. And the only reason they visited at all was if they were short of cash.

The irresponsible pair came from an equally irresponsible mother. Diana's sister-in-law was a widow, and seemed to believe he was responsible for their welfare. He wasn't. Freddie and Jane were the late Diana's relatives, not his, and he was heartily sick of them disrupting his household. He didn't like the unfair way they'd treated Fanny, or Sara.

He had, in fact, discussed them with their mother while he was in London, and she'd agreed with the plan he'd come up with. He hadn't intended to mention it to the pair until the New Year had come in, but now they were here he'd bring it forward.

Back in his room, and Oscar was unpacking his bag. 'Is everything all right, Oscar?'

'All is in order, sir. Miss Finn is extremely efficient.'

Finch nodded and went downstairs to the study. Judging by the snap and crackle of kindling and the faint smell of smoke, the fire had recently been lit and the coal was just beginning to catch. As yet there was no warmth from it. Carefully, he reached out to where the lamp usually stood and felt the heat of it against his palm. Sara would have lit it when she'd lit the fire.

He remembered the room as having warm, reddish brown panelling. One wall was devoted to shelves of books embossed with rich gold lettering, on fine red, green and brown leather. He missed reading.

He edged around the room, refreshing his memory of it. His fingers slid along the polished edge of the desk, and touched against his initials carved under it. Further up were his father's initials, both sets carved there in a moment of defiance when they were boys. He'd stood in front of the desk many times, studying the bookcases and day-dreaming while his father, who'd done exactly the same in his time, lectured him on his short-comings.

On a couple of occasions he'd been hung over the back of the leather chair like an old coat while his rear end was flogged with a strap for his sins. A pity Frederick's father hadn't lived long enough to do the same for him, he thought. Frederick was right, though. They were far too old for an official reprimand.

Beyond the desk, five steps took him to the bookshelves. He took out a book, positioned his nose against the leather cover and drew in a breath. The book had a faint smell of brandy on it, as though the last person to handle it had left their own breath there. Himself perhaps.

He idly ran his finger over the indentations of the embossing. After a while he thought he could feel the outline of a letter. It was a capital *E*. He tried the next letter. It was harder, not so big. He stood his finger on edge and traced it round the embossing. It was a *b*. No, wrong way round. It was actually a *d*. Ten minutes later he tugged on the bell pull.

Before too long Sara Finn's footsteps tripped across the hall. 'Yes, sir.'

He handed her the book and said, 'What's this called?'

'*The Fall of the House of Usher* by Edgar Allan Poe. I have a volume of his poetry on my own bookshelf, a gift from Mrs Pawley. Do you want me to read this to you, sir?'

A small sense of triumph centred in him, one almost to the point of smugness. 'No, Sara. I love his work, and know the stories and poetry by heart. I read them when I was a boy. Pass me another book. I want to show you something.'

He concentrated as he slowly moved his nail round the indentations, murmuring the letters of the first word, before saying quickly, '*Two Years Before The Mast. Henry Dana.*'

'If you don't mind me saying, sir, you only touched on the first two words. You guessed the rest.'

He experienced a sense of disappointment. 'So I did. You know, Sara, you could have humoured me.'

'I could have told you what you wanted to hear, you mean. Would that have given you a greater sense of achievement when you realized your mistake for yourself?'

'I might not have.'

'You've got too much intelligence not to have missed the obvious.'

'Being unable to see frustrates me sometimes.'

'Me too, because there are so many things I'd like you to see. Maggie's new hat . . . the robin that comes down to the kitchen for scraps. You're missing so much and I'm sorry for that, but feeling pity for you won't help. If it did I'd sell it and make a fortune.'

She moved to the fire, placed a shovel of coal on it and gave it a few prods with the poker. An explosion of sparks crackled up the chimney, such a normal domestic sound, and he could almost see the brass poker and the leaping flames making the shadows on the wall dance. 'There, that's more cheerful. Is there anything I can get for you, Mr Leighton?'

'No, nothing, but you were right, you know. I am lucky in being able to see before I went blind. I've been remembering this room from when I was a boy.'

'I hope the memories were good ones.'

'Apart from having my backside tanned a couple of times, mostly I had a happy childhood. The odd thing is, Sara, in the years to come this room could be painted a different colour and the furniture could be refurbished, but I will always retain a memory of the same room. I've read most of the books on the shelves. The work of Edgar Allan Poe used to scare the wits out of me as well as fascinate me, and I used to go to bed with my head under my pillow. Is Diana's picture still on the wall in here?'

'I dusted it this morning.'

'She'll never grow old.'

'Because she no longer physically exists. All you have is a picture on the wall, one you can no longer see. It's only paint layered on a canvas. In time the portrait will crack and peel with age, and she'll look old because of it. The time will come when there won't be anyone left who remembers her, or even cares about her.'

It was surprising how detached from Diana's memory her words made him feel. 'That's something to ponder on. You surprise me sometimes, Sara.'

'I'm sorry, I shouldn't have said that . . . not to you, when I know how much you cared for her and blame yourself for her death.'

'No . . . you're right. That's exactly what will happen. I like your way of thinking; it has twists and turns in it that surprise me.'

To change the subject she said, 'We . . . the staff . . . have a surprise for you tomorrow if it's not raining.'

'What is it?'

She heaved a sigh. 'I'm not saying, and don't think to ask Oscar because he doesn't know what it is. You're to present yourself in the hall about eleven if you would, sir. Make sure you wear something warm.'

'Stop being a mother hen,' he said, and she laughed.

The hall clock began to chime. 'I'd better go, since you're expecting your relatives. I'm sorry I was rude to your niece and nephew. I'll apologize if you wish.'

'An apology would certainly be in order, I think. But not now, Sara, off you go, girl.'

As Finch expected, the Milson pair were childishly, and deliberately, late, but not late enough to anger him.

'Sit,' he said when Jane and Frederick came in. 'I talked to your mother while I was in London. Because I'm not willing to support the pair of you indefinitely, we have to come to a decision about your futures.'

'Surely that's for us to decide,' Frederick said, sounding bored.

'Not while you're living off my money. You might decide to indenture yourself to a profession suited to a gentleman, one that will support you in the future. Accountancy perhaps. As I recall you were good with figures. I know someone connected to the East India Company. I might be able to secure you a posting abroad as a clerk after you've trained. Or I'm willing to buy you a commission in the army.'

'But, sir. We have the allowance you pay us.'

'And we are your heirs, after all,' Jane said delicately.

'My heirs? Where did you get that idea from?'

'From Aunt Diana. She said, and mother said, that when you died . . . when she died . . .' Her voice became shrill. 'Well you have nobody else to leave it to, have you? Besides, Aunt Diana promised me I could have her jewellery. We are your only relatives, except for the Bishop, but he's old and has enough money of his own. Besides, you told Aunt Diana he didn't want it, and had in fact made you his heir.'

So Diana had made it her business to conspire with her ne'er-do-well family to manage his fortune. Much good it would do them now. 'It's true that the Bishop doesn't want it, but after the accident I decided to change my will. After deliberation, and unless something happens to change the course of my life, that's what will happen. I decided that the bulk of it would be better spent supporting a charity, and unless something happens to change that, it will.'

'What do you mean by that? Are you dying?' Jane asked him.

'Sorry to disappoint you, Jane, but no. It may not have occurred to you, but I may decide to marry again and a desirable outcome would be children of my own.'

'But it's not likely, is it? I mean, who would want you when you're—'

'Do be quiet, Jane,' Freddie said. 'Take no notice of her, sir. I'll certainly think about this for a while. I don't think I'm cut out for soldiering. The East India Company sounds promising though, and Jane can come and visit me when I'm settled somewhere.'

Jane said, 'Surely you don't expect me to work as well, Uncle. Doing what, pray? Should I follow the example of Florence Nightingale and take myself off to be trained to look after the sick?' She shuddered. 'Everyone is gossiping about the woman. I suppose you think that's a suitable profession for a young lady, to put herself at risk of catching a deadly infection.'

'Since you ask, I think such a profession is a calling, Jane, and that you lack the intelligence, the dedication or the altruism required to nurse the sick back to health. My suggestion is that you find yourself a husband as soon as possible. When you do, I'll settle ten thousand pounds on you.'

'A year?' she said, her avarice all too apparent to him.

'In total. If it's managed properly it will bring you an income.'

'Oh, how mean to give the bulk of your fortune to strangers,' she said, clearly disappointed, and going on to further display her greed. 'What about your homes? Are you going to leave one to mother? She was rather counting on it.'

'I see no reason why she should be, when her husband left her provided for.'

'Oh, mother was forced to mortgage it, and she couldn't pay the loan, so she sold it to the lender, and now leases it back. If you settled ten thousand on me now I could start my own business,' Frederick suggested.

'And watch you gamble it away. I think not, Frederick. But you'll get the same amount when you marry and settle down. Plan your futures carefully, since this is all you will get.' Even that was too much, and it would be worth it to get rid of them. 'Now I've made my intentions perfectly clear, Jane, you may go and apologize to Miss Finn, and to Fanny, as well. I don't want my staff upset. It makes for a bad atmosphere.'

'Oh, don't worry, Uncle, we'll be catching the morning train to London. We want to be in the capital for the Christmas season. We have invitations to balls and the theatre to attend. I did so hope I could persuade you to lend me some of Aunt Diana's jewellery for the season. There was a sapphire set that would go well with my new gown.'

'I think not, Jane. Off you go.'

Frederick lingered after Jane had gone. 'Uncle, could I prevail upon you to make me a small loan.'

'How small, Frederick?'

Frederick tossed the figure out casually, as if he thought Finch was used to carrying large sums with him. Like the other loans he'd made him, Frederick would never get around to paying it back. 'Oh, three hundred will do to carry me over to when my allowance is due. If I'm to work for a living I'll need a new suit.'

'When that time comes I'll have you outfitted with a new wardrobe. I will advance you one hundred pounds.'

'That will have to do then.'

There was no word of thanks and Frederick moved towards the door, pausing to say, 'I must go and sweet-talk that spirited little housekeeper of yours. She's a little beauty, where did you find her?'

'Miss Finn was recommended. She's a hard worker.'

'Yes, I've noticed the change in the house. You know, Uncle, you should be careful of her. She acts as though she owns Leighton Manor and her manner towards you is too familiar. You'd be a good catch for someone like her.'

'Nonsense, Frederick. Miss Finn is far too young for me, and even if she were older I have no inclination to marry at the moment.'

'Well, you don't have to marry her to make use of her, do you?'

'What are you suggesting, that I take my housekeeper into my bed? I'm not interested in her that way. As I said, she's far too young for me.'

'You wouldn't think that if you could see her . . . oh, well, if you're not interested I might have a bit of fun and make an advance on her myself before I go. Who knows, though she's socially beneath me, she might be the means of getting that money out of you. Your last housekeeper married for convenience as I recall. I'll make an effort to be nice to this one and bring her round to my way of thinking.'

Finch felt like roaring with laughter. He hadn't known Sara Finn very long, but long enough to suspect that she had more sense than to fall for the tricks of someone as shallow as Frederick. 'I would advise against that, Frederick, I really would.'

But Frederick didn't want his advice, and Finch knew he had to offer the girl a little protection as the door closed gently behind Frederick. He called Oscar in.

Sara was in the dining room, her mind on her task as she set the table for dinner. Mr Leighton had pretty things, she thought, polishing an engraved wine glass. The letters F D L were entwined within a vine of leaves and grapes. The *D* belonged to Diana, she supposed, and she wondered if the suite of glasses had been a wedding gift.

She set three places. Oscar would stay with Mr Leighton throughout dinner, cutting his meat and unobtrusively helping him. She sometimes wondered if her employer felt embarrassed being treated as a baby.

She jumped when somebody touched her arm, and spun round.

'I've come to apologize for my behaviour, Sara,' Frederick said, giving her that insincere smile of his.

She had no choice but to accept it. 'Thank you. I'm sorry too. I shouldn't have spoken out of turn.'

'No you shouldn't have. My uncle was annoyed about it. I only just talked him out of dismissing you from his service.'

Her face fell. She would hate to lose her job. 'I haven't got any relatives, so I'd have nowhere else to go if he did.'

'Then you owe me a favour. I told him I was interested in you.'

'Why should you tell him such a thing, when it's not true?'

'Oh, but it is true. You're the most beautiful woman I've met in a long time.' Reaching out he ran a finger down her breast.

She blushed and pushed his hand away. 'Leave me alone, Frederick Milson.'

He took a step closer, pushing her gently against the table, trapping her there with his hips and his hands either side on the table. 'You don't mean that, Sara. Just give me a little kiss as a reward, then I'll leave you alone.'

It wouldn't stop at one kiss. She shuddered at the thought. He was loathsome. 'You'll leave me alone now. I've got work to get on with.'

When he stooped to kiss her, her hand closed around a fork and she brought it down on his hand. At the same time she stamped on his foot.

He leaped back, his face contorted with anger. 'You little bitch, you've drawn blood.'

Sensing he was about to slap her, Sara dropped to her knees and scrambled under the table to emerge on the other side.

She kept a wary eye on him as he glared at her. 'Don't think you're going to get away with that, you ungrateful little bastard.' Napkin clutched to his wound, he began to edge around the table, coming between her and the door.

She threatened him with the fork, waving it in front of her. 'Keep away from me.'

Frederick laughed and threw himself across the table, scattering plates and cutlery everywhere. His plan failed when he collided with a chair and it toppled over with him on top of it but he managed to snatch the fork from her hand on the way down.

Crying out in fright with the suddenness of it when he sprang to his feet, Sara dodged round the table again and jerked on the bell pull, hoping Maggie would answer it, because Fanny wouldn't be of much help in this situation.

To her relief it was Oscar who arrived, and it was almost instant. His glance flicked from one to another, then at the table, summing up the situation. 'I was just passing when I heard a crash and a cry. I've come to help you, Miss Finn.'

'What the devil d'you mean by that?' Freddie said.

'That the table is in disarray and that Mr Leighton will be down shortly. In fact he has sent me down to assist Miss Finn. Have you injured your hand, Mr Milson?'

'Not that it's anything to do with you, but I accidentally pricked it with a fork.' Frederick threw the fork into the corner followed by the bloodied napkin, and examined the wound. 'It's just a scratch.'

'Of course, sir,' Oscar said blandly. 'Miss Milson requests your presence in the drawing room. Allow me to help you to prepare the table, miss.'

Frederick pushed past them, limping slightly, his face dark with anger.

Oscar smiled at her after Frederick walked away. 'You'll be all right now, Miss.'

She was trembling. 'Thank you, Oscar. He tried to . . . well, he was overly *familiar* so I stuck a fork in his hand.'

'As I observed. By his own admission it happened quite by accident. However, would you like me to mention the incident to Mr Leighton?'

'I'd rather you didn't. Mr Leighton comes here to relax, and there's been enough trouble. Frederick said Mr Leighton was going to dismiss me over what happened earlier, but he talked him out of it. If he hears of this I'll be dismissed for certain.'

Oscar lowered his voice. 'Mr Leighton had no intention of dismissing you, and never conclude that he's fooled by the Milson pair. I must go and help him dress for dinner now. I doubt if

Frederick will be back.' Oscar cracked his knuckles. 'They'll be gone early tomorrow, but if he bothers you again before they go, let me know and I'll take him outside and give him a good thumping.'

She laughed at that because Oscar was only a small man. 'Thank you, Oscar.'

Eight

The atmosphere had lightened the moment that the Milsons and their slobbering lurchers had disappeared down the drive. Fingal had appeared in the kitchen, still nervous and twitching. Instead of disappearing into the safe hiding hole he'd found for himself during the visit he curled up in his rightful place on the rocking chair in front of the stove, giving Maggie the opportunity to hang his hated bell collar around his neck.

Just before they'd departed the Milsons had offered Sara black looks, so her back quivered from the mental daggers they'd stuck there. There was a warning in the smug smiles they exchanged. Their leaving brought relief, but Sara was left in no doubt that there might be an unpleasant surprise in store for her somewhere.

However, nothing was going to be allowed to spoil this moment later in the morning, even though the sky was threatening rain and the wind shivered through the shrubs in sudden little gusts. When Giles returned from the station they gathered in the porch at the appointed time.

As instructed, Mr Leighton was warmly dressed. He had a mystified half smile on his face as she led him forward. 'Sorry, but you can't wear gloves, and I expect your hands will get cold.' She removed them, picked up the slack of the rope and placed it in his palm.

'What is it?'

'Rope.'

He smiled. 'Ah, a length of rope, something I've always wanted. Is it one of those trick ropes that stand upright, and if I climb up it I'll disappear?'

'That would be a sight to see.' She giggled. 'Be serious, Mr Leighton. It's a guide rope. You keep your hand on it and you walk round the garden from post to post without having to have someone with you. There are wooden benches here and there in case you want to rest, or to stop and smell the flowers . . . not that there's any to smell at the moment, but come spring there will be.'

'And you can plant your own flowers if you've a mind to,' Joseph Tunney said, 'and you can sit on a bench under the oak tree.'

Maggie broke in, 'Let Sara tell it, Joseph. It was *her* idea.'

'But we wouldn't have done it without Joseph and Giles doing all the hard work,' she reminded Maggie. 'Now, Mr Leighton . . . every now and again you'll find a wooden notice with your location carved on it. The one to the left of your hand on the post says front door. The letters are quite large so they shouldn't be any trouble.'

He reached out for the notice, located it, and his finger tips traced round the carving. He chuckled. 'It actually says front odor.'

'It was getting dark when I did that'n, and I got the letters back to front,' Giles said defensively. 'But you know what it means, I reckon, you being clever and learned and all.'

'Yes, of course I do, Giles. I wasn't making fun of you. I didn't think you knew how to write your letters.'

'Miss Finn has been teaching me, Jassy and Fanny to read and write.'

'I can write my name,' Fanny said, beaming proudly at everyone.

'Well done, both of you. Now, let me try this contraption out. You'd better follow me this first time, Oscar, in case I lose my bearings.'

'It goes around—'

'Not now, Oscar, it's a voyage of discovery. I'll find out the destination when I get there, and the route will reveal itself to me as I go. Fetch the umbrella if you would; it feels like it's going to rain.'

When Mr Leighton walked out of doors he usually put a hand on Oscar's shoulder. Now he kept his hand on the rope, while the stick he usually carried was held in his other hand. 'Thank you for the surprise, everyone. I'm truly touched that you thought of me with such a practical idea in mind. I'm off now.'

He looked vulnerable as he cautiously started out, unaided, his stick skimming the ground in case of obstacles in front of him, such as tree roots. When he stopped to read the next signpost he seemed to gain some confidence. Mouthing the letters as he traced and understood them, he smiled.

'He'll soon get the hang of it,' Oscar said as he hurried past. 'I just hope we can get all the way round before the rain starts, because it looks like a storm is building.'

They did, but only just. Mr Leighton came back in, his face glowing from the cold, and raindrops spattered across his shoulders. His smile was a mile wide. The pleasure he'd found in such a simple device touched her, and tears came to her eyes.

Adam's journey had quickly become a nightmare. The soreness in his throat had worsened. The rain pelted down, driven by a cold wind that lashed both himself and his horse. Soon he was soaked through to the skin, and the horse he'd hired was skittish.

He had no choice but to dismount and stand against a wall under a dripping bush that hung over it. It offered little shelter to either man or horse. The wall surrounded the grounds of Leighton Manor, since according to the directions given to him it was the only dwelling along this lane past the farmhouse.

The horse whinnied and sidestepped when there was a rumble of thunder overhead.

'Easy boy, I'll have to find us shelter until this is over. If you allow me to remount you, it will be quicker.' Although taking shelter at Leighton Manor would suit his purpose, which was to get a glimpse of Sara Finn . . . alias Serafina, he regretted the thought that he might have to reveal his hand too soon.

The next few yards revealed a gate, left open, and beyond that a curving drive. His skittish mount was hard to control and he whinnied shrilly and sidestepped all the way. An answering whinny from the stable block made the gelding prick his ears forward, and brought a young man to the door. He took hold of the gelding's bridle and led them inside, talking soothingly to the horse all the while.

As Adam dismounted, he said, 'Have you got business with Mr Leighton, sir? Don't you worry about Red Robin, he's been here before and knows us; don't you, my lovely? He'll soon settle. You come here to Giles now, Red. A good rub down and a feed will see you right. In the meantime you can chat to old Curruthers over there. Likely he'll enjoy your company for a while and you can have a good old gossip.'

The horse settled down in a vacant stall next to Curruthers, whickering his complaints while he waited to be fussed over.

'Thank you,' Adam said.

'If you'd like to follow me I'll take you in through the kitchen, sir. Miss Finn won't like you dripping water all over the place, and might prefer you to dry off a bit before she takes you through to Mr Leighton. It's warm in the kitchen.'

Adam drew in a deep breath, acknowledging the deep chill gnawing at his core and thinking that a hot stove and a drink to match wouldn't go astray. He should have ignored his curiosity and gone home two days ago.

Giles introduced him to Maggie the cook, who took one look at him and exclaimed, 'Glory be, you look cold enough to be a corpse risen from the grave!' which did nothing to reassure him. 'Go and fetch Miss Finn, Fanny, and be quick about it.'

Miss Finn came in a flurry of skirts to entrance him. The young woman he'd been seeking stood there before him, all eyes, which were large, brown, soft and captivating. They widened even more at the sight of him, her lashes giving an unconscious feminine flutter. 'Mr Leighton didn't say he was expecting anyone; do you have an appointment, sir?'

'I'm afraid not. I was seeking shelter from the storm.' Over his chattering teeth he said, 'I'm sorry to be such a nuisance, I'm so very cold.'

'So I see. You're also very wet and making a puddle on the floor. Maggie, give the man a towel to dry himself with, and some coffee, with a measure of brandy poured from the bottle you've got hidden away in the dresser. I'll go and tell Mr Leighton.'

She gazed at him for a long moment of indecision, head to one side, assessing him, rather like a blackbird contemplating a worm for breakfast. There came a moment when she reached a conclusion that he might be harmless, and she relaxed. 'What shall I tell him your name is, sir?'

His smile brought a slightly frosty look from her, as though it was one liberty too many. 'Adam Chapman.'

'You have a card to present, do you not?'

She was still measuring his standard to protect her employer.

All reputable gentlemen presented their cards, after all. He fumbled in his waistcoat pocket. The card was sodden, rendered halfway towards pulp again. It was just about readable. 'It's not in very good condition, I'm afraid.'

'As I see.' Oddly, she handed the card back to him, then turned and left.

'How the devil did she know about that brandy,' Maggie grumbled to Fanny as she placed a generous measure in a glass and added coffee from a pot steaming on the stove. 'Cream, sir?'

The cream turned out to be of the rich, thick variety, manufactured no doubt from the lush and luxurious pastures hereabouts.

After a while, the delightful Miss Finn returned. Now she did smile at him, her lips slightly pursed, letting him know the smile was designed for the sake of politeness only. There was an independent air to her that fitted neatly into the Honeyman sisters' mould, but there the resemblance stopped.

She had a sweet curve to her mouth and the bottom lip had a slight, but natural pout to it that was wholly delicious. 'Mr Leighton has agreed to give you shelter. I've told him how saturated and cold you are, and he's ordered me to hand you over to his man, Oscar. So *if* you have finished your coffee, follow me.'

He wasn't going to be allowed to linger, he thought, as he swallowed the last mouthful and thanked Maggie. He smiled at the girl called Fanny, who'd been observing him with her mouth open, and followed Sara Finn out of the kitchen, along a dimly lit corridor and into the hall. The stairway they ascended was of the wide, sweeping variety, with brass rods keeping the red and blue patterned carpet in place on the risers.

He followed her up, his hand on the highly polished banister, admiring her small waist and the smooth sway of her perfect rear. She was petite, her movements quick and economical.

She stopped abruptly, then turned, catching him unawares. He was two steps below her when he realized. He stopped, and found her face level with his.

'There's something I should tell you, Mr Chapman,' she said.

Uncharacteristically he voiced his thoughts out loud. 'You're very pretty.'

Colour seeped under her skin but she didn't remove her gaze. In fact she ignored his statement and said, 'He's afflicted by blindness.'

'Who is?'

'Mr Leighton.'

Her lack of reaction to his previous overture puzzled him. 'Did you hear what I said?'

'Yes, of course, I heard. Men tend to make personal statements on first acquaintance. My immediate reaction was that it was presumptuous of you, so I ignored it. Imagine if I said that to you on such short acquaintance. You'd be shocked, and would think that I was quite forward.'

'I wouldn't. If I happened to be a woman I'd be quite flattered.'

'But you're not a woman, so nobody would call you pretty. And unless you've been a woman you wouldn't know if you'd be flattered or not. You haven't been a woman, have you?'

He was quite bewildered by her reasoning. 'I can't lay any claim to that.'

'There you are then.' Her smile had a trace of mockery to it. 'I admit though, you *do* have pretty eyes, like those of a hawk.'

Laughter filled him, even though the comparison pleased him. 'And your mind is as sharp as your wit.'

She heaved a sigh. 'Let's stick to the business at hand, Mr Chapman. You are here because you're wet and cold, not to exchange compliments or engage in a flirtation that will come to nothing. This time, did *you* hear what I said to you?'

'About Mr Leighton's lack of sight? Yes, and thank you for warning me.'

'I'm only telling you so you don't ask him to look at things, and make a fool of yourself.'

He wanted to laugh; the whole conversation was ridiculous. 'I daresay Mr Leighton is used to people doing that, and doesn't take offence.'

'Oh, he's a very kind man and he wouldn't take offence. But you might feel a bit silly if you didn't know, because he doesn't look as though he's blind, you see.'

'So you were thinking of my feelings being affected, not Mr Leighton's. That's kind of you. I apologize if I made you blush.'

'I didn't blush, you must have imagined it.'

He chuckled. 'I've never met a woman who didn't appreciate a compliment before.'

'Then this will be a new experience for you, Mr Chapman, and you might learn something from it. Kindly remember that you're a guest in Mr Leighton's home, and you're dripping water on his stair carpet.'

He couldn't help it. He pressed both of his hands against his heart and said, 'I'm totally contrite.'

'You don't look in the least bit contrite, let alone totally. Come . . .' She turned and sped off, leaving him staring after her, slightly disconcerted. She had won this round, he realized.

'Yes, your majesty,' he murmured, and could have sworn that a breathless giggle floated back to him. Adam trotted after her like a well-trained dog called to a whistle, thinking, this was a woman worth pursuing.

He was introduced to the manservant, Oscar, who listened to her instructions with a faint grin.

'This is Mr Chapman. He's to be made comfortable while his own clothing is being dried. Mr Leighton said he may need to stay the night, so I'll make the second-best guest room ready and light a fire in there. Call me when he's ready.'

'Yes, Miss.'

'I'm sorry to be so much trouble—'

'It's no trouble. It's what I'm paid to do.'

Before too long Adam found himself expertly processed and warmly clad in a morning suit that was slightly larger than the one he usually wore. But Adam could still feel the cold gnawing at his core, and now and again he was wracked with shivers.

He followed Sara down to a small sitting room, where a fire burned cheerfully in the grate.

His host turned towards the door when they entered, and he got to his feet and held out a hand. 'Welcome to my home, Mr Chapman. I don't often entertain visitors here, even unexpected ones.' The man's handshake was firm.

'Thank you for your hospitality; I'm grateful. Please sit down, sir. Your housekeeper has informed me of your disability and I have no wish to put you out.'

'I'm not in the least put-out. In fact, I've been looking forward to meeting you.'

'Me, sir? You've heard of me?'

'I practise law, Mr Chapman. Leighton & Jones. Of course I've heard of you. Most of the lawyers in London have. Word of mouth is a fine thing, sir. Perhaps you'd care to pour us both a brandy.'

'Shall I do it?' Sara said.

'Are you still here, Miss Finn? You must have realized by now that Mr Chapman is a decent young man who wishes me no harm. You don't have to act as my guard dog. If there's anything more you wish to know about him, just ask him before you leave.'

'Well,' Adam asked her with a grin. 'Is there?'

Her brown eyes mirrored her chagrin and Adam felt guilty when she murmured, 'You're of no interest to me whatsoever.' She left, her face burning with embarrassment.

Leighton sighed. 'That was cruel of me.'

'And me. The young woman is more sensitive than she appears. I will apologize to her.'

'Oh, she will bounce back with a vengeance, I daresay, since she always does.'

Adam put out a feeler. 'Do you know anything about her past?'

'The same as you do, I imagine, Mr Chapman. Sara Finn is a good, honest and hard-working young woman. That's all I need to know about her.'

Pouring them a drink, Adam said. 'Where do you want this brandy?'

'In my hand, please. I understand we have a mutual acquaintance in Edgar Wyvern.'

Adam chuckled. 'No wonder you've heard of me if that's the case. Edgar is much more than an acquaintance, though. He's very generous with his patronage, and will become my stepfather at the end of January.'

'Ah . . . I wondered if matrimony was in the offing. I met your mother when she was hosting a dinner for Edgar. She's a charming and gracious lady.'

'Yes, she is.'

'Since I lost my sight I've developed a good memory, along with acute hearing and touch. In fact, my loss of sight, which you considered a disability, has allowed me to discover, and more importantly, bring my other abilities to the forefront.'

'My pardon if I offended you.'

'You didn't. What I want you to know is that I can still reason, and can smell an evasion from a mile away.' Then came the question Adam was dreading. 'You were not passing by, since the road outside my gate leads nowhere. And it seems that you had no intention of visiting me. But you were loitering outside my house for a reason. Now you're enquiring about my housekeeper, which has intrigued me. I can only come to the conclusion you were spying on her. Why?'

Adam quickly decided on the truth. 'I had no intention of intruding. I was hoping to get a glimpse of Miss Finn before I returned home, for identification purposes. I was about to turn back when the storm came on.'

His host raised an eyebrow. 'Identification?'

'To see if she resembles those seeking to prove kinship to her. My enquiries are on behalf of a man who thinks Miss Finn may be his daughter. I was not about to approach her at this stage though, since he's abroad for several more months and I don't like giving anyone false hope.'

'May I ask who this man is?'

'That I won't reveal, since it's a confidential matter.'

'Of course you can't . . . and now you've seen my housekeeper do you think she's the young woman you're looking for?'

Hating himself for doing it, but knowing that curiosity often overcame a man's natural instinct for discretion, Adam employed a tiny amount of subterfuge. 'I've tracked Serafina over four counties. She certainly could be the girl I'm looking for, but she bears very little resemblance to the family concerned.'

Leighton's alert posture told Adam that his host was familiar with the name in connection with his housekeeper. 'Serafina?'

'That's a name we call her by. Her file name, if you like.'

'Because . . . ?'

Adam gave a faint smile. Leighton played things close to his chest. This was a man after his own heart, but he dealt with facts and it wouldn't be wise to tell him that it was a name the wind on the heath had once blown into Marianne Thornton's pretty ear. 'We believe she was named after an aunt with that name, who ran an orphanage on the outskirts of Dorchester. Constance Serafina Jarvis her name was.'

'My housekeeper does admit to having a name such as Serafina, but she can't quite remember some things from her past, since she's been moved from pillar to post. She has an ambition . . . to reach old age with enough money to own a house with two bedrooms, so she can board a respectable lodger to help her make ends meet.'

He imagined a white-haired Serafina in a little cottage like Ham's mother had. Adam's heart went out to the girl for having such a modest dream. Had she been allowed to remain within her family Serafina's expectations and desires would surely have been much more advanced.

'A laudable plan.'

'That's if she doesn't marry and have children in the meantime, or so she tells me. I think she has a need to feel secure, which accounts for the forward planning.'

'We all do, and having a background, however humble, gives us a sense of belonging. I may be able to provide her with that. Do you have any children, Mr Leighton?'

'I suggest that we use first names, Adam. No children unfortunately, my wife . . . *died*. It was an accident and I had the reins.'

'Oh, I'm so sorry, that must have been hard to live with.' Adam's head spun and he remembered little Annie at the cottage, with her flushed face and faint pink rash. He dismissed it. She'd had a childhood disease, one he'd probably suffered in childhood himself, therefore giving him immunity. Another fit of the shivers attacked him and his glass chattered against his teeth.

'Are you feeling unwell, Adam?'

'I was chilled to the bone and I'm shivering now and again.'

'It sounds as though you're coming down with a fever.'

'It's probably just the cold. I should be all right by morning, though I'm enjoying your hospitality so much that I might fake an illness just to stay here longer.'

Leighton laughed. 'You'd be quite welcome.'

As it was, Adam didn't have to fake an illness. He woke the next morning with a sore throat, a soaring fever and a rash. He staggered to a chair, rang the bell and was rewarded by the patter of feet, followed by a knock at the door. It was Serafina's voice – a voice as clear as a crystal bell. 'Mr Chapman?'

'Don't come in,' he said.

Contrarily, she did the opposite. The door opened and she advanced upon him, stopping a few paces away to accuse him, 'Your voice is croaking; are you feeling ill?'

He was at a disadvantage, sitting there in his host's spare robe with his bare feet sticking out of the bottom. 'Go away, Miss Finn. I think I'm infectious since I have a sore throat and a rash.'

She advanced the rest of the way and gazed down at him, concern in her eyes. 'After living in the workhouse I've been exposed to every infection going. Show me your rash.'

He showed her his neck, where the rash was a blotchy red tide spreading up to his face.

'Is it anywhere else?'

'On my stomach,' and he clutched his robe tightly against it. 'I'm not going to allow you to inspect it. Do you know what the cause is?'

'Ah, I see that I have you at a disadvantage now, Mr Chapman.' She laid the back of her hand lightly against his brow. It was a well-worked hand, but cool and soothing . . . almost motherly. 'Yes, I know what ails you.'

'Tell me then. Am I infectious?'

'I'm afraid so. But we'll wait for the doctor. He's a man, and won't approve of me diagnosing your illness before he does.'

He wanted to smile at the thought that this chit of a girl would take advantage of his infliction to criticize the learned doctor. 'You're infuriating, Miss Finn. Perhaps you could offer me a prognosis instead.'

Her head slanted to one side and she smiled. 'If you stay in bed and rest, drink plenty of fluids, behave yourself, remain calm and do as you're told, you should be ready to return home in about a week's time.'

Finch Leighton sent Oscar to London to inform Adam's family that the man of the family was suffering from German measles and would be his guest for as long as it took him to recover.

Oscar returned the next day, accompanied by Adam's sister.

'Oscar said you wouldn't mind if I came down to look after

my brother. I do hope that's true and you'll forgive the intrusion,' she said. 'My mother will worry less if I'm here to look after him, and Mr Wyvern tells me you're a gentleman of good reputation. Are you? I will try and stay out of your way.'

Her voice was calm and unhurried, like moonlight on water. The hand Finch took in his was warm, the skin like silk. She smelled of honeysuckle.

Finch had never believed in love at first sight. When he'd fallen in love with Diana it had been her looks that had gradually attracted him, but that hadn't been enough after a while and her faults had come to the fore.

It struck him as ironic that he'd had to wait until he was blind to discover that love could be instinctive, and it was a perfectly feasible concept to be attracted to a woman sight unseen, even for one such as him.

He sensed in Celia Chapman a rare perfection that he was totally at one with. At the same time he felt like weeping. A woman like her could have no interest in a man such as himself . . . so flawed.

Yet he found he could be no less than gallant and manly in his reaction to her presence. 'I'm glad you're here, Miss Chapman; your brother talked so much about you last night that I feel as though I already know you. As for staying out of my way, I'll never forgive you if you deliberately deprive me of your company. I will, however, forgive any presumption or trespass you wished to make,' he said, and when he kissed the soft feminine hand he held, she drew in a sharp intake of breath.

As he was readying himself for bed later that evening he asked Oscar, 'What do you make of Miss Celia Chapman?'

'Oh, very nice, sir. She's a sensible, well-mannered young woman. Her bearing is graceful, her manner polite, if a little diffident. Her shyness is appealing, I thought. She's not the type of woman who would push herself forward to be noticed in a crowd.'

'That was the impression I formed, too.'

'Oh, by the way, sir. I found the key you lost the last time you were here. It was in the drawer of the bedside cabinet. I can't imagine how we missed it.'

'Odd . . . I could have sworn I'd lost it in the London house.

Are you sure it's my key and not the housekeeper's?' He hoped it wasn't Sara's. She would have to learn to curb her curiosity and her instinct to clean everything in sight, and he'd specifically told her to leave Diana's room as it was.

Nine

Adam was still asleep when Celia woke. Over breakfast in the kitchen with the gossipy cook, Celia quickly discovered that everyone at Leighton Manor had recovered from this mild version of measles at one time or another, usually in childhood.

'I'm so pleased my brother won't be able to pass it on,' she said to Maggie.

'Would anyone mind if I went for a walk, do you think? Compared to London, it's so lovely and fresh here.'

'You go, Miss Chapman. I'll tell Miss Finn, and Oscar will see that Mr Chapman is comfortable. He's a good sort.'

The morning was beautiful, though cold along the country lanes while the dew was still rising from the ground. Then the sun came out to dispel the frost and everything sparkled. It was such a pretty morning, the air fresh and crisp. Rabbits raced across the fields, birds of prey hovered overhead and a hedgehog trundled across in front of her. Celia had fallen in love with the peacefulness of her surroundings. Leighton Manor was a handsome, yet homely building.

The long-case clock in the hall was chiming eleven when she got back and she guiltily sped upstairs to see her brother.

His face brightened when she went inside. 'Serafina said you'd gone out.'

'It's such pretty countryside here, and I was tempted to go further than I meant to.'

'It has done you good for your cheeks have a healthy glow to them.'

'Mama said she can't imagine how you didn't catch this disease when you were an infant, and that she hopes you soon recover in time to take her to the altar,' she told her brother.

'I'll try. How is the agency coping?'

'You don't have to worry. I've put Andrew Parsonage in overall charge of the agency, and Edgar has promised that either he or his clerk will visit every day to advise them on any legal problems that might arise.'

'That's good of him.' He smiled. 'Have you been introduced to Miss Sara Finn yet? She's been looking after me wonderfully well.'

'That dark-haired young woman?' She lowered her voice and smiled at him. 'My dear Adam, I think you've made a conquest there. She was taken aback a bit when she learned I'd come here to care for you, until I revealed that I was your sister, then she was all smiles. Even then she told me quite firmly that I wasn't to tax your strength. At this very moment she's probably hovering outside the door to make sure I don't.'

'Then you'd better do as you're told. Sit in that chair by the window because I have something to tell you about her. The young lady is the object of my search, and although she doesn't know it I have confided in Finch Leighton. So be discreet, and befriend the girl if you can.'

'Sara Finn is the missing sister! From looks alone I'd never suspect that she's related to Charlotte and Marianne. Not that she isn't quite lovely in her own way . . . she is. Such big eyes, and a sweet little face . . . and she has quite a provocative way with her.'

'She certainly has.'

'Sara Finn,' Celia mused, and smiled. 'The name is so very nearly Serafina when run together. Do you think she deliberately changed it so she wouldn't be found?'

'Why wouldn't she want to be found?'

'Obviously she's a bright young woman. She has a job that she seems to like, and judging by the appearance of the house she does it very well. She has an employer who is kindness itself, and he treats her with respect. She is earning a living. Why would she want to change that when the chance of her background being beneficial to her is practically nil?'

Celia was right. Why should she? Adam admitted to himself that he'd missed the similarity of name entirely. That couldn't be a coincidence, surely. He gazed at his sister with new respect. 'Actually, there's a chance that her name could be Mary Fenn. Our Serafina lived on a farm with a family called Fenn. There were two girls about the same age and most of the family was lost to cholera . . .' He began to shiver. 'Sorry, this happens now and again. I was thoroughly soaked and chilled to the marrow.'

Pulling the blanket up to his chin she plumped up his pillows and gently kissed him. 'Enough talking, Adam. I'll read your note-book while you try and sleep.'

Eventually her brother's teeth ceased their chatter, but he was restless. There came a knock at the door and the housekeeper came in. She carried a tray with a bowl of broth. The aroma made Celia's mouth water.

Waking with a start, Adam said apologetically, 'I'm not hungry.'

Celia observed the way the young woman handled herself. 'Just a spoonful or two to warm you up inside,' Sara Finn said gently and she tucked a napkin under his chin. 'Maggie made it especially for you, and since a chicken lost its life in the quest to help you regain your health, the least you can do is oblige all concerned – especially the chicken – by eating it.'

When Adam opened his mouth to protest the housekeeper put a spoonful of broth inside and he had no recourse but to either swallow it or spit it out. Adam would not resort to the latter, he was too much the gentleman, Celia thought, and she grinned when he swallowed it.

'There's a good boy,' Sara Finn cooed, something so unexpected that Celia was forced to stifle a giggle when her brother's eyes widened.

'Damn you, Miss Finn, you're taking advantage of my good nature and mocking me,' Adam said weakly.

'Yes, I know. Now do stop feeling so sorry for yourself and eat,' she said, and managed to slide another spoonful in.

Celia's chuckle brought a grin to the girl's face. 'Luncheon will be served in the dining room at half past the hour. Mr Leighton said he'd be honoured if you would join him, Miss Chapman.'

Colour flushed her cheeks. 'But I'm here to look after my brother.'

'He'll be taking a nap as soon as he's eaten this broth, won't you, Mr Chapman? Doctor's orders. Besides, you've got to eat. We can go down together if you wish.'

'Thank you for being so good to my brother.'

'It's a pleasure.'

Celia sucked in a breath when Adam gazed up at the house-keeper through feverish eyes and murmured, 'Is it a pleasure?'

'Didn't I just say so, Mr Chapman? Now, do open your mouth and eat this before it gets cold.'

'I'm quite capable of feeding myself.'

'Then why am I doing it?'

Helpfully, he offered, 'Because you've trapped my arms under the sheet and have given me little choice.'

After her brother obediently opened his mouth for the next spoonful, Sara stood and held out the bowl. 'Prop yourself up on the pillows, then.'

When Adam freed his arms and shuffled himself into a more upright position, she handed him the bowl and warned, 'I'm staying until you've eaten every morsel, mind.'

'Bully,' he grumbled, and when her brother's grey eyes engaged those of Serafina, the girl gave him a quick, shy smile and a faint flush appeared on her face. 'You must tell me if I become too overbearing. It's my greatest fault.'

'Is it? It seems to me to be a rather endearing characteristic.'

When a smile lit her face at the compliment a sudden affection for the young woman surged through Celia. If anyone could nurse Adam back to health quickly it would be Serafina.

Not only did Celia share a pleasant lunch with Finch Leighton, he made it clear that he expected her company for dinner, and she could only oblige him.

He looked handsome in a dinner suit. And she was pleased she had her lavender gown to wear, even though he couldn't see it.

'How is the invalid?' he asked her.

'Sara has him organized. He's regained his appetite and is eating a light dinner at the moment.' She laughed. 'Maggie has made him an apple pie for pudding, and Sara won't let him have it until he's eaten his broth,' Celia told him. 'Not that Adam minds. I think he's rather enjoying being made a fuss of.'

'As most men do when they're indisposed. There's nothing like a woman's concern to make a man feel . . . *wanted*.'

'Adam should be ready to travel in a few days if the doctor is agreeable. I feel as though I've intruded by coming here. It was silly of my mother to panic.'

'If she hadn't I would have been denied the pleasure of meeting you, and of enjoying the pleasure of your company. You must see the week out, at least. I'm given to understand that your mother is to marry a colleague of mine, Edgar Wyvern.'

'Yes, at the end of January. My mother and I were addressing the invitations when your servant arrived with news of Adam's illness. I recall that you were on Edgar's guest list. The invitations are in hand and one will be sent to your London address.'

'My thanks.'

'It's short notice, I know, but my mother and Edgar saw no need for a long engagement. I do hope you'll be able to attend. It will be an afternoon wedding service followed by a buffet and a reception at Edgar's home. Then the following week we've been invited to the theatre to see the play *The Thirst For Gold*. Have you seen it?' Celia softly laughed. 'I'm so sorry, I do hope you'll forgive that slip of the tongue.'

Finch aimed a grin with unerring accuracy in Celia's direction. 'People do it all the time, my dear, and they usually embarrass themselves over it more than me. As a matter of fact I have seen the play, many years ago. It's about a group of people seeking their fortunes in the new world. It has many a dramatic tableaux and I found it to be completely tedious.'

'Then I shall take your word for it and decline the invitation.'

'Good, because on that very night I'm having a supper, followed by a social evening of my own. You and Adam must join me.'

'But I haven't said which evening it is yet.'

'Well, tell me, so I can arrange my evening to interfere with your theatre engagement. You will then have a legitimate excuse.'

Colour touched Celia's cheeks. 'Mr Leighton . . . you are quite devious by nature. Are you always so adroit at arranging matters to suit yourself.'

The laugh he gave was natural and open. 'No, but it's a long time since I've met anyone whose acquaintance I'd like to pursue more.'

'You're referring to my brother, of course.'

'I'm actually referring to you, Celia, but it certainly includes your brother. You have a lovely speaking voice, you know; it's soothing. Can you sing as well?'

'I can sing in tune, but that's about all.'

'Then perhaps you'll sing for me after dinner.'

'My voice doesn't have much volume, I'm afraid.'

'I will not allow you to wriggle out of it for that reason, since my hearing is extremely sharp.'

'Mr Leighton,' she protested, and her eyes sparkled with laughter. 'I'm here to look after my brother.'

'Sara is looking after him competently I imagine. She's very diligent. Tell me more about yourself, Miss Chapman . . . are you spoken for, perhaps?'

Celia began to laugh, 'Perhaps I am . . . or perhaps not. Now you're being outrageous, as well as too personal for such a short acquaintance.'

'Then I must change my approach. That green gown matches your eyes perfectly.'

'It's lavender, and my eyes are grey . . . stop this at once, Mr Leighton. I will not allow a complete stranger to tease me in such a manner.'

'Alas, I'm not quite complete, but a thousand apologies. I promise to behave myself from now on. You sound like a woman who can play chess.'

'Now there's a challenge. Adam taught me to play. Are you good?'

'Yes. I have a photographic memory, but you'll have to move the pieces for me, otherwise I knock them over.'

Mr Leighton was flirting! Amazed, Sara exchanged a grin with Oscar, then she began to clear the dishes away. Oscar helped her.

'Is the fire lit in the main drawing room, Sara?' her employer asked.

'It is, sir. I'll serve the coffee there, shall I?'

'Thank you.' He got to his feet, made his way to Celia's chair and held out his arm. 'If you would take my arm I'll escort you to the drawing room.'

'Thank you, Mr Leighton.'

'You are quite at liberty to address me as Finch,' he said firmly as he led her away, 'because from now on I intend to address you as Celia.'

Sara couldn't help but laugh after they'd gone. 'I'd never have expected Mr Leighton to act in such a manner.'

'Oh . . . he always had a lot of charm with the ladies. They used to like it . . . but that was before Diana Milson got her hooks into him. Wrapped him up good and proper, she did, like a fly in a spider web.' He lowered his voice. 'Mr Leighton intended to open a branch of the legal practice in Taunton. He thought that if he parted her from the fast company she kept she'd settle down and provide him with a family. She wouldn't have it.'

'He said there was an argument?'

'Yes, there was . . . and he always blamed himself for her death.'

'What do you think of Miss Chapman?'

'I think she's a sensible young woman who is a little on the shy side, and intelligent. Mr Leighton always liked females who can hold up their end of a discussion. He's taken quite a fancy to Miss Chapman, I feel. I haven't seen him so relaxed for a long time.'

'And her brother?'

'A pleasant young man with a great deal of integrity.' Oscar's lips pressed together and he fixed her with a sly grin. 'I think he's got his eye on you. He always talks about you?'

She blushed. 'Why would a professional gentleman like him take an interest in me?'

'For the same reason Frederick Milson took an interest in you, I suppose. You're an attractive young woman and men will be men, especially if women encourage them by trifling with their affections.'

'I'm not trifling with any man's affections, especially the affections of that sly Freddie Milson.' Sara felt quite put-out by the remark. Picking up the tray of dirty dishes she flounced off, leaving him to follow.

When she took the coffee through to the drawing room Celia was seated on the piano stool.

'Leave it on the table, Sara. Miss Chapman will see to it. I've persuaded her to play the piano to provide me with some entertainment. She might even sing for me.'

And she thought Celia had come to look after her brother! Then Sara chided herself. Celia Chapman had wrought a change for the better in her employer in the short time she'd been here. Still, she didn't mind caring for Adam Chapman. Sara told herself that she was merely doing her duty in nursing him. It wasn't as though he was seriously ill. After a couple of days rest he would begin to mend fast.

Sara felt self-conscious in his presence though, aware that he was watching her, and bestowing smiles on her whenever she caught his eyes – and more than aware that her heart went all of a flutter when he did.

Well, however charming he was to her, and however much her heart fluttered when she saw him she was not going to fall in love with a man who was so far above her on the social ladder. Oscar had been right. Men would be men, and what's more they should learn how to control themselves, the same as women did. Well . . . most women, she thought and her gaze went to Diana Milson's portrait and she gave a disparaging, 'Pffff!'

The next morning Sara found the invalid out of bed and seated by the table in front of the window.

When she tut-tutted, he curled her a grin and said by way of excuse, 'Oscar has just shaved me in honour of your visit.'

A little twist of happiness bounced about inside her. 'So I see, Adam.' She could smell the shaving soap, and his skin was smooth and soft. His hair gleamed in the light coming through the window and it curled like strands of dark, sun-kissed honey against his temples.

'Allow me to stay here in this chair, Serafina,' he said.

Her mouth dried. 'Why did you call me Serafina?'

'I understood it to be your real name. It's very pretty.'

Mr Leighton must have told him. 'It's too good a name for a servant.'

'That's not true. It's a lovely name, and it suits you.'

She remembered Oscar's warning. She was not going to be trifled with. 'Most people call me Sara; I prefer that.'

'I've upset you . . . why?'

She didn't know why . . . perhaps because the name unearthed something in the far reaches of her past that she still craved for. There had been an old woman, and there had been something fine and warm about her. When Sara's mind reached out to her she was elusive. She closed herself around the memory as she placed the tray down on the table. 'I'm not upset, and it's not up to me to tell you what you can do and what you can't.'

'Why do you look upon me with such disapproval?' he said gently, which immediately disarmed her.

Sara recognized something in him that connected with something in herself. Was it because she liked him more than she should, and didn't quite know how to handle it? She retreated behind a brisk, no nonsense approach. 'Eat your breakfast, Mr Chapman, then go back to bed and stay there until the physician says you may rise.'

'Ah . . . so it's back to Mr Chapman, is it?' and before she could answer, 'Do you like living in the country?'

'I lived on a farm when I was a child.'

'With the Fenn family?'

'Yes . . .' Her nose wrinkled as she remembered the dirt and the smell, and despite that how she'd wanted to belong to them, especially Mary who told her they were secret sisters and she would love her forever. 'We all caught a bellyache one day and my ma and pa . . . at least I thought they were my ma and pa, even when it wasn't my turn, because sometimes things got confused in my head. Anyway, they died, except for myself and my uncle.'

Now Adam was confused, something that didn't happen very often to him. 'Your turn . . . what do you mean by that?'

'It was a game Mary and I played. Sometimes she pretended she was the orphan child, and sometimes I did. We would change our names and pretend to be each other, especially when we went to the village school. It confused everyone. We looked alike, you see.' She gave a faint, sad smile. 'We were going to be princesses when we grew up.'

A game that had proved to confuse her, he surmised, since Serafina wasn't totally convinced of which child she was. All her memories could have stemmed from two unrelated little girls with fertile imaginations playing a game of make-believe and sharing one set of parents between them.

'Your uncle . . . was his first name Tyler?'

'I don't know, we just called him uncle. He came to stay a few months before we were taken ill to help with the farm chores. He was . . . *mean*. After they died he told me that I didn't belong to the family any more because I wasn't kin. And he told me to collect my things. We went a long way on the cart, and he left me outside this building and he told me to wait there and he'd come back for me. Only he didn't.' She gazed down at her hands and there was no self-pity in her voice. 'When it was dark somebody came out and took me inside and I was there for two years.'

Her eyes came up to his, all at once wary. 'How did you know they were called Fenn?'

So she'd picked up on his mistake and was now playing him at his own game, Adam thought. 'I assumed they had the same name as you.'

'But my name is Sara Finn.'

He shrugged. 'So it is. It was a slip of the tongue.'

'Was it? You haven't come about the doll, have you?'

'What doll is that?'

'The one I took from Mary. I thought it was mine at first, but Mary said it was her doll and I stole it from her. We decided to have half each and share her. Because Mary had died I didn't see any harm in taking the doll with me when I left the farm. I missed my friend and wanted something to remember her by. How do you know about the Fenns . . . unless Mr Leighton told you? Why do you want to know so much about me?'

She was more astute than he'd expected her to be. 'Perhaps it's because I like you.'

'Perhaps you do . . . but no, it isn't because you like me. You appear to be friendly, and you are, but your questions have a purpose behind them. It's about the doll isn't it? Uncle Fenn wants it back and he sent you here to get it. He wanted everything, the farm and everything in it, except for me. But I didn't think he knew about the doll. It was part of our secret game, and we kept her hidden. I put her in the bottom of the sack with my change of clothes on top.

'After they died uncle kept shouting at me to tell him where the money and the will was. I didn't know what he was talking about. Then one day he found a box with some papers in it, and he burned them in the grate. They curled in on themselves, went black and flew off up the chimney on a draught. They looked like bats. I often wondered where they ended up.'

Interesting how her memory came in fragments, as if she'd built a wall around her past, and bits kept escaping. But then, this girl was adept at settling into her environment, like a broody hen sitting on an egg. It was obvious that she liked to feel secure, however tenuous her hold was likely to be.

He should put her mind at rest over this. After all, what bearing could a doll have on the puzzle that was her life? 'No, it's not about the doll, but I should perhaps tell you that I'm a detecting agent and I'm investigating your background so I can restore you to your rightful place in society, Miss Serafina.'

The giggle she gave had a breathless quality. 'You mean I might be a lost princess after all?'

The truth often threw people off guard if they weren't expecting it, and her expression told him that she didn't believe him. But she would remember him telling her that she didn't belong in the comfortable little niche she was settling herself into if, or *when*, the time came.

Although he was quite sure she could play the part of a princess to perfection if she found herself dressed in satin and visiting a palace, he said, 'I haven't met many princesses employed as country housekeepers, have you?'

Laughter burst from her. 'Oh, you . . . behave yourself. I'll be back for the tray in a little while.'

'Will you bring the doll to show me?'

'If you like. She's precious to me because she's all I've got to remember Mary by, so I don't want to lose her.'

'You won't lose her.'

'Her name's Charlotte.'

Adam's breath nearly left his body. Now who was thrown off guard? It felt as though she could see right through him and was playing some sort of game. This was too much of a coincidence. 'Charlotte? How did the doll come by that name?'

She shrugged and gave a secretive grin. 'You'll know that when I show it to you.'

And he did discover something when she brought it back for him to inspect – firstly that it was an expensive doll in the same style of one Celia had when she was growing up. A wax composite face and limbs were attached to a sawdust-stuffed body. The doll was dressed as an infant in a lace-trimmed, flowered nightgown, and she wore a frilly bonnet with ribbons over a brown wig. Her glass eyes were opened and shut by a wire mechanism at the waist.

His second surprise came when he saw the ragged remnant of shawl the doll was wrapped in. Embroidered in the corner was the name, Charlotte H.

'There, you see . . . Charlotte. I called her after the name on the shawl.'

'Was the doll wearing this shawl when you got her?'

Instantly, the answer came back. 'No, I always had the shawl. I was six when I got the doll for my birthday. At least, I thought the old lady gave it to me for my birthday, but when it was Mary's turn to be the orphan she said the old woman gave it to her.' She shrugged. 'Does it matter? We went to the farm shortly afterwards. I remember that better.'

'When you want to.'

'Not all memories are pleasant to remember, are they?'

'You guard yours well.'

She shrugged and they gazed at each other longer than was comfortable.

There was the sound of a carriage outside. 'That's the doctor; your sister will bring him up in a moment, no doubt. I'd better tidy you up.' She bade him lean forward and pounded his pillows into shape, her breasts moulding against her bodice with just a few heartbeats of space between. 'Lean back, now.' She began to tuck the bedclothes in, her movements economical. Her hair was as smooth and glossy as a yard of melted chocolate and her mouth was slightly pursed in concentration, so her natural pout was pronounced. She was so kissable that Adam could almost taste it.

All he had to do was move his head an inch or so and . . . He closed his eyes, enjoying the anticipation and barely resisting the temptation. The atmosphere between them was fraught with possibilities.

Quietly, he said, 'What would you do if I kissed you, Serafina?'

She moved away from him in a flurry of alarm. 'I stabbed the last man who tried it.'

'Stabbed him?'

When his eyes flew open he just caught the remnant of her quick smile before she told him, 'In the hand with a fork.' She gazed at the door with relief written all over her. 'Ah, here's Miss Chapman with the doctor. Good morning, Doctor. Miss Chapman.'

Only a female with a touch of wickedness in her could tell him she'd stabbed a man with a fork, then sound so totally angelic the next second. Serafina fascinated him.

'Good morning, Miss Finn. How is my brother this morning?'

'As lively as a flea on a dog's tail.'

When Celia hiccuped with laughter the doctor smiled benignly at her before turning a disapproving look upon Sara. 'Not exactly a kind description to apply to the afflicted, Miss Finn.'

'But a true one,' she argued.

'Then perhaps it's time we allowed Mr Chapman out of bed.'

Allowed him out of bed? she thought. Adam Chapman was a law unto himself. Fancy asking her what she'd do if he kissed her, when if he'd just kissed her without warning, as she was sure he'd wanted to, he would have soon found out what she'd do.

She would find out too, come to that. She fought off a threatening grin and her mouth tingled as the idea of Adam kissing her took hold. She'd never been kissed – at least not a proper kiss where she wanted to kiss in return, just the wet dribbly forced kiss from the reverend's son and Frederick Milson pushing himself against her like a fevered dog.

Not that she wanted Adam to kiss her, she told herself. The very idea . . . wasn't as objectionable to her as it should have been, she realized. What was she about, thinking such confronting and uncomfortable thoughts?

'Hah!' she said, then she realized that everyone was looking at her.

Colour rushed to her cheeks. 'Happen I'll give you some privacy then. Ring if you need me.' Scrubbing her lips against the back of her hand she picked up the doll, gave the grinning patient a bit of a glare and departed.

Ten

Sara made sure she wasn't alone with Adam, since she didn't want to encourage him. On their last evening before the Chapmans were due to return home Mr Leighton had arranged some entertainment for staff and guests alike.

They put on their best clothes for the occasion. Sara had an outfit that had been placed in the church charity bag when she'd worked for the Pawleys. Elizabeth had repaired the tear in it and shortened the hem before giving it to her to take with her. She'd also given her the cape that Frederick Milson's dogs had shredded, and which he'd promised to replace. Needless to say, he hadn't. It was past repair, so thank goodness she had a shawl to wear if she needed to go outside.

'The gown will be warm to wear to church in the winter, and the material is long-lasting,' Elizabeth had said of the outfit.

It was also ugly, but Sara had no choice but to wear the brown checked skirt and velvet jacket over a cream-coloured blouse. Its only decoration was a small piece of lace at the neck. She wished she had a brooch to wear, but she didn't. Instead, she took a star made from small glass beads from the Christmas tree and pinned it to her hair. The beads shivered as she moved and sparkled like diamonds in the candlelight. Maggie and Fanny wore different shades of blue, and Giles and Joseph Tunney looked self-conscious in their Sunday suits.

All of them had been rehearsing something for the evening, and could be found in odd corners, muttering to themselves in the lead up to the social event.

Sara had gone into the dining room early to help Maggie bring the supper through. They placed it on the sideboard so people could help themselves, and they opened the dividing door that led to the drawing room. Oscar had opened the wine and decanted it, and there were jugs of lemonade.

Mr Leighton had told them that he'd prefer candles tonight. Sara had set them out exactly where he'd told her, because he had a remarkable memory when it came to such things. There were sconces along the sideboard, several in trays so the wax wouldn't drip on to the furniture, and on the piano, too, secured in candle holders. When her employer came in to check, she said, 'Everything is where it should be, Mr Leighton.'

'Good . . . what are you wearing, Sara?'

'A brown check skirt and a brown velvet jacket.'

He screwed his face up. 'Brown! How very sensible of you.'

'It's all I've got.'

'Well, at least it matches your hair and eyes. Hold out your arm.' When she did he gently stroked her sleeve. 'You feel like a lioness.'

'When did you last stroke a lioness?' she said, trying not to laugh at such a description.

'You have me there . . . I was going to say you felt like a camel, but it didn't seem quite so complimentary.'

Now Sara did laugh and her employer joined in.

'Would you take a glass of wine with me before the others join us. Needless to say, you'll have to do the pouring.'

She poured him a glass of red wine with the space of a thumb left empty at the top, so he wouldn't spill it. She took some lemonade for herself.

'Firstly, I want to thank you for all you've done this week. Mr Chapman and his sister are very appreciative of your care.'

'It was no trouble, Mr Leighton. It wasn't as though he was dangerously ill, thank goodness, and I like having plenty to keep me occupied.'

'I know you do . . . tell me, what do you think of Celia Chapman?'

Ah . . . so this was the real objective of this little tête-à-tête. She managed to keep her amusement under control when she said, 'More to the point, Mr Leighton, what do *you* think of Miss Chapman?'

'Highly . . . and what's more I seem to think of her all the time. Does she appear to be the type of woman who would encourage attention from a man . . . one like me, I mean, whose vision no longer exists?' He shrugged. 'Perhaps not.'

'Did Miss Chapman give you an impression that she would?'

'I felt perfectly at ease with her, you know, Sara, and I thought that perhaps my liking for her was reciprocated. But then, I imagined that it was just kindness on her part, that I was reading more into her attention because I couldn't see her expression.'

Fiercely she told him, 'You can see better than most men who have sight; some of them can't see past the ends of their noses. Would you like me to find out if Miss Chapman would encourage your attention?'

'If the opportunity arises, but be discreet. Discover if she'd welcome me calling on her when I get back to London. I wouldn't like to approach her directly here since she is under an obligation and might feel awkward.'

'From what I observe, Miss Chapman has a sigh in her eyes every time she looks at you, and she lights up when you walk into the room. And no wonder, you've been flirting with her.'

'Have I?' He chuckled. 'I do so enjoy her company, you know. She makes me feel alive.'

Sara finished her lemonade and rose to her feet. 'If there's nothing else, sir? I thought I might go upstairs and offer my services to Miss Chapman.'

'How very devious of you, Sara. Off you go then.'

Celia was seated at the dressing table when Sara knocked and entered. Her gown was a pretty pale-lilac colour, and she had a silver pendant around her neck. 'Is there anything you need helping with, Miss Chapman?'

Celia turned, a genuine smile on her face. 'I've never been able to afford a maid so I'm used to fending for myself. Shall we go down together? I've never felt confident of walking into a social gathering by myself. Adam says I'm too shy, and the more often I do it the easier it will become.'

And here was she thinking that, because Adam Chapman had an air of confidence about him, he was also wealthy. He was a professional working man, after all, and for that he went up in her estimation. 'May we talk for a minute or two first, Miss Chapman?'

'Of course . . . is it something to do with Adam.'

'Adam . . . ? No it's nothing to do with him,' and she grinned. 'It's Mr Leighton?'

'Finch?' Colour flooded Celia's cheeks. 'He hasn't caught the German measles from Adam, has he?'

'No, but I'm on a mission for him. He wants me to discreetly find out if you'd encourage him if he called on you when he returns to London.'

Celia Chapman gave a nervous laugh, then she giggled. 'That wasn't exactly discreet, Sara.'

'I know, but you strike me as the type of woman who would like to know where she stood in the affections of a man. If I may offer recommendation, Mr Leighton is a lovely man. He's kind and thoughtful, and he thinks he's not good enough for you because of his blindness.'

'What utter nonsense!'

And Celia said it so vehemently that Sara began to laugh. 'I'll tell him it's yes then, shall I?'

'I've only known him a week, so you may tell him that I will promise only to think about encouraging him, and will give him my answer in due course. Tell him I will not be approached through a third party, but thank you for the recommendation, Sara. I will seriously bear that in mind.'

Sara said with a groan, 'Poor Mr Leighton. I can see that you're interested in him.'

'And I can see that my brother is interested in you, Sara. What do you have to say to that?'

'That you needn't worry, since we're on different social levels and he is merely trifling with my affections, as men do with housemaids on occasion.'

'Worry!' Her eyes widened considerably at that. 'Good Lord, where do you get your strange ideas from? I'm not worried, my dear . . . what if I told you that Adam was definitely interested in you?'

It wasn't normal that a man like Adam Chapman would be looking for a serious relationship with a housekeeper, even if he wasn't wealthy enough to hire a maid for his sister. 'I'd say that he's made that perfectly clear, but I'd like to know *why* he's interested in me. I get the feeling there's a motive behind his questions, but he uses evasions.'

'You can trust Adam, you know.'

Sara didn't answer, and she was not about to discuss her feelings towards Adam Chapman. A man like him would attract many women. He'd be gone tomorrow and he wouldn't give her another thought after the door closed behind him. She'd get over him.

Celia took her hands, turned them over and gazed at the palms. 'Did you get these calluses at the workhouse?'

'Yes.'

'Poor you.'

Feeling a kiss soft against her cheek, Sara experienced a moment of sadness, and she wanted to cry for what she'd never missed before, a mother's love. Who had the woman been and what was she like to have left her daughter at an orphanage? But then, perhaps she'd had no choice.

Celia's hands were soft and white in contrast to her own, and she pulled away, saying more sharply than she intended, then immediately regretting it, 'They were caused by hard work. It's nothing to be ashamed of; I'm used to them.'

'Of course it's nothing to be ashamed of. Nevertheless, I'll smooth some balm on them to help soften them.'

She opened a small jar and massaged some of the contents into Sara's hands, working it into her palms and her finger-tips. 'You know, Serafina, if you keep on doing this they will improve.'

Did everyone know her proper name? She grinned; it did make her feel a bit grand though. 'I can't afford such luxuries. I'm sorry, I didn't mean to sound sharp earlier. The hand balm smells lovely.'

'I make it myself out of beeswax, almond and lavender oil. I'll leave you this little pot if you'd like. If you wear it to bed with cotton gloves on, it works much quicker.'

'Thank you, Miss Chapman. That's kind of you.'

'Please call me Celia, after all, I do call you by your first name.'

'I will then, Miss . . . Celia,' and they looked at each other and laughed.

Everyone was in the drawing room when they went downstairs.

Adam moved forward to meet her, kissing her hand as though she was a grand lady, and murmuring, 'You look lovely, Princess Serafina.'

Let him play his games, she thought, but she grinned as she said graciously, 'Thank you.'

His glance wandered to her hair, which she'd drawn back into a bun, as best she could, and he smiled. 'The star looks prettier on you than on the Christmas tree.'

'Do you always notice details such as stars on Christmas trees?' She absorbed his easy smile and told herself to beware . . . to *beware!*

'Usually I do . . . that one fell from Orion's belt.'

'Yet there are still seven stars left up there. How odd.'

'How odd that you should know such a thing.'

'No stranger than you knowing about it. Mr Leighton has books in his library that explain such things as the position of the stars in the sky. I read them in my spare time. I'm afraid that this one did not fall from the sky, but I borrowed it from Mr Leighton's festive decorations.'

'You have no romance in you, Serafina.'

She chuckled. 'Oh, I do, I just don't let it run away with me.'

The wine relaxed everyone, and the entertainment began. Oscar consulted a piece of paper in his hand. 'Ladies and gentlemen, first up on the programme is—'

There came a jingle of bells. Fingal suddenly jumped up on to the piano keyboard and stomped along it with a loud discordant tune, stopping only to scratch behind his ear when he reached the middle. When he leaped off at the other end everyone began to laugh and clap. He sidestepped across the floor to where Maggie sat and jumped into her lap.

'Show-off,' Maggie said.

'For the benefit of Mr Leighton, that was Fingal playing the cat concerto. Now, we have Fanny, who will recite and act out a short rhyme titled Incy Wincy Spider.'

Fanny leaped to her feet, grinning at everyone and wriggling her fingers about in anticipation.

'Incy wincy spider climbed up the water spout . . . along came the rain drops and washed the spider out . . .'

Fanny managed the nursery rhyme without too much trouble, until she got to the last line. Then she faltered and looked towards Sara. Sara wiggled her finger at her and Fanny gave a broad grin and copied her actions, shrilling out with great confidence, 'Wincy incy spider climbed down the spout again.'

She retired pink-faced and smiling after her effort and Mr Leighton clapped loudly and called out, 'Well done, Fanny.'

Joseph Tunney played the fiddle while Giles sang a folk song in foot-stomping style. Then it was Sara's turn and she played a Bach Sonata followed by a piano duet with Mr Leighton, one that he'd taught her when he'd been home before.

They stopped for supper.

Afterwards, Oscar and Maggie recited a poem between them, then Adam played the piano while Celia sang, her voice sweet and tuneful. Sara turned her gaze on Finch Leighton. He had a faint, but tender smile playing around his mouth as Celia sang, and when she'd finished he said, 'Bravo, Celia, you have a truly delightful voice.'

'Thank you, Finch,' she said, the praise bringing colour whipping into her cheeks.

Christmas carols around the piano finished off the evening. Sara couldn't remember enjoying herself so much.

She helped Maggie take the dishes into the kitchen afterwards.

'There's a meat fork missing,' Maggie said.

'I expect I'll find it in the morning when I clean the dining room. Let's get off to bed. I've had a grand time.'

'Aye, me too. Having visitors to stay has perked Mr Leighton up no end, and he hasn't done any moping for a long time and is getting his interest back in everything again.' Maggie took off her apron, folded it over the back of the chair and grinned. 'You want to watch out for that Mr Chapman. He's got his eyes on you, my girl . . . you mark my words. Goodnight, Sara.'

'Goodnight, Maggie.' Sara made sure that the door was locked and the candles were extinguished, then retired to her own quarters. She'd forgotten to light the fire and her rooms were cold. Not that she ever used the small sitting room, except when she was teaching her pupils their letters. She was proud of them, especially Fanny, who had managed to retain the nursery rhyme she'd taught her. Undressing as quickly as possible she pulled on a patched flannel nightgown, climbed into her narrow bed and pulled her knees up to her chest. Wrapping her arms around her body she promised herself she'd find an extra blanket tomorrow. It was too late to go and look for one now. She pretended it was Adam Chapman's arms around her, and she gradually warmed up.

Was this how she'd spend the rest of her life, she thought,

never really knowing who she was, spending her nights shivering alone in a servant's bed with an imaginary lover, and spending her days polishing somebody else's furniture and wondering if love would ever come her way? Perhaps she'd marry for convenience in the end, like Elizabeth Pawley, who didn't seem to mind her lot in life, or Mrs Cornwell, who'd seemed resigned to hers, and had been desperate enough to answer an advertisement in a newspaper.

The widower got the best of such an arrangement. As well as a wife for his bed, he'd get a mother for his orphaned children, a housekeeper, a cook, and in Elizabeth Pawley's case, a tutor – and all for no expense except the food she ate to keep her alive and working.

Sara believed in love, and she was enjoying the romance enfolding before her eyes. Mr Leighton deserved someone shy and sweet like Celia, especially after the disappointment of his first wife. That reminded her that she'd not told Mr Leighton what Celia Chapman had said yet. He would interrogate her tomorrow after their guests had left, no doubt, and she grinned as she fell asleep with Adam's imaginary arms still about her.

Morning departure. It was not Sara's place to stand outside and farewell the guests as if she'd been their hostess, so she got on with her work.

Celia had said goodbye to her earlier and given her a hug. 'I do hope we meet again, Serafina. I've enjoyed my stay, and enjoyed meeting you.' She handed over a note. 'This is for Finch. I'd be obliged if you'd read it to him.'

'Thank you, Celia, I will,' and she slid it into her apron pocket. 'I've enjoyed meeting you, too,' she said, and that yearning filled her again . . . one that said she wanted to belong to someone. But she mustn't feel sorry for herself. There were people worse off. At least she was strong and healthy, had food in her stomach, a fine roof over her head and an equally fine employer to match.

She heard Adam in the hall and felt disappointed when he didn't come to say goodbye. Lingering in the drawing room she heard Giles bring the horse and cart around and heard them talking, laughing and exchanging pleasantries.

'I've forgotten something; I won't be a minute.' Adam's footsteps came swiftly across the hall towards the drawing room she was in, and her heart began to beat so fast she thought the top of her head might fly off.

She pretended to be busy, and was looking under the cushions when he came in. 'We've lost the meat fork and I'm looking for it,' she said, feeling the need to have an excuse for her actions before he asked.

He came to where she stood, took her hand in his and placed the fork in it. 'I have it.'

'What are you doing with it?'

'You told me that you stabbed the last man who tried to kiss you, with a fork. I wanted you to have something to defend yourself with.'

'Defend myself . . . whatever do you mean?'

'This.' Taking her face between his palms he stooped and captured her mouth. His lips were a soft tender caress against hers, and she seemed to lack the will to pull away. She felt growing inside her the very emotional connection with him that she was trying to avoid. She should be fighting against him not encouraging him.

Then it was over, and she wanted more so she kept her eyes shut and couldn't look at him in case he saw it in her eyes.

'Mr Chapman, you shouldn't have done that,' she whispered, and his name was almost a sigh.

'Well, don't expect me to apologize. We'll meet again, Serafina, and that's a promise,' he said, and was gone.

She didn't open her eyes again until the sound of the horse and cart had died away. When she did open them it was to find that the fork had dropped to the ground. Her captured breath expelled from her in little puffs and gasps. Truly he'd bewitched her, and she must get a grip on herself.

Mr Leighton came in. 'Sara?'

She pulled herself together. 'Yes, I'm here.'

'Are you all right? Your voice is shaking.'

She sucked in a breath to steady it. 'I'm fine.'

'Come into the morning room. I want to speak to you.'

She grinned. 'Certainly, Mr Leighton. Miss Chapman has left a note with me for you.'

Eagerness filled his voice. 'What does it say?'

'It says that if you can be patient and wait until the appropriate time, your housekeeper will open it and read it to you.'

She made a big show of opening it, rustling the paper until he growled, 'Have you ever felt like strangling someone?'

'Often . . .' She grinned and cleared her throat.

> *Dear Finch,*
>
> *On behalf of my brother and myself, our heartfelt thanks for your hospitality over the past few days. Adam's illness could have become more serious without your intervention and the dedicated care of your staff, especially Miss Serafina, to whom we have both become attached.*
>
> *I do hope you'll call on us when next you are in London. Please feel at liberty to visit us at the agency, which is not far from your London home, and will be more convenient for you than travelling to Chiswick, I feel.*
>
> *With best wishes from us both.*
>
> *Celia Chapman*

Sara gazed at her employer, a suspicion growing in her mind. 'What agency is that, Mr Leighton?'

'Adam Chapman has his own detecting agency in London. He's becoming well thought of in legal circles, and will no doubt do well for himself in the future. Didn't he mention it to you?'

'Yes . . . yes, he did . . . he was teasing about it; said I might be a princess he was looking for.' She gave a faint smile. 'I'd forgotten.'

'Do you think you *are* Adam's lost princess?'

She stared at him for a moment then chuckled. 'You know that could never be, but you might be Celia's lost prince.'

'I hope you are right. Was that all Celia said in her letter?'

'Yes . . . but she mentioned to me in private that she'd rather you had approached her directly with your request.'

'I deserve a reprimand. Did she say anything about my lack of sight being a factor.'

'It was more of a retort really. She snorted and said, Utter nonsense!' Placing the letter in his hand she was about to walk away when she thought to ask him, 'Did you know that Adam Chapman ran a detecting agency before he came here?'

'I'd heard of him.'

'He asked me questions about my past.'

'He's curious about people, that's his nature. I believe he's very good at what he does, and is both thorough and discreet.'

Sara was satisfied by his answer to a certain extent because she instinctively trusted Finch Leighton. 'Sometimes I thought there was a definite purpose behind his questions.'

'Perhaps there was. He seemed attracted to you.'

She was glad he couldn't see her blush as she remembered Adam kissing her – and of her allowing him to. Nevertheless, she dismissed the suggestion with a sharp retort. 'I'm a servant and he was flirting. Adam Chapman is a handsome man who would attract women – not me of course,' she added hastily. 'He would have forgotten me before they got to the station.'

'Perhaps you're right, my dear,' he said with a smile, and slipped the letter into his pocket. 'Would you fetch my coat, Sara. I'm going out for a walk around the garden. There are certain things I need to think about and later I'd like you to write a letter for me. It's of a private nature.'

'You know, Mr Leighton, you wouldn't have forgotten how to form your letters, so I'm sure there's a way of writing you could learn if you needed to keep matters private, as long as you don't mind using a pencil . . . well, at first, anyway. Mastering pen and ink might be a bit messy.'

'How?' And he said it so eagerly that she smiled.

'If I can find some cardboard I'll show you when you come back.'

While he was out she cut a slot in a piece of cardboard, making it wide enough to fit inside a frame of cardboard and slide up and down.

He was surrounded by an aura of cold when he came back. Impatiently, he said, 'Have you done it? Explain it to me.'

She waited until he was seated. 'Feel in front of you.'

His fingers ran around the cardboard. 'It's a frame?'

'Yes. It's the same size as your notepaper and will fit over it and form your margins. Your notepaper is in the right-hand drawer.'

When she rustled a piece of his notepaper he took it from her and placed it under the frame. His fingers went around the edges making sure it was lined up. Picking up the small piece of slotted cardboard he frowned. 'What do I do with this?'

'You place it inside the frame, write your words inside the slot, then when you reach the end of the row you turn it over and down for the next line. You're going to have to use feel and memory, and make allowances for spaces.' She placed the pencil in his fingers. 'Try it . . . write your name.'

She could almost experience his concentration as he applied himself to the task and wrote, My name isfinch Leighton.

She told him, 'You've forgotten the space after is, and the capital letter of your first name, but it doesn't matter. It's readable and you'll get better at it if you practise. I've sharpened a couple of pencils and they're in the holder on your right.'

'How did you think of this?'

'I didn't think of it, Elizabeth Pawley did. She used the slotted cardboard to help the children in the workhouse reduce the size of their letters, but it was on a slate and with chalk. I adapted it, that's all. It's better than nothing. I believe she did charity work, visiting the blind at home and teaching children their alphabets. She said there were books with raised letters in for blind people to read.'

'There are, but they're clumsy and heavy, and take a devil of a long time. Mrs Pawley sounds like a worthy and pious woman; how did she end up in the workhouse?'

'When her father died he was deeply in debt. He was a church cleric too, which is probably why she was content to marry a man like Reverend Pawley, and grateful that he had motherless children for her to care for. I think you would like her if you met her.'

'I'm sure I would. You know, you have a good heart, Serafina.'

She smiled, for the name had stuck with her since they'd called her that at the social evening. She might as well make it her own now she was grown up.

'What does my writing look like?'

'It's a bit wobbly, but readable, and it will improve with prac-tice as you grow in confidence. Now . . . I'd better get on with my work. I'll check on your progress in a little while.'

Finch hadn't expected to fall in love and wondered if his letter to Celia Chapman was too premature, since he didn't want to frighten her off. He was man enough to know that somebody else might sweep her off of her feet if he left it too long. Only God knew what it looked like, he thought as he sealed it. What he *did* know was that his words were more fluent than they would have been if he'd dictated the letter, and he'd apologized to Celia in advance in case it was hard to read.

The more he learned of Serafina the more he liked her, and she had a sensible head on her shoulders despite her youth. Although he didn't want to lose her he hoped the young woman would turn out to be what Adam wanted her to be. And if she didn't . . . that Adam would accept her for what she was, a hard-working, intelligent and loyal young woman.

Eleven

Christmas and New Year had come and gone quickly. Gifts had been exchanged and Serafina had been the recipient of a warm coat with a shawl collar and a matching bonnet and muff.

'I heard your teeth chattering in church, and Maggie told me that Frederick's dogs had ruined your cape,' Mr Leighton said by way of explanation for such a handsome gift.

Mr Leighton went to London to attend a wedding in January. He was due to return in April. Then the skies were wreathed in sunshine one minute and weeping all over the landscape the next. The daffodils were a moving ocean of lambent yellow and the trees newly born in tender shades of green. Catkins swung in the breeze like velvety golden tassels buzzing with bees – and in the eaves, house martins were busy with their nests and offspring.

Serafina allowed the spring air to circulate through the windows.

It was to be a month of wedding announcements. First Giles and Jassy. 'We're getting married next month,' he'd said, and had turned a bright red. 'Jassy's got a young'un inside her, she reckons. Anyway, I'm going to live at the farm and work for her pa, because the farm will be ours one day and I've got to learn how to run it, like.'

'You'll have to give Mr Leighton proper notice, mind,' Maggie said. 'He's been good to you, giving you a job when you was down and out and didn't have a roof over your head.'

'I'm not daft. I knows that, don't I, Maggie? Now I can write I reckon I'll put it down on paper, so it's legal, and private from the likes of you. I'll give it to him next time he comes down from London and I'll stay until he finds someone else.

'In the meantime you can mind your own business and stop being so bossy.'

Maggie retorted, 'You might have learned to write, but you're still a cider sucker if you think he can read it. He'll need someone else to tell him what's in your legal note.'

'Cider sucker yourself,' he said triumphantly. 'I'll read it to him messell, won't I?'

Finch Leighton arrived unannounced at the beginning of May. His face was wreathed with smiles as he gathered the staff together and said, 'Miss Celia Chapman has accepted my proposal of marriage. We're to be wed in July, and will travel to Italy for a month before returning here to Leighton Manor in August to live.'

After accepting the congratulations he headed off to the morning room. 'Serafina, I'd like to talk to you. Bring coffee for us both, please.'

Her employer was in his usual chair when she went in. She placed his coffee on the table and took the seat opposite.

He said, 'What's that perfume? It's making my throat a little husky.'

'It's blackthorn blossom. Is the fragrance too strong?'

'It is a little, but it's lovely . . . move it to the mantelpiece if you would.'

She did as she was told and seated herself again. He cleared his throat. 'Adam Chapman is coming to visit you next week.'

Her heart gave a jolt. 'Why should he want to see me? I'm nothing to him.'

His forehead creased into a frown. 'This is business, not personal.'

'Business . . . what business can he have with me?'

'It's complicated, but he's asked me to prepare you.'

Bewildered, she gazed at him. 'I don't understand; prepare me for what?'

'Of course you don't understand, since I haven't explained, yet,' he said testily. 'Don't keep interrupting else I'll be here all day. When Adam Chapman was taken ill he was looking for you.'

'Me?'

'He had no intention of approaching you. He just wanted to take a look at you when he got caught in that storm . . . you know what happened next.'

She took a deep breath, exaggerating her sigh as she set it free.

He grinned. 'He's traced your progress from the day you were born, through an orphanage in Dorset where you were left as a newborn baby. The orphanage was supported by an elderly woman called Constance Serafina Jarvis, who Adam believes was your relative. She made certain arrangements, and when she died you went to the farm in Gloucester with two of her trusted servants and their family.'

She remembered his questions and felt dismay. 'The Fenns.'

'Yes. From there you went to the workhouse, then into the Pawley household before coming to work for me.'

Adam had told her about his job . . . but he'd made light of it to put her off guard and trick her into answering questions about herself. Anger trickled through her and she stood. 'I see, thank you for telling me, sir.'

'Sit down, Serafina. I haven't finished.'

'My name isn't Serafina, it's Sara Finn.'

'Oh, for goodness sake, don't get your hackles up with me. Adam doesn't know if you are Serafina, but the name Sara Finn is so similar and you are familiar with it, so it's not likely to be a coincidence. The alternative is that you're Mary Fenn. You told Adam yourself that you used to swap names and parents.'

She grabbed at the familiar. 'Yes, that's it, I remember now . . . I'm Mary Fenn. Can I go now?'

There was a short silence then he said. 'Yes, go.'

'A pity you're being so stubborn,' he said when she was halfway to the door. 'If you'd stay you'd discover that Serafina Honeyman has two sisters. There is also a man who thinks he may be her father, and would dearly love to discover his daughter's whereabouts, and find her.'

Dear God, a family . . . her own family after all this time. Her heart began to ache and her knees weaken. 'This man who says he might be Serafina's father, tell me about him.'

'He's a seafaring man who has employed Adam Chapman to find you. One of Serafina's sisters was called Charlotte, the other is Marianne.'

She began to tremble. Could this be true? 'Why didn't Adam tell me? Why did he pretend to be interested in me for my own sake. He . . .' She pulled herself together. 'You said Adam doesn't know for certain, and this man only *might* be Serafina's father. That means that he might not be.'

'It means exactly that. Serafina might share a father with her sisters, she might not.'

'What of my mother? What type of woman would have both husband and lover . . . then give away her infant?'

'A woman who married for convention's sake, and who fell in love with someone else, my dear – one who lost her life giving birth to her third beloved daughter.'

She was responsible for her mother's death then. 'Then how . . . ?'

'Everything pointed to her husband. The sisters were told that Serafina had died with her mother, but recently the younger of the pair got it into her head that you might be alive.'

Everything inside Serafina seemed to collapse and she dropped into the nearest chair. 'What if I'm Mary Fenn?'

'And what if you *are* Serafina Honeyman? Adam wants to take you to meet the man who might have fathered you, in case there is a family resemblance.'

'And if there isn't?'

'Then no harm is done. I thought you'd be pleased to know that you might be part of a family.'

'No harm done! For the first time since I can remember I am truly happy. Sara Finn knew her place in life. Now you tell me I'm not her, and I'm probably not Mary Fenn either, but I could be – in all likelihood – a woman called Serafina Honeyman, who was responsible for her mother's death and was cast from the family home because she was born a bastard. And you expect me to feel pleased about it.'

Hadn't she often imagined herself as part of a family, of having siblings and a mother and a father? Though she took a deep breath, the panic rioting inside her didn't subside. Now she was faced with it she didn't think she'd be able to handle it. Illusion was one thing, reality another. They were strangers. What if they didn't like her, or her them? 'What if Serafina Honeyman had died after all, and this family finds out later and accuses me of being an imposter?' she said.

Mr Leighton snapped, 'Stop talking about yourself as if you're a third party you invented. If you can't discuss this without getting emotional and feeling sorry for yourself, you can go away until you can.'

The hurt she felt hit her like a blow, so her throat swelled with the ache of unshed tears. 'Sorry . . . I'm sorry.' But she hated him for wounding her, and rising from the chair she opened the door and went through it, slamming it behind her.

'Serafina, come back here!' he shouted.

'Leave me alone. My past is none of your business,' she tossed at him in reply. She left the house at a run and pounded through the garden, going past an astonished Joseph Tunney who was bent to a flower-bed, his fingers gouging into the crumbly earth to loosen the hold of the spring weeds. She headed for the copse as though a hound from hell was after her. Ignoring the small wooden bridge she splashed across the knee-deep stream on the way and tripped up the muddy bank. Her skirt was now slimed with mud and flapped wetly against her legs. Her boots filled up with cold water that slopped over the top with every step she took.

She stopped, gasping when she ran out of breath, and she sank down on a fallen log covered in brightly coloured layers of fungus. It was cool in the shade of the copse and the long bracts of thorny blackberry bushes plucked at her clothes. Underfoot, the layer of compressed leaves oozed water left there from the showers, and the air smelled of mould, mushrooms, bruised pine needles and decay.

The old woman had smelled of mould. She'd been dressed in a nightgown, her hair spread around her.

'Kiss your aunt goodbye, Serafina.'

Her skin had been grey, and patched with brown liver spots, her lips purple. Close up they were surrounded by downy grey hairs that brushed against Serafina's lips. The long, silver hair that Serafina had been allowed to brush when the woman was feeling old and tired, was fashioned into a severe braid wrapped around her head.

Why won't Aunt Constance talk to me? Where is she going? She's so cold.

'The dead are always cold because they have no soul to warm them. God has claimed her soul and taken it to heaven. Be glad you don't look like her with that gypsy face and coarse skin. You're coming to live with us now, on a farm far away from here. That's her legacy to you, to all of us. We will be your family. She wanted you taken away where nobody will know about you and the shame you brought down on the family. You're unclean, and from now on you'll be Sara Fenn.'

After that, Serafina had lost herself. She didn't want to be unclean and bring down shame on anyone.

She leaned forward, her breath rattling harshly in her throat. She had never known what unclean meant until now. The Reverend Pawley had told her that cleanliness was next to godliness, and if she worked hard God would take that into account when she died. So she had scrubbed and polished his floors on her hands and knees, and she'd kept herself clean and prayed every day with his family.

But now she'd discovered that she was the result of a sin, and she had killed her own mother and been cast out by her family. What was worse, she'd met Adam Chapman and now knew the control her emotions exerted over her body and her will. Now she understood why her mother had sinned in the first place, and she couldn't blame her for it.

Tears coursed down her face. Mr Leighton was right. She had to face up to this . . . but not yet. She was happy here . . . he would understand that, and he would send Adam Chapman away.

Adam had said her father was a seafarer. Curiosity tickled at her. 'Damn it, stop thinking about it!' she yelled.

There was a whirring sound as a startled bird exploded out of a bush.

'Serafina?' It was her employer, with Oscar.

'Yes . . . I'm here.'

'Typical of you to have ended up in a patch of brambles,' he grumbled as a thorn caught at his trouser leg.

'I didn't ask you to come looking for me.'

'You sound low down.' He stretched his hand out. 'Where is she, Oscar, in a rabbit hole?'

'You're treating me like a child,' she said.

'Because you're acting like one.'

'It's not very gentlemanly of you to remind me.'

Oscar led him forward. 'Miss Finn is sitting on a fallen log, sir.'

'Thank you, Oscar. You may go back to the house.'

'Yes, sir.' Oscar turned and walked away.

'There's no need to be so churlish. Aren't you going to invite me to sit down?'

'It's your log.' She sighed. 'Two steps forward, turn and sit. Where's your stick?'

'I forgot it . . . which of us is going to apologize first?'

'You are.'

'Because?'

'You're a man, you were insensitive and I feel betrayed by you
. . . and by Adam Chapman, as well.'

'Ah, you're going to take the gender approach. A good stance,
since it's manly to shoulder the blame in such a situation.'

'Unless you weren't to blame in the first place, then it's
stupid.'

'Men are often stupid, I'm afraid. I'm sorry for being insensitive to your feelings. You're always so sensible, and I forgot that
you think and feel like a woman. In no way did I betray you.
As for Adam Chapman, he can make his own apology. Now you
can apologize to me.'

'For what?'

'Slamming the door to start with. A lump of soot fell down
the chimney and scattered all over the drawing room.'

'I just cleaned that room yesterday; now I'll have to clean it
all over again,' she wailed.

He chuckled. 'It serves you right for getting into such a paddy.'

'Ah . . . but if the soot had stayed in the chimney it might have
caught fire and burned the house down.' There was a moment
of silence then she sniffed and offered, 'I'm sorry I was rude to
you, even though you deserved it. None of this is your fault.'

'You don't give much quarter, do you? If it's not my fault then
it must be yours.'

'I can't help what I feel.'

'Then we'll blame it on Adam, since he's not here to argue
with us.' He reached out and his fingertips brushed against her
face. 'You're crying. Did the news that you might not be Sara
Nobody from Nowhere upset you that much?'

'I like my life just as it is. I love it here and I like being Sara
Finn and working for you. I don't want it to change, and I'm
scared.'

A beam of sunlight shafted down through the tree canopy and
fell across his eyes. He flinched and closed his eyelids.

'Why did you do that?'

'Do what?'

'You screwed your eyes up against the sunlight.'

'Did I? Sometimes I can see light and shadows . . . I told you. It doesn't mean anything.'

'It must mean something. What did they tell you after the accident?'

'The doctor said he could see no damage to my eyes and it was possible I could get some vision back in time, but he strongly doubted it.'

'What would you do if you did get your sight back?'

He sighed. 'I'm trying to avoid wanting it too much, a concept that you're totally familiar with. Getting my sight back would be a *truly* life-changing event, don't you think, but frightening since I'll be able to look in a mirror and see myself.'

'Ah . . . you're leading me back to where you want me to go. I can never get the best of you in conversation. Out with it, Mr Leighton.'

'The point of this conversation is about *your* life changing, and of course it will change. It did for me. I never thought I'd meet another woman I wanted to marry, but in Celia, I have. You will just have to adapt, you know, as I've had to, and will have to again if my condition reverses.' He held out his hands to her. 'Let's go home, Serafina.'

'Promise you'll not make me do anything that I don't want to.'

'Only if you promise that you'll listen to what Adam has to say, and think the situation over carefully, using that good mind of yours. You'd have friends to support you if you decide to go ahead, whatever the outcome.'

Reluctantly, she murmured, 'I promise to listen,' and she was filled with an odd flutter of excitement at the thought of seeing Adam again.

She led her employer around the bramble patch and they made their way out of the copse. She expected him to place his hand on her shoulder like he did with Oscar, but he took her hand in his instead, turned it palm up and ran his fingers over it. 'Celia has sent some more salve down for your hands. It seems to be working. They're smoother than they were when you first came here.'

'That was kind of her. It does help. I'm glad you fell in love with her . . . she's so sweet and calm, and kind.'

'So am I, and yes, Celia is all of those things, and more besides.'

It began to rain, one of May's soft surprise gifts to the country-side. He laughed and said, 'I should have brought an umbrella. We'll be soaked.'

'I'm drenched already. I waded through the stream instead of over the bridge, and it was deeper than I thought.'

'I used to do that when I was a child and it reached to my chest. It was fun and it used to annoy my governess, because she had to wade in to get me out.'

'And I thought you were perfect.' She laughed and her hand closed around his. 'Can you run?'

'Rather clumsily, because I can't see the ground coming to meet me.' He huffed with laughter. 'It sounds like a challenge, so I'll try not to fall on my face.'

They galloped down the hill in an undignified manner, leaving behind them the scent of bruised and broken plants, and she led him sploshing into the stream. The breath left his body in a whoosh. They began to laugh, splashing water over each other before wading the rest of the way across.

'I have very little sense of distance or direction and I didn't expect that, though I did enjoy it, since there's something satisfying in being . . .'

'Childish?'

'Yes, hmmm . . . I should have expected you to claim retribution for that remark.'

The sun came out and once again he screwed his eyes up against the direct light. He said wistfully, 'What does everything look like?'

'Everything is covered in quivering, silvery drops. The meadow is full of daffodils, marsh violets, primroses and butterflies and the hedgerows are enamelled in red, gold and green. There's a rainbow arching across the sky . . .' A small lie to colour the picture wouldn't hurt. '. . . and some swallows darting after the insects.'

'It's exactly as I remember it always being in early May. You're good at painting a scene with words, better than Oscar. I could almost see it.'

'I'm not as good at painting a scene with a brush in my hand though.' The argument about her name no longer existed. Oscar must have seen them coming from the upstairs window because he was in the kitchen when they entered, grinning all over his face as they emptied the water from their footwear.

'Miss Finn tried to drown me, Oscar.'

'How very odd, sir. From my observations I could have sworn it was the other way around.'

'Have you been spying on me then?'

'Yes, sir. I considered your behaviour to be most undignified. I have some dry clothes ready for you to change into; we don't want you to risk catching a cold.'

The laugh Finch Leighton gave was spontaneous. 'Oscar, if I do catch a cold, then that little excursion will be worth every snuffle and sneeze. There's nothing like being childish to cheer yourself up. You should try it.'

'If you say so, sir,' and the sniff Oscar gave was so stuffy that Serafina giggled when the manservant winked at her and said, his voice laced with disapproval, 'I don't know what Miss Chapman would make of such odd behaviour.'

'Celia would have joined in I expect. Stop being such a bloody schoolmarm, Oscar, else I'll tell Miss Finn about the time you got yourself inebriated on my brandy and I found you in the fountain minus your—'

'Mr Leighton! That is not something to shock a young woman's ears with.'

'Perhaps you're right, Oscar, they might drop off, and that would be a pity. Off with you then, Miss Finn. I can hear you dripping from here.'

As she squelched off towards her quarters Serafina heard Oscar say, 'Giles is waiting to see you, sir. I told him to come back in half an hour. He was wearing his best suit.'

'Oh, dear, it must be something serious then.'

Adam was still living in his Chiswick house. Mostly he ate out, and his housemaid came in twice a week to do the cleaning and his washing. The idea of putting tenants in the house and renting gentlemen's rooms elsewhere had been discarded by Adam the very moment he'd met Serafina.

It amazed him that a chain of events that had initially started life as a search for the orphaned child, John Barrie, had widened into ripples that had led him to the Honeyman sisters, their husbands, and from there to an ever-widening circle of friends and acquaintances, until eventually he'd met the young woman who'd stolen his heart.

Even his mother and sister had found love and happiness within the circle. Adam was happy for both of them, but especially for his sister, who had almost resigned herself to spinsterhood. Finch Leighton was perfect for Celia, since they would be intellectually compatible. Finch wasn't the type of man who'd measure Celia's use in terms of household duties. Even when the man was in the company of Serafina – who was to all intents and purposes Finch's servant – there was lively conversation as he encouraged her to exercise her mind.

Celia also loved Leighton Manor, and was looking forward to settling there and being a companion to her husband. Adam just wished that Finch could see her because he'd appreciate her quiet elegance, especially now she was glowing with the happiness she felt inside her.

His own home was lonely without Celia and his mother for company, though he received many social invitations. Unexpectedly, due to the elevation of his position to Edgar Wyvern's stepson the interest in him as a possible suitor for somebody's daughter had also increased. His heart belonged to Serafina though.

He hoped she would learn to cope with the social side of things, though she was not backward at having her say once she'd found her confidence. Her education was patchy, but better than most females, especially one who'd spent time farmed out and who'd been moved from one place to another.

Serafina had unexpected depths though, and she was curious about things and wanted to learn. She would find her security here with him if she'd have him, and he'd encourage her to blossom. Here was the house she coveted, a comfortable nest, bigger than she'd planned for, but not big enough to scare her. She'd keep it in order, because that was her nature, and that would also suit him. But that was for the future. It didn't strike him as odd that he was planning in advance, since it was part of his nature to do so, and he could change direction if he needed to, as long as he kept his goal in sight.

Adam spent a few days at the office to consult on cases and

to make sure everything was in hand and running as it should. He then travelled to Poole to see Marianne and bring her up to date with events. He hoped to bring this particular case to an end within the month.

From Marianne he learned that Erasmus was due back in port in two weeks' time, and he promised her he would try and bring Serafina to meet them by then.

He wasn't at all confident though. The more he knew of Serafina, the more Adam learned that behind her confident veneer was a frighteningly vulnerable young woman – one who'd experienced rejection from the moment she was born.

He would have to be patient with her, and gently pace the pressure he placed on that quick mind of hers, as well as appeal to her emotions.

Twelve

Finch Leighton intended to move into the family home after his marriage. He'd accepted an appointment as a local magistrate, and had gone with Oscar to sit in on a court session and make the acquaintance of his future peers.

It was a bright day when Adam arrived at Leighton Manor. He led a horse with a wicker basket attached to either side of the saddle. There was an overnight travelling bag clutched in his other fist. His honeyed curls bobbed about his hat, and his stride carried him over the ground fast. He nearly took Serafina's breath away.

When Adam lowered the baskets Joseph took the horse round to the stable. He must have walked from the station to enjoy the day, Serafina thought, though there was very little room left on the horse for a passenger, as well. Like many tall men he wore his clothes well, and his short flared overcoat was a dark contrast to his pale-grey trousers.

There was a surge inside Serafina, like a spring tide relentlessly pushing the water over the sand into an empty space, then swirling around and taking everything back with it as it receded. She felt her body separate into swirling fragments that were drawn towards him like metal to a magnet. He was here to put pressure on her, she knew.

Glancing at herself in the mirror she sighed at the sight of her unflattering servant garb and her untidy braid. She'd been tidying up the linen cupboard. Now she hurriedly straightened her apron and pinched some colour into her cheeks, then reminded herself that Adam could have no interest in her beyond her relationship to one of his clients. Well, perhaps he could, she conceded, but that didn't mean she should encourage it.

A seafaring gentleman, Mr Leighton had described her father as. She imagined him scowling, his long facial hair streaming in the wind. He was heading into the boiling sea, his boat laden down with gold, and with a skull and crossbones flapping at the mast.

'Heave to, me hearty tar,' she muttered, and placing a mental dagger between her teeth she swaggered down the stairs when the doorbell jangled, hand on hip.

But no, her mind's diversions didn't work this time. She stood poised on the bottom step, and, seeing Adam's outline beyond the frosted glass she forgot her imaginary pirate father, forgot Adam was socially above her, and remembered instead his parting kiss in every sensuous detail. Her traitorous body reacted accordingly.

'Damn,' she said, conceding that the sensations rioting into her were gloriously pleasurable. She hadn't allowed herself time to think about the personal problem Adam represented – hadn't actually *given* herself time, since she'd been attacked by spring cleaning fever of late. Not that there was much dirt around these days, except for *that* room, and her palms itched every time she passed it. She wondered what Celia would think of it when she came to live here. Still, as Mr Leighton had made quite clear to her, his former wife's room was none of her business. She supposed, nor were his future wife's thoughts.

Shading his eyes with his hands, Adam pressed his nose against the glass like an inquisitive boy. He wouldn't see her in the shadows.

'The doorbell has rung, answer it, Serafina,' she reminded herself, and lifting the edge of her skirt she trotted across the hall with some anticipation.

She sighed as she opened the door. Adam's mouth had curved into a smile of great charm at the sight of her. She kept her happiness at seeing him again carefully controlled, but if she'd been a puppy dog she'd have run around his ankles in circles of yelping delight.

'Mr Chapman,' she said calmly above her inner turmoil. 'Do come in. Mr Leighton isn't at home at the moment, but he shouldn't be much longer. You know where the drawing room is; I'll bring you some tea.'

Adam placed a basket on the floor. Within seconds he was in front of her, gazing at her through eyes shining like winter sunshine.

She gazed back at him, feeling more flustered by the minute, and breathless with anticipation. Don't look at me like that, her thoughts begged, as if scared by her reaction to him.

The day darkened as though a cloud had moved over the sun. His mouth didn't move but she clearly heard her name whispered in one, long husky breath, so it sounded as though it had been carried on the wind.

'*Serafina* . . .'

Dust, leaves and hawthorn petals swirled in a circle on the tiled floor of the porch. The day lightened and she felt as though something momentous had happened.

His eyes widened and the black irises in his eyes intensified. 'Did you say your name?'

'No . . . I thought you did. It must have been the wind.'

'So it's true . . . Marianne was right and she did hear your name on the wind. Perhaps you're being called back to the place where you were born . . . did you know you have gypsy blood in your veins? It came through your mother's line.'

And practical Sara Finn remembered the old woman when she was still alive – her aunt, whose eyes had been sometimes strange and full of wisdom, her tongue full of lore as she'd told her tales of travelling folk, and of a gypsy princess called Serafina after whom she'd been named.

She'd thought of her aunt in the copse just a week ago when she'd run from Mr Leighton, and Serafina knew she'd been running away from the old woman too.

'They told me I was unclean,' she whispered.

Now she couldn't deny what was in her blood. She could feel it inside her, pulling at her . . . and in the nature of the landscape around her, as if they were tied together and her soul had a connection with it. It was no good running from it because it was part of who she was. The good thing was she was no longer afraid of it, and that alone had a cleansing effect.

'You remember, don't you?'

He could see inside her, make a connection to where it mattered. 'I remember that my name is Serafina and that a long time ago my ancestors were gypsies. At least, I think I do. You will tell me the rest, no doubt, and I'll decide whether in my heart I am what I want me to be.'

'I spoke to your sister Marianne, and she wants you to come home. She has sent you a gift.'

Home? She closed her eyes . . . was home the place where she'd been created in an act of love . . . or of hate perhaps. If so, it was the place where she'd been born, with mother, father, sisters . . . death, grief and . . . pain, that had become a lost memory.

Or was home being with someone she loved and who loved her in return? Someone like . . . *Adam*. But hadn't she learned that hoping for too much from people could disappoint?

'Tell me of Charlotte . . . what does she want of me?'

He hesitated. 'Charlotte has shouldered a great deal of responsibility over what happened in the past. When your mother died it hurt her badly, and she needed to hate somebody for what had happened.'

'Dear God . . . it's me she hates, isn't it? All this time Charlotte has hated me.'

He didn't deny it. 'She despises the man who hopes you are his daughter. It's hard for Charlotte to reconcile herself to the fact that you might be alive after all this time. She knows she's being unfair and is trying not to be. She has much to commend her.'

'The seafarer . . . what's his name?'

'Erasmus.'

'What's he like?'

'Straightforward, and a bit taciturn. He's been at sea since he was a child. As a result he's superstitious. He's of above-average height, and muscular. Erasmus has eyes that can see a long way. He enjoys the sea and his ship *Daisy Jane*, and has only ever loved one woman in his life . . . and she happened to be married to someone else. He would have given up the sea for your mother, I think.'

'I pictured him as a pirate with flying whiskers and a dagger between his teeth, like the murdering rascal *Blackbeard*.'

Adam's chuckle curled softly into her ear. 'Erasmus could very well be a pirate at heart, but he's an honest man. Don't build your hopes up too high . . . you bear very little resemblance to the Honeyman sisters as far as I can see, and there's still doubt about who fathered you. All the same, you're entitled to claim the birthright of knowing your name and where you came from.'

'But I could be rejected all over again.'

'There is that possibility.'

When tears began to trickle down her cheeks she was pulled

gently into his arms. 'You will not be rejected by me, Serafina . . . never by me. I promise.'

Adam had learned on his recent visit to Poole that even if Serafina refused to meet them at the last minute, there was no way she would escape Marianne now. Marianne was eager to meet Serafina and she couldn't understand why she hadn't accompanied him back to Somerset right there and then, to introduce herself.

Adam smiled as he remembered the scene . . .

Nick had laughed at the notion. 'Have patience, my sweet. What about Alexander? He needs you . . . I need you. We'll be lost without you. Besides, Charlotte's new baby is due to arrive any day now, and God forbid that you should miss the event because you'd never forgive yourself. The girl must be introduced to Erasmus first.'

Marianne's blue eyes had beguiled him. 'Why must she, Adam? I'm so dying to see her.'

'Nick's right,' he said. 'This can't be rushed. Serafina is very unsettled about all of this. She's happy where she is, and she might take it into her head to bolt.'

'How can she be happy? She's pretending to be, because she's scared she might turn out to be someone else – that other girl you told us about, the one who belonged to our aunt's servant. Mary someone.'

'Mary Fenn.'

'It was more likely that Mary tried to steal Serafina's identity because there might have been something in it for her. Then she died and left Serafina all mixed up.'

'They were too young for that sort of subterfuge, just little girls, friends who played imaginary games together.'

Which reminded Adam of something he needed to check while he was here. 'Do you know the name of your aunt's lawyer, or have a copy of her last will and testament?'

'Lor, no. The will is probably at Harbour House, unless pa destroyed it.' Her eyes began to shine. 'Is it important? Charlotte might allow me to dig around in the attic . . . though she might not. She's gone infuriatingly dignified on me and is secretly hoping you'll fail so she can say, I told you so. You should go and ask her yourself, Adam. You can be irresistible when you turn on the charm, you know.'

He grinned when Nick winked at him, and turned her delicious little nose away from that particular scent. He was not about to indulge her in any sisterly rivalry. 'Not at the moment. I can soon find a copy of the will, and anything else that had been duplicated and filed. I think acceptance of Serafina might come down to family recognition in the end, which is all the more reason to take things slowly with her.'

'Nonsense, Adam. In my heart I know the girl is Serafina Honeyman, and so do you, else you wouldn't be here.'

'Or a Thornton,' Nick thought to add, something that had brought him a quick gleam of a smile from his wife.

'Or a Thornton,' she agreed. 'I keep forgetting that we're all interrelated. I must send her something nice to make her feel welcome.'

Nick tipped Marianne's chin up and placed a kiss on her mouth. 'Go to the emporium and pick out a nice gift for the girl, so she knows she's welcome. Adam can take it with him when he leaves.'

Marianne kissed Nick in return. 'I'd miss you if I went away, even for a day, Nicky darling, and of course I must be here for Charlotte's lying in, so you needn't worry that I'll run off with Adam.' She'd kissed Adam's cheek. 'You must tell me all about Serafina, Adam. What colour are her eyes?'

'Brown . . . they're large with the longest of lashes, and she has dark straight hair and the sweetest face with a pointed chin and a captivating little dimple to the left of her mouth when she smiles. She's a little bit taller than you, but shorter than Charlotte, and is . . .' Without him thinking about it, his hands outlined her in the air. 'Neat . . . but womanly, I suppose.'

'Hmmm,' Nick offered, grinning. 'I like her already, and you obviously have an eye for the technical details. Now those are dispensed with, what's the girl like?'

Marianne offered Nick a frown. 'He means, who does Serafina resemble the most, the Honeyman family or the Thorntons?'

Adam shrugged. 'That you must decide for yourself. I see no resemblance to any member of either family that I've met so far.'

'Oh, never mind that now, there's bound to be some resemblance, it just won't be noticeable until we're together. You said that Serafina is working as a servant. Is there anything she needs?'

'Just about everything. Apart from what Mr Leighton supplies in the way of uniform she has very little else. One best dress and a few books I believe.'

Wrong answer, since Marianne obviously decided that *everything* was what she'd send Serafina, and she sent the maid running to fetch her coat and bonnet and set off with great haste to shop.

Nick roared with laughter when she returned and he set eyes on the pile of clothing and accessories that had arrived back with her in the emporium carriage. Alexander threw himself at the parcels, giving squeals of delight as he ripped the packaging from them.

Nick picked his son up, sat him on his lap and gave him his watch and chain to play with. 'Do you think Adam's a packhorse, Aria?' Dark eyes sought him out. 'You know, it serves you right, really. By now you should know better than tell Aria that the girl has nothing.'

Adam knew he wouldn't be able to carry it all, and gazed ruefully at it. He didn't want to upset Marianne. Nick was ruthless in helping him out, though. In the face of his wife's protests he ferreted out the ornaments, several pairs of slippers, a travelling beauty case, picnic set and some half a dozen dresses, books, mirrors in frames and bed linen. They were able to pack the rest into two wicker baskets.

Nick picked up a pair of silky pantelettes with pink rosettes and ribbons from the pile. He ran them through his hand and gazed at them, grinning. 'These would look good on you, my love.'

She blushed, and half-laughing, snatched the garment from her husband's hands and threw them back at him. They landed on his head with the legs dangling down the front as she scolded, 'Nicky Thornton! Not in front of Adam, you're embarrassing him.'

Nick drew the legs aside and gazed through them at Alexander.

'*Boo!*' Alexander yelled at him, and began to laugh when Nick tossed him in the air and caught him again.

'Oh, I imagine Adam has seen a pair of pantelettes before, and will see them again before he's an old man.'

This time it was Alexander who parted the legs, and he laughed in anticipation when Nick's lips pursed.

'*Boo!*' Marianne snatched the garment from Nick's head and scolded him over Alexander's giggles. 'Behave yourselves, the pair of you. Nick, you should be setting him a good example,' to which warning the males of the family paid no attention whatsoever.

'I've never seen them displayed so becomingly like that; you should wear them more often, Nick,' Adam said with a laugh, and got a cushion in the face for his trouble.

Marianne found room for the pantelettes on top of the largest of the two wicker baskets and she and Alexander sat astride it while Nick buckled a strap tightly around it. Marianne gazed doubtfully at him afterwards. 'Two of them does seem rather a lot for one man to carry. Perhaps we should go through it all again.'

'After you fought me over every scrap that went into them?' Nick said in disbelief.

Marianne giggled and batted her eyelashes at her husband. 'I'm teasing.'

Enjoying the banter between the Thornton couple, Adam grinned. 'I'm sure I'll manage with the help of porters.'

From there Adam had made a quick visit to Dorchester and had learned the name of the lawyer who was the trustee of the orphanage.

The man's initial suspicion was dispelled when Adam told him that he wasn't interested in challenging the Jarvis will. 'I'm trying to prove the identity of a young woman, believed to be a relative of the Honeyman family. She was given into the care of Constance Jarvis, then brought up by a family called Fenn. It would have been about eighteen years ago.'

'Ah . . . my father would have handled that one.' He gave him a sharp look. 'Will anything in your enquiries be detrimental to the orphanage?'

'I shouldn't think so, and that's not my aim.'

'Then I'll set one of the clerks to find a copy. My father was very meticulous with detail. What is this girl's name?'

'Serafina Honeyman.'

He looked thoughtful. 'The two Honeyman nieces inherited

under the Jarvis will, as I recall. I was given to understand that their legacies were squandered by their father. Where does this girl of yours fit in?'

'There was the third daughter born to the family, one whose paternity was in dispute. She was believed to be dead by the family, but there is no record of her death as far as I can find. She has a strong claim to family kinship, including being named after Constance Jarvis. Serafina was her second name.'

'Ah yes, I thought the name was slightly familiar, and I've heard the rumours, of course. If you could come back in an hour I'll see what I can find for you. The Antelope serves a good lunch.'

The man's face was wreathed in smiles when Adam returned to the office. 'There was an addendum to the Jarvis will, added not long before Mrs Jarvis died – she was ill at the time, and it concerns the young woman you mentioned. The Fenns were trusted and loyal servants. Serafina was adopted by the Fenn family just before Mrs Jarvis died. In exchange Mrs Jarvis provided the family with accommodation, a farm, which would also bring them in an income. They were provided with cash for livestock, and a trust fund from which to draw an allowance for Serafina's needs.

'The property deeds were drawn up in the name of Christopher Fenn. If Serafina died the property would become his. If he died before his wife, then Serafina would inherit, and the family could remain living on the estate and drawing an income from it until Serafina reached the age of twenty, when she would also inherit the principal sum of the trust. After that, her estate was to go to her descendants. If she died without issue, the estate was to become the property of the orphanage.' His eyes scrutinized the paper. 'That's fairly straightforward.'

When Adam nodded and said, 'It seems so,' the man smiled.

'There is a letter in the file from a local solicitor stating that three people died from a cholera epidemic in that house. It was Mrs Fenn and her two natural children. Mr Fenn is still living at the property with the girl and providing for her by drawing on the trust account. It's all above board. I'm afraid your young lady might be imposing a fraudulent claim, sir.'

'There was a woman there when I visited, but she was older, about thirty. As for my young lady, she is making no claim at all . . . yet,' he thought to add, because Serafina might well decide that she was entitled to the property and put up a fight for it. Just now, Adam could do without this extra complication. 'At the moment I'm trying to establish her parentage for a would-be relative. If you would listen to what I have to say, you can then decide who is the fraud. To start with, I'd beg to differ with the solicitor who sent you the information regarding the graves. There are *four* in the cemetery, including that of Christopher Fenn, husband of Emmy Fenn, who was also the father to her deceased children. They all died within the same two-week period. I have seen the grave with my own eyes.'

The man's eyes sharpened. 'And the man living on the estate and drawing on the trust fund?'

'His name is Tyler Fenn. He claims to be a relative.' Adam told the man all he knew, then finished by saying, 'If you don't mind my advice, I'd suggest that the matter should be properly investigated by the county constabulary.'

'I think you are right, since it seems that something dishonest is going on, and it might involve the local legal representative. Thank you for bringing it to my attention, Mr Chapman. Perhaps your young woman has a valid claim against the estate under the will, after all. If she doesn't, the orphanage will put it to good use.'

'The exchange has been enlightening for both of us, I think. I'll leave it in your capable hands, but would be obliged, should you discover anything that might prove useful to my client, if you'd let me know of it.' Adam handed the man his card. 'I'll be quite happy to share my knowledge with the authorities, but would rather shield my young lady at this moment.'

He'd just readied himself to leave the district when a message came from the Hardy home that the expected arrival was well on its way, so he waited, and was relieved to hear that a healthy son had been born, who would be called James.

Now back at Leighton Manor Adam wondered what Serafina would make of the pantelettes . . . especially since he had every intention of enjoying the sight of her wearing them, one day. He doubted if she'd ever had much in the way of women's fripperies.

But although he'd already made his intentions perfectly clear where Serafina was concerned it wouldn't be wise to make a move towards her – not until this business was settled. She had enough to deal with at the moment.

So he took a step back and handed her his handkerchief.

'I seem to be doing a lot of weeping, lately,' she said, mopping at her eyes and trying to get some normality back into her voice.

'The tears make your eyes look luminous.'

'Not just red?' and there was a forlorn mockery of a laugh from her. Her curiosity was raised though, when Joseph brought the second basket in.

'That's heavy, allow me to take it from you,' Adam said to the struggling Joseph, and he lowered the burden of the heavy basket to the floor.

'Goodness! We'd better move them before Mr Leighton arrives home and trips over them. What's in them?'

Adam's lips twitched at the thought of one particular intimate garment. 'I have no idea. They are a gift to you from Marianne Thornton. Would you like me to take them through to your quarters?'

'A gift? Why should she send me a gift when she doesn't even know me?'

'Because Marianne is a generous person who wants you to feel welcome, and who is so longing to meet you that her husband had to tie her to a chair to stop her following after me.'

Serafina laughed. 'So why do I feel so embarrassed by her generosity?'

'Because you're an ungrateful creature with no graces, and I wonder why I'm bothering with you.'

'Why are you?'

Because I love you, Serafina, he wanted to say, but he didn't have the courage, not yet, when all her defences were still up and she was bristling with caution. 'Because it's my profession to bother with you. I'm being paid to.'

He caught the tail end of the grin she tried to hide, one which said she knew he was lying. 'Oh, I see. Thank you, Adam; are you staying for a while?'

He reached out and took her hand in his. 'Long enough to persuade you to journey to Poole with me in two weeks' time,

I hope. Captain Thornton's ship should be coming into port about then.'

'If I agree to go with you now, you'll leave right away, so I'll reserve the right to detain you a little longer than five minutes.'

She had no idea how those words warmed him. 'That's the nicest thing anyone has ever said to me, but I hope to stay overnight, at least.'

'Since you're practically one of Mr Leighton's family now I'm sure you don't need an invitation, Adam. You can let go of my hand, now.'

He gazed down at it, knowing it wasn't the prettiest hand he'd seen on a woman, but her history of hard work from an early age was written on her palm and he felt an extreme tenderness towards her because of it. 'Must I?'

'Yes, you must . . . *eventually,*' and she gave a breathless little giggle. 'How's Celia?'

'Planning her wedding and looking forward to her life here as Mrs Leighton. I have a note in my waistcoat pocket for you.'

'I'm sure they'll be happy together. Have you eaten yet?'

'Not since breakfast.'

He let go of her hand when Giles came into the hall.

'Joseph sent me to take them baskets off you, sir. Mr Leighton will give me what for if he trips over them. He gave me a right wigging last time. Giles, says he, you should know better and be glad I don't send you packing.' He shrugged. 'Now I'm sending myself packing and I'll be my own man – and a family man at that. It's funny what life throws at you?'

'It certainly is,' and Serafina slid a glance towards Adam, and her smile along with it.

'Where shall I put them, Miss?'

'In my sitting room please, Giles.'

'A gift for you from Mr Chapman, is it? Just asking, since Maggie will wonder,' and Giles gazed at her, his curiosity plain to see.

'No, Giles, it isn't a gift from Mr Chapman. Tell Maggie that Mr Chapman will require some lunch. Perhaps some chicken broth, followed by a slice of that delicious pork pie she made with some new potatoes, and pickles. Serve it in my sitting room, along with mine. You won't mind, will you, Adam? The dining room floor has just been scrubbed and it's still damp.'

'It suits me fine. Don't you want to open your gift from Marianne?'

'I haven't decided yet that I'm going to accept it. We're complete strangers, so it's a little premature, and the gift seems overly generous, so I'll never be able to repay her kindness.'

He was disappointed. 'Marianne finds pleasure in the giving. If you'd seen how excited she was at being able to offer you this gift, you wouldn't be so cruel,' and he chuckled. Marianne Thornton was a force to be reckoned with, despite her sweet nature. If the gift were refused she would probably descend on Serafina like a swarm of hornets and give the hapless girl a good telling off.

'Why did you laugh?'

'There was twice as much to begin with and Marianne's husband made her whittle it down. When he took something out she put up a convincing argument that every woman had great need of such an item. Luckily, he overruled her, otherwise I'd never have been able to transport it . . . it nearly broke my back getting it here. The horse's back as well.'

'Then I'm being ungrateful, and shouldn't put you to so much trouble a second time by sending it back.' Her husky chuckle made Adam's hairs stand on end.

'No, you shouldn't.'

Taking a step forward she gave him a quick, tentative kiss on his cheek. 'Thank you, Adam.'

She coloured a little afterwards, when he commented, 'Is that the best you can do?'

'I don't know; I'm not used to kissing people . . . I didn't mean to kiss you.'

'Then why did you?'

An odd, embarrassed little laugh flopped from her. 'I don't know; because you've been kind, I suppose. Was it so awful and shocking?'

'Not in the least. Will you allow me to kiss you in return?'

Her eyes widened and a grin came and went. 'I didn't expect you to *ask* . . . now I don't know what to say.'

'Yes will do.'

She sounded flustered when she said, 'I'll think about it. Let's go through to my sitting room; you can take the straps off the baskets for me if you like.'

He followed her down a dark corridor to where her rooms were situated. What had she said — that she hadn't expected him to ask?

Her sitting room was next to the kitchen and faced north. It was a dark, gloomy cavern with high thin windows that let in light, but not the sunshine. Sitting, Serafina wouldn't be able to see out of them. A row of well-thumbed books leaned against each other on the shelf. There were feminine touches; a vase of wild flowers on the table, an embroidered cushion, and a bowl of pot-pourri that gave off an elusive perfume of summers past. The fire grate was inadequate for such a large room. Through a door he could see her bed, narrow with an iron headboard and a faded bedspread.

As soon as the door closed behind them he turned her round, drew her into his arms and gazed down at her. Her eyes were pulled to his, as beautiful and as innocent as those of a fawn.

'Adam, is this wise?'

'Of course it's not wise, but life's about risk.' He could see himself drowning in the shining brown depths of her eyes and felt her heart beat against his. She made a soft mewing sound in her throat that was half in protest and half-pleasure, and she laid her head against his shoulder.

He should never have allowed himself to fall in love with her, he told himself, and now, because he was encouraging it, she was discovering what she had inside herself — the need to be loved. Her hair smelled of lavender and his nostrils flared to capture it.

There was danger in this innocent hug, their arms clasping them together so warmth and emotion flowed from one to the other, making them as one. Adam reacted to her womanliness, felt her breasts become aware and push against his chest. She was new to the complications of love, and had no idea that the surge of him against her was of her own creation. Heat filled him and he wanted to drag her to her neat virgin bed and ravish her perfect little body until he evoked so much lust inside her that they'd end up as a heap of naked tangled limbs tied together by the rumpled sheets — and then she'd beg for the release they both craved.

She looked up at him, knowing that nature had changed him somehow, but unsure why. What she was feeling was registered in her eyes, so they were sleepy with lust for an instant, like a purring cat unable to resist the ecstasy of its chin being caressed. She was shy nevertheless, especially when he grinned at her.

He contented himself by kissing the end of her nose, seeing in its shapeliness a resemblance to Marianne's nose.

'Goodness . . . someone might see us, you had better let me go, Adam,' she said breathlessly, and when he did – for his own comfort rather than hers – she opened the door to the corridor then walked the length of the room and closed the door to her bedroom, as if the sight of the bed was unsettling because she'd just remembered that there might be another purpose it could be used for, apart from sleeping the sleep of the innocent.

He grinned as he bent to the wicker baskets and bent himself to the task of loosening the straps that Nick, with his strong and dextrous hands, had so efficiently tightened.

A few moments later both Fanny and Maggie drifted in, drawn by Serafina's exclamations of surprise and delight.

Hearing the rumble of Finch and Oscar's voices above the feminine clamour, Adam left the females to it and headed off towards the drawing room.

Thirteen

A thin and wiry-looking lad from the workhouse had been hired to replace Giles, and he underwent a week of training before Giles said he was satisfied that he knew how to look after the horse, and what his duties were.

Thomas Stark was respectful to everyone, and a willing worker, though when he'd first fallen on his food like a starving wolf Maggie had rapped him on the knuckles with her spoon.

'We haven't said grace yet, and we employ good manners in this household. You eat with your mouth closed, chew your food, don't speak when your mouth is full and you say please and thank you.'

'Yes, ma'am.'

'Then you may say grace if you wish, Thomas.'

'Thank you, God, for smiling on me. You must be, else why should Tommy Stark, who was sent packing by his kinfolk because they could no longer afford to feed him, end up with a position in a house that has the best cook in the world?'

Maggie smiled benevolently upon Thomas then. 'Poor boy, you're as thin as a sparrow. I reckon you didn't get much to eat in that place, at that. I'll need to fatten you up a bit as well as teach you some manners.'

'Thank you, ma'am,' Thomas said humbly, though with a gleam of mischief shining in his eyes. 'May I eat now?'

'You may.'

Serafina stifled a giggle.

The following month Giles and Jassy were wed in the same church that Mr Leighton and Celia would use . . . only Mr Leighton's relative, the bishop, would officiate at their nuptials.

Serafina had felt like a queen in her new skirt and day bodice with its wide bell sleeves. Fashioned from glowing bronze taffeta with cream lace trim, it had a matching bonnet with a posy of red and yellow silk poppies sewn to one side.

Fanny wore Serafina's cast-off bonnet decorated with new blue ribbons. Maggie had admired a Kashmir shawl amongst the other treasures Serafina had been sent. As there had been two of everything enclosed in the wicker baskets, Serafina didn't see any sense in not sharing her pleasure and good fortune. Adam had assured her that the gift need not be returned if it turned out that she was not the missing Honeyman daughter, though she'd allowed herself the luxury to hope that she was.

After the service they had gone to the farm and eaten the feast provided by Jassy's mother, and drank her dandelion and elderberry wine. Giles was left at his new home, looking awkward, and with Jassy clinging possessively to his arm.

With stomachs straining at the seams they'd walked the wedding feast off on the way home, where Serafina changed into her working clothes, rather than spoil her new ones. The morning had been humid and the afternoon had become overcast. They were in for a thunderstorm, she thought.

Her employer had been suffering from a headache all through the service, and had not eaten much at the wedding feast. He looked pale and had gone upstairs to rest as soon as they got back to Leighton Manor.

'I'll make you a compress,' Serafina said, and to relax him she prepared a cloth dampened with cold water to which a few drops of lavender oil had been added.

'I hope Mr Leighton is not sickening for anything,' she said to Oscar as she handed it over. 'I'll bring him up some tea after he's rested.'

The sky darkened ominously. The air grew still, and there was a sense of waiting about it. There was no work to be done. Maggie fell asleep in her rocking chair with Fingal curled on her lap. After the big midday meal they were having cold cuts for supper, so she didn't have anything to do at the moment. Fanny lit a candle and practised her letters at the kitchen table, singing softly to herself.

Thomas and Joseph were probably in the stable. Serafina didn't know where Oscar was; watching over Mr Leighton, she supposed.

She went to her sitting room, lit a candle and took out Marianne Thornton's note, reading it for what seemed like the one hundredth time.

Dearest Serafina,

I do hope you won't mind me calling you by your first name, but why should you when we are in all likelihood, sisters. My heart has always told me that you survived your birth.

From what Adam has told me I know your life has not been easy, so please accept my gift in the way it is offered, not as a charitable act but a gift of love between two sisters who were never destined to grow up together. If by chance it proves that we are not related, then I hope we will find a way to become good friends instead.

I'm looking forward to the day we meet.

Yours sincerely,

Marianne Thornton

Kissing the letter Serafina folded it back into its creases and placed it in the book box Mr Leighton had given her for her treasures. There was the pretty purse with her money in and the key to Diana Milson's room, which she had also hidden there so she wouldn't be tempted. She slid the box back into the shelf of books and smiled. It was the first letter she could ever remember receiving – a letter from her sister . . . *one* of her sisters.

'My sister, Marianne Thornton,' she said out loud. But what of the other one, Charlotte Hardy? Would she prove difficult to know?

The temperature dropped suddenly and the storm hit them without warning, a squall of hailstones flung with some force by a gust of wind.

Serafina checked that all the doors and windows were secure, then went upstairs. Lightning zig-zagged out of the sky and snicked about the boiling clouds. She stood on the stairs landing and allowed the fury of it to explode around her. Outside, the limbs of the trees thrashed and cracked and the sky was flooded with great flashes of light. It was a magnificent sight – strength against fury.

There was a cracking noise upstairs. Serafina went up the rest of the stairs at a run. The door to Diana Milson's room stood open. She could smell the stale dust from the top of the stairs and her nose wrinkled. It offended her.

The room itself seemed the same, only different . . . the difference was something she couldn't quite put her finger on.

Finch Leighton stood at the window. He wore no jacket, just a waistcoat over his shirt. 'Serafina?' he said without turning round.

She smiled at this uncanny ability of his to sniff people out. 'Is your headache better?'

'It's gone, thanks to you.'

'I heard something crack.'

'Yes, so did I. Tiles have fallen off the roof, I expect. I'll have someone investigate it when the storm has passed.'

'It's cold. I'll get your jacket for you.'

'No, leave it be. Oscar ate too much at the farm and has fallen asleep in the chair. Besides, I like to feel heat and cold against my skin and imagine what's causing it.'

'You don't need much imagination for this storm; it's so full of rage that the thought of the elements losing control so completely is awe-inspiring.'

'So, you think the elements are governed by reason?'

She smiled. He was in the mood for one of their discussions. 'I know nothing about science, but I imagine it's like getting in a temper. You can take so much tension and if it's not expressed it builds up until there's no room to contain it all, then it just bursts out of you.'

'Then again, the same thing can happen with joy, or love, only the end result is different, and can be just as spectacular.'

'Are you saying that love and hate are the same emotion?'

The next flash of lightning showed a smile on his face. 'I wish such emotions could be explained that easily. It's the anniversary of Diana's death today.'

She didn't know quite what to say except, 'Would you like me to leave?'

'Tell me about this room that I've turned into a shrine, Serafina, and don't spare my feelings. I know you'll be honest.'

She gave a small huff of laughter. 'Are you sure you want me to be honest?'

'I'm positive.'

'This room is not a shrine. To my mind it's a tomb you visit when you know you're beginning to forget your late wife and feel guilty about it. You need this room to use as a stick to flog yourself with.'

'Like a penitent? That's too harsh a judgement. You have no idea how I feel.'

'Perhaps, but I think Celia deserves better than being expected to take second place to a memory.' Tears pricked her eyes and she said quietly, 'You told me once that you liked the poetry of Edgar Allan Poe. Do you know the poem called *The Dream?*'

'In visions of the dark night I have dreamed of joy departed, but a waking dream of life and light hath left me broken-hearted . . .'

She took up the next verse. *'Ah, what is not a dream by day, to him whose eyes are cast on things around him, with a ray turned back upon the past.'*

After a short silence he said, 'Come here, my dear, and forgive me if this seems too familiar.'

When she joined him he reached out, and, locating her face he very gently ran his fingers over it, tracking through her tears and following the contours of it. When he'd finished, his hands fell to his side. 'How does someone as young as you possess so much wisdom? You cry for me, yet you want me to abandon the last sight that my eyes remember seeing, and embrace . . . ? How do the last lines of that poem read?'

'You know how they read. *What could there be more purely bright in truth's day star?'*

'And Celia is my *truth's day star*, even though she resides in my darkness. You're right, Serafina. When the storm has abated we shall rid the house of Diana's ghost, and you can scrub her away so she can no longer mock me. Everything must go. Her bed and bedding, her clothes and her portrait, chairs, and ornaments. I shall give her jewellery to Jane . . . she has long coveted it.'

There was a whiff of sulphur in the air. A vicious slash of light-ning speared to earth and was followed by a crash and flying sparks. Everything rattled. It brought a small scream of fright from Serafina.

Finch jumped, then he sniffed. 'I can smell burning, and wonder if this is a message from beyond the grave. Are we both being roasted on the devil's spit?'

'He can go and stick his fork in someone else or he'll get a kick in the seat of his britches,' Serafina said shakily. 'As for the lightning strike it's merely coincidence. We agreed that we don't believe the elements are governed by reason . . . remember.'

'I'll allow myself to be governed by the fact that the storm is a random act rather than Diana's ghost displaying its displeasure, then.'

It was revealing that he unconsciously referred to the devil rather than connecting his former wife with heaven.

A prolonged rumble of thunder set off a harmonious hum around them as she gazed out of the window, and there was a muted jangle of noise, of metal jiggled in the drawers, wood rubbing against wood and the crystal in the lampshades offering up a melodious tinkling tune. Her palm pressed against the window glass absorbing the vibrations as she looked outside.

The ground was covered in a thick mush of ice, except for around the oak tree.

'I think the oak tree was struck. The tree seems to be intact, but the trunk is scorched and there's smoke coming from it. There's steam rising from the ground, too. The heat must have melted the hailstones.' Her glance went beyond the tree. 'The seat has been thrown across the garden and it resembles firewood.'

Oscar came in, carrying Finch's jacket. 'Ah, there you are, sir. You'd better put this on since it's become quite cold. The oak tree has been struck by lightning.'

'Thank you, Oscar. After the storm has passed over would you help Joseph and Thomas check for any damage. I think we've lost a few tiles . . . check the attics for leaks and we'll put containers to catch the water.'

'Yes, sir.'

'And Oscar, we're going to clear out this room and remove my late wife's portrait from the drawing room downstairs, since I want the future Mrs Leighton to feel welcome in her new home and secure in her role as mistress here. I'd be obliged if you'd give the ladies a hand. I'll want it done before Serafina is claimed by Mr Chapman and goes off to discover herself.'

It was an odd way of putting it, but true on both counts, Serafina thought. She *was* hoping Adam would claim her and that she would discover herself. For a moment she allowed herself to imagine the moment when she met the man Adam thought was her father, and a little chill went through her. If only she was as self-contained as people seemed to think she was.

What if this sea captain didn't like her and he denounced her as an imposter? If he did there would be no sisters and she'd be sent away and forgotten about. No, not forgotten, because the abandoned infant had always been a skeleton in their family closet. Adam would then look for another young woman to fit into the family mould – and that might be her friend, who was dead and buried as Mary Fenn. Did her childhood memories really belong to her, or did they come through Mary during the childhood games they played, when being a mysterious orphan had seemed so romantic?

Would Mr Leighton allow her to come back here? And what about Adam . . . he might decide she was not worth knowing after all? How could she stay here when Adam was bound to visit his sister often . . . and with each visit her heart would break into a thousand pieces?

Panic hit her again and her heart began to pound.

What her eyes had seen and ignored before, suddenly came to the forefront. Diana Milson's diamond ring was missing from the table and the bracelet and pendant were gone.

'Mrs Leighton's jewellery?'

'What about it, Serafina?'

'The jewellery . . . have you moved it, sir? The ring, bracelet and ruby pendant have gone.'

He reached out to explore the empty spaces, his touch so delicate that he didn't even disturb the dust. 'I haven't moved anything . . . when did you last see it?'

'The last time I was in here . . . when you told me not to come in here again.'

'And you haven't been in here since?'

'No, sir.'

'Are you sure? Oscar found the key to this room in my bedside table. I was going to ask you about it; I thought you must have been in here, even though I told you not to.'

'No, and it isn't my key. I keep that in that little treasure box you gave me.'

He shook his head. 'Are you sure?'

'Of course, I'm sure . . . it was there an hour ago when I read the letter inside it – one that Mr Chapman brought me from Marianne Thornton. Shall I fetch it?'

'No . . . Oscar will.'

It pained Serafina that he didn't trust her to fetch it herself and although she could understand it, a lump filled her throat. She tried to keep the hurt from her voice when she said, 'It's amongst my books on the shelf, Oscar.'

He was back a few seconds later with the box. Serafina opened it. 'Here's the key to the room, here's the note, and there's the purse you gave me with the money in . . . my wages from Reverend Pawley.'

Serafina looked on, bewildered when Oscar opened the embroidered purse, and said, 'The purse contains two of Mrs Milson's handkerchiefs, with her initials embroidered on them, and there's something hard inside them.'

He shook the handkerchief open and the ring tumbled back on to the table, nearly settling into the same spot from where it had been taken. A flash of lightning found its core and sent a myriad of cold gleams twisting from its heart as it rocked back and forth.

If it had a heart, Serafina thought morosely. She'd read somewhere that the diamond was the hardest natural substance known to man. Serafina's own heart plunged suddenly, as though a void had opened up underneath her. Her hand sought out the bedpost for support and she whispered, 'You think I stole it, don't you?'

Finch Leighton gave a tired sigh. 'I don't know what to think at the moment.'

Serafina couldn't think of anything convincing to say, except, 'I didn't put the ring there, and I'd like to point out that my money has gone. Only three of us knew that the money was in there.'

'Is the tortoiseshell jewellery box still there?'

'Yes, sir . . . and so are the pearls.' She shrugged. 'I've never looked inside the box, so I don't know what's in there.'

'There's an inventory in my late wife's desk drawer,' Finch said, and he opened the drawer and took out a satchel with papers in. He handed it to Oscar. 'Damn and blast it to hell, Oscar! Nothing like this has happened before. I shall have to ask the constabulary to investigate.'

Oscar suggested limply, 'Perhaps it was a jackdaw.'

There was a flare of hope in Serafina, then it fled and she said miserably, 'I doubt if a jackdaw would have wrapped the ring in a handkerchief, flown into my sitting room and placed it inside a purse in the secret box. Besides, how would it have got in, when the window here has been closed tight all this time?'

'She's right. It was taken from this room and placed there. But where is the rest of the jewellery?'

There was a moment of charged silence, then Finch said, 'As soon as the storm dies down you'd best go and fetch the constables, Oscar. They will want to take statements from the staff and search some of the rooms. They will soon get to the bottom of it, no doubt. In the meantime you'd better go and find something to do, Miss Finn. Oscar and I will go through the inventory and make a list of anything else that might be missing.'

'I didn't take that ring . . . I promise . . . I wouldn't do anything like that.'

'I haven't accused you, but you must agree that someone did, and that the affair does have to be investigated. In the meantime get on with your work. Hand Oscar the key to this room if you would, then leave us.'

The joy seemed to drain from Serafina as she left.

The house was plunged into an atmosphere of gloom when it was discovered that there was more of the jewellery missing; several rings, a gold snake bracelet with a ruby eye that went with the pendant, and several brooches and earrings.

They were all interviewed, including Giles, Jassy and Oscar, and the newcomer, Thomas. A search was made of their belongings. Nothing turned up.

Serafina was singled out for special attention, and the constables didn't seem that interested in the fact that her money had been stolen too, until Mr Leighton suggested, 'It's possible that the ring slid off the thief's finger after he'd stolen the money, when he was padding the purse with the handkerchiefs.'

Finch Leighton spent an hour or so shut away with the constables, while Serafina gnawed on her nails. She had a feeling that she was about to be arrested and charged.

Instead, she was called in, and a stern-faced constable said, 'I believe we have enough evidence to charge you with the theft of the jewellery, Miss Finn. However, Mr Leighton has decided not to press charges at this time. We will still be pursuing evidence, so if you have anything to tell us I suggest you do so now, and save us a lot of work.'

Gazing at her employer, she whispered, 'I didn't steal it . . . why don't they believe me?'

Fourteen

When Adam arrived at Leighton Manor he was called into Finch's sitting room, and informed of what had taken place.

After a while anger replaced his initial shock. 'You think Serafina has stolen it . . . that's nonsense.'

'There's no other explanation, Adam.'

'Of course there is, there has got to be . . . you just haven't found it, and the constables are pursuing the easiest and most obvious suspect. Where *is* Serafina?'

'She's either in her rooms, or doing the laundry work, or perhaps she's gone up to the woods. She avoids me and only comes out to clean when I'm out. I feel so guilty when I run into her. Maggie and Fanny are looking after me. Maggie won't hear a word against her, and Fanny keeps snivelling. Even Oscar has a disapproving tone in his voice. Damn it, Adam. It's not my fault that this has happened.'

'Isn't it? If the jewellery hadn't been left in plain view to tempt people, it wouldn't have been stolen. How do you know I didn't take it while I was here?'

'Did you?'

'No . . . but if I had I wouldn't have hidden it in Serafina's purse, or in a storage box disguised as a book . . . especially one that you'd given her, since it would be the first place you would have looked for it. Didn't you wonder about that?'

'Wonder about it?'

'For God's sake, Finch, stop being so bloody obtuse! You're a barrister, soon to be a magistrate. Where's your brain? The person who stole the jewellery could have borne Serafina a grudge.'

Colour touched the man's face. 'Don't think I haven't considered that aspect. Serafina said she cannot think of anyone. I did have the feeling there's something she's not telling the constables though.'

Heaving in a steadying breath Adam asked him, 'Do you intend to have her charged?'

'No . . . but I won't be able to keep her on here now. It was going to be impossible anyway, since Celia likes her and deals with her as a friend rather than an employee. My fault; I grew up here and was always closer to the staff as a result. Joseph taught me to ride. Maggie was employed when I was about ten and at boarding school. I used to look forward to the holidays so I could fatten up on her cooking. My staff in London are much more formal, and I've decided that it would be too awkward for my wife and housekeeper to be close friends.'

'Oh, I don't think you need to worry too much about that,' Adam said with a reluctant smile. After all, if all went well, Serafina and Celia would eventually be on an equal footing.

'The constables are still making enquiries, but they haven't found anything yet. They tell me that they've given a list of the missing jewellery to local gem dealers in case it was sold.'

'Serafina wouldn't have been that stupid, as to sell it locally.'

'That's what I keep telling myself.' Finch placed his head in his hands and groaned. 'I keep going through it.'

'Go through it again for me.'

'Serafina wanted to clean my former wife's room the moment she arrived here, and she more or less told me that keeping it as a shrine was macabre.'

'It is.'

'I know, but she was the first person who had the guts to tell me so. When I met your sister and fell in love with her, I realized how right Serafina had been about what I was doing to myself. She quoted Edgar Allen Poe at me, you know,' and he gave a faint smile. 'We had some wonderful conversations. She has a good mind that seems to absorb everything, like Celia, I suppose, though Serafina argues from an instinctive emotional standpoint, while Celia is more logical in her reasoning.'

Noting Finch's tone of voice Adam leaned forward and touched his wrist. 'You don't have to tell me about Celia. I've known her all my life. When did you notice that the jewellery was missing?'

'I'd decided that it wouldn't be fair to Celia to keep the room as it was any longer. Serafina found me in there watching the storm from the window. I was giving her instructions about cleaning the room out when she noticed the jewellery was missing.

It was lying about the room before, you see, as Diana had left it on that day. She was untidy.'

'Your late wife didn't take it with her to the station, then. I find that odd.'

'I never gave it much thought. Diana left the house in a fury of passion and without any luggage, so she could catch up with her friends. Most of her belongings were in the London house, anyway, and I was instructed to send the rest on. I wish I'd put my foot down and stopped her from going now.'

'Your former wife sounds as though she was unstoppable,' Adam said, trying not to feel sorry for the man.

The smile he gave was wry. 'I was a fool, and Diana was wilful and demanding, but it's no good castigating myself about it now. Many a man has been taken in by a pretty face and lived to regret it.'

Adam smiled and said, 'By your expression this is the first time you've admitted it to yourself.'

'It's the first time I've said it out loud. That's something Serafina taught me . . . to live my life in the present instead of the past. I can't believe she would steal from me, yet . . . ?'

'Yet?'

'Oscar fetched the treasure box that she kept in her room, and he found one of the rings in there. It was a ring Serafina had admired before, not very expensive, but a pretty stone. I'd decided to give the jewellery to my late wife's niece. Diana had promised Jane Milson she could have it if anything happened to her, or so Jane said.' There was uncertainty in his voice now.

'What is it, Finch?'

'I'd forgotten that Jane had wanted to borrow some of the jewellery just before Christmas. She specifically asked for a sapphire set, and that is missing from the jewellery box.'

'Then before you do anything else, you might suggest that the constables look further afield, perhaps while Serafina is away meeting her family.'

'I think I would prefer to keep this matter private. If she's involved in this, Jane will bow under pressure. Freddie has a sly way of getting around things though, and he was sent packing by Serafina as I recall. I sent Oscar after Freddie to rescue Serafina when I realized what his intentions were, and he said she'd managed quite nicely on her own. Apparently she'd stabbed Freddie with a fork. She doesn't encourage liberties, which is why she lost her last job. She slapped the son of the house, I'm given to believe.'

Giving a smile Adam remembered the delightful laugh Serafina had given after he'd kissed her. She hadn't minded the liberty he'd taken with her.

'I was going to ask you not to bring Serafina back here,' Finch said. 'I intend to offer one of my London staff the position.'

'Does Serafina know?'

Finch looked ashamed. 'I was hoping you'd tell her.'

'What did you expect me to do with her, leave her at the railway station like a piece of abandoned luggage? Hasn't she been through that before?'

'You're too fond of her to do that. I thought her family might give her a home.'

'If they *are* her family.'

'It's a cowardly way of doing things, I know.'

Adam decided that Finch needed hauling over the coals a little. He said brutally, 'It's like leaving an unwanted puppy in the middle of nowhere to starve, hoping someone else will happen along and take pity on it. Serafina needs stability in her life. She thought she'd found it here, and this will tear her apart.' He lowered his voice. 'Serafina holds you in high esteem; you're like a father figure to her.'

Finch winced. 'I suppose I could just slide into that age group if I had to. I didn't want Serafina's fate to become the cause of dissent between Celia and myself. Your sister is fond of her.'

'I doubt if Celia would think any the less of you since she's quite capable of understanding the position you find yourself in.'

'What else can I do, Adam? If you've got a solution, let me hear it.'

'I have a vested interest in this, and I think you know exactly what that might be, which is why I can't help solve the problem for you. But I will think of a way to let both you and Serafina down lightly. If I were you, I wouldn't let the matter drop though. I'd pursue it privately and make sure that all avenues are covered until you discover the truth – for your own peace of mind if no one else's.'

'Rest assured, I'll take that advice.'

'Allow me to ask you something, Finch. Do you honestly think Serafina stole the jewellery?'

He reflected for a moment, then said, 'My heart tells me it's something she wouldn't stoop to. I desperately want to believe that.'

'Good, then I'd be obliged if you'd let her know that before we leave in the morning, so it doesn't weigh too heavily on her mind. May I see her now?'

'Of course you may. Try her sitting room first; she spends a lot of time alone there now. If you happen to run into Oscar send him to me if you would. If not before, I'll see you at dinner then, Adam, though I warn you, the atmosphere is barely tolerable in the house since this business started.'

The door to Serafina's sitting room was ajar. She was seated in a chair with a book in her lap, but she wasn't reading it, she was staring at the wall. Her down-turned mouth and the abject misery in her face shocked him. She seemed to be drained of spirit. The flames in her eyes were dulled, her shoulders slumped.

'Serafina.'

She turned towards the sound of his voice, her eyes still filled with her thoughts. A smile of welcome fleetingly touched her lips, then fled as she stood and faced him. Coming aware that he'd been told of the charge against her, she buried her face in her hands and whispered in a voice so quiet that he strained to hear her, 'Adam . . . I didn't expect to see you after what has happened. I feel so ashamed because people will think I'm a thief. I don't know what to do.'

He was across the floor in two seconds, and his arms came around her and pulled her against him. Clinging to him, she began to weep.

It was a full ten minutes before Serafina was strengthened enough to look up at him, her eyes crushed and drowning in tears. The desperation in her face told him that she was nearly at the end of her tether. 'I'm sorry . . . whatever must you think of me, Adam?'

'The same as I thought of you the last time I saw you.'

'What will I do?'

'Exactly as we planned. You'll accompany me to Poole, where we'll unravel the mystery of your family connections.'

'Even if there's a connection, they're respectable professional people, and won't want to know me now.'

'You underestimate them. Besides, they won't know about it unless you tell them.'

'You want me to deceive them?'

'It's not deceit. It's up to you to tell them what you want them to know, and you're allowed to be private about some things. We both know you didn't steal that jewellery. In his heart, Finch Leighton doesn't believe you took it either, and he's not going to press charges. The investigation must continue though, and he's following another lead.'

'All the same, it will be intolerable for Mr Leighton and Celia if I come back here to work, won't it?'

She was reaching the inevitable conclusion, as he'd hoped she would. 'Yes, I imagine it would be awkward. All the same, he feels bad about what's happened.'

Fiercely, she told him, 'Mr Leighton has been good to me and I don't want him to feel bad, or awkward. Perhaps I should make it easy for him and leave his employ, otherwise he might feel obliged to dispense with my services.'

'That's a possibility. It would be a good idea, because I expect your family will want you to stay with them for a while.'

'And if they don't?'

'We'll cross that bridge when we come to it. I have need of someone to look after my home in London, you know.'

Their closeness was becoming uncomfortable for him and he put some space between them. When colour rose to her cheeks he placed his hand against its warmth, smiling when she un-expectedly turned her face into it and kissed his palm. He brought up his other hand, took her lovely face between his palms and scrutinized it. Her mouth was the colour of crushed raspberries.

She said, 'Why are you taking my side?'

'Because you need someone, my love.'

'Am I your . . . *love*?'

As an answer to that Adam's mouth sought the soft pliable curves of hers. A moment later she was kissing him in return. Her laughter when they pulled apart had a husky awareness to it. 'We shouldn't have done that.'

'Why not?'

'Because I have problems enough in my life without adding any more to them.'

'I see no problem in kissing you.' He kissed her nose and then her mouth again, just to demonstrate.

'I also like you too much . . . and in ways I shouldn't, and kissing leads to one thing and then another.'

He couldn't help but tease her. 'And we might end up naked in your bed making love to one another just for the enjoyment of it. Would that be a problem?'

She struggled on valiantly, her cheeks flaming. 'Well, yes . . . you know it would be a problem . . . not for you perhaps because you're a man, but definitely for me. I don't know whether to welcome your attention or be afraid of it.'

'These sort of problems have a way of sorting themselves out, Serafina. Nature designed us to feel this way about each other, and the time may yet come when we're unable to resist each other.'

'Well, if you would just stop kissing me it might help.'

'How can I stop when I find you irresistible?'

'You have a glib tongue, Adam Chapman, but I do enjoy your company.' She began to laugh when he grinned at her.

'There,' he said, 'you look so pretty when you smile,' and he eyed the wicker baskets. 'Are those ready to go?'

'Yes . . . I thought Thomas, the new stable hand, might take them to the station in the cart.'

She was a neat figure in her servant's gown, but it was the last time she'd have to wear it, and for that he felt only pleasure. 'Do you have something ready to travel in?'

'Yes, one of the gowns Marianne Thornton sent me.'

Relief filled him. 'I was worried it might be that brown checked garment with the velvet bodice.'

'I gave it to Fanny.'

'Good . . . we'll catch the early morning train.'

The reluctance was back in her eyes again. 'It will be all right, won't it, Adam? I've made so many friends here, and I don't want to leave them.'

'I know, but friends don't disappear just because you part company. I've a notion that you haven't seen the last of Leighton Manor.'

'I hope not. Will you help me to tell Mr Leighton that it's possible I won't be returning to my position here. I don't know how to talk to him since that jewellery was stolen.'

Not possible? It was *certain*, he thought.

Later that afternoon they found Finch back in his sitting room. Oscar announced them and he got to his feet and cleared his throat.

'Serafina, I understand that you wish to speak to me, and in the presence of Mr Chapman. I do hope you're not about to tell me something that I don't want to hear.'

'Like confess to a crime I didn't commit? No, I'm not going to do that.'

Her opening gambit was good, and cleared the air for what was to come.

'You're aware that I'm travelling to Poole tomorrow.'

'Yes . . . I wish you the best of luck, and hope everything turns out well for you.'

Assuming the role of observer Adam was keen to see how Serafina performed under pressure. He only intended to step in if he had to.

Serafina ignored the niceties. She made an impatient little humming sound in her throat and waded directly into the conflict. 'I was thinking that perhaps it might be better if I didn't return here, because until this business is cleared up it will be awkward for both of us.'

Adam noted the effort Finch was making not to show his relief. 'It's all right, Serafina. I'll be sorry to lose you, of course, and I'll make sure that your wages are paid up to date, and the savings you lost are reimbursed.'

'My savings were not lost. I didn't have that money when I came here, and you secured it for me. Now it's stolen, and since you are not the thief, I would rather not take advantage of your generous offer.'

It was a good thrust, one that left her pride intact, and made Finch Leighton's mouth twist at the irony contained in her statement.

She went on, 'Just my wages will do, since I do feel that I'm entitled to the money I earned . . . I'm sorry to leave it until the last minute to give notice. It's not the done thing, really, and I won't expect a reference under the circumstances.'

She'd gone for the throat, not once, but twice, as though she'd known all along that he intended to dismiss her.

Adam grinned when Finch visibly squirmed, but he recovered fast with, 'Oh, don't be so holier-than-thou, Serafina, it doesn't suit you,' but then he overcompensated with, 'and of course I'll provide you with a reference, since I have no quarrel with your work.'

'Thank you.'

'I'm going up to London on business the day after tomorrow, so I'm sure Maggie and Fanny will manage by themselves. There's a maid on my London staff who might consider being my house-keeper, an older woman. She has relatives living hereabouts and I'm sure she'll suit the position. Now we have cleared that matter up, perhaps you'd like to go to the kitchen and fetch me some tea. Will you join me, Adam?'

Serafina sniffed, as if annoyed by the thought that she could so easily be replaced in the household of this man she almost idolized.

However, she'd routed Finch so neatly that Adam had to admire her strategy, and he began to wonder if she hadn't anticipated and planned the whole battle in advance.

Fifteen

They'd left the train on the other side of the harbour and had taken a cab across the toll bridge and through the town. Their boarding house was positioned quite a way out of town and situated on a hill, which afforded it a view of the harbour and the islands it contained.

A fine house was under construction just a little way below them, but it was far enough away for the noise of the comings and goings of the workmen not to be a bother.

Now Serafina had left Leighton Manor and its peaceful surrounds, where she'd been constantly aware that she was under suspicion of theft, the sense of bustle about Poole energized her. Living in a busy town might have its compensations, she thought, since she was interested in everything going on around her.

'I've made a decision to tell Captain Erasmus Thornton about my problem,' she told Adam. 'If I'm related to him, in all fairness I cannot join the family under false pretences. With such a title he sounds like an important man, so he'll be the head of the household, will he not?'

Adam murmured something about Marianne being the head of that household, but his accompanying grin told her that he was teasing.

'When I tell him I imagine he'll send me packing and that will be the end of that, don't you?'

They were sitting on a seat in the garden. Adam, who had a small telescope to his eye, laughed at such a notion as he lowered it. 'We'll see.'

Now she gazed at the tangle of masts in the harbour and said, 'Which ship belongs to Captain Thornton?'

'*Daisy Jane* isn't in port yet. I understand from the agent that she had cargo to discharge at the Isle of Wight.' He pointed. 'You can just see the island on the horizon through the haze.

The ship will arrive some time tomorrow.' He handed her the spyglass. 'Here, you'll be able to see the ship through this when she comes in.'

She placed it against her eye and gazed through it at the grey rippled sheet of water that was the harbour. 'There are ships coming and going all the time. How will I know which one belongs to Captain Thornton?'

'Her name is painted on the prow and she'll have the company flag flying from her mast. The flag is dark blue with the company initials intertwined, TSC. It stands for Thornton Shipping Company.'

How odd that a small flicker of pride tweaked at her. 'How fine it must be to have a ship named after you. Was Daisy Jane his sweetheart – the name of the woman who gave birth to me?'

'Your mother's name was Caroline Honeyman, née Jarvis. Daisy Jane is Erasmus Thornton's sister. She's married to Reverend Phipps.'

Serafina made a face. 'It must be boring to be married to a reverend and have to do what he tells you, even if you do have a ship named after you.'

Laughter bubbled from him. 'They're not all like the Reverend Pawley. Nobody would tell Daisy Phipps what to do, I assure you, and her husband is quite jolly and has a good sense of humour. I'm sure you'll like him when you meet him.'

Serafina hoped so. 'Can you see the house I was born in from here?'

He gave her a quick smile. 'Not from here, but it's a nice afternoon so would you like to take a trip to Dorchester with me? I can hire a rig and you'll be able to take a look at the countryside. We'll be back in time for dinner.'

'You changed the subject very quickly, Adam.'

'That's because I know that your curiosity is piqued, and you are going to plague me with questions if I encourage you.'

'Can you see Marianne's house from here, then? You don't have to tell me which one it is.'

'Yes. And no, I won't then.'

'You're infuriating. You just don't want me to run around like a ferret trying to get a glimpse of people who might be my relatives, that's all . . . so you can laugh and feel all superior.'

'I imagine Marianne is doing the same thing,' and he gave a little laugh. 'She will be on the lookout for someone wearing one of the gowns she sent you.'

'We came past their emporium, didn't we?'

'I wondered if you'd noticed.'

She laughed at him and teased, 'What will you do if I escape from your vigilant eye and go into the emporium and introduce myself?'

'Will you?'

'I might if the opportunity arises. I hate being kept in suspense.'

'You're like Marianne in that regard, you know.'

Jealousy stroked a finger over her heart. 'You mention Marianne often. Are you in love with her, Adam?'

'I do love her, and Charlotte, as well, but I'm not *in love* with them. I imagine you can understand the difference?'

'Oh, yes . . . I loved Mr Leighton in exactly the same way. He's such a fine man, one who is everything that a gentleman should be. I'm sorry we parted under such awkward circumstances, but I'm pleased he fell in love with Celia. They will be happy together and she'll make him forget Diana Milson, who didn't deserve to have him for a husband from what I've heard.'

'Finch couldn't bring himself to believe you were guilty, you know. I told you that he was following up another lead.'

'Frederick and Jane Milson, I imagine. Did you put that in his mind?'

He looked astonished. 'How did you know that?'

'It was obvious to me right from the beginning, but how could I tell Mr Leighton that they might have been the culprits, when they're his first wife's relatives?'

'His fault is that he likes to think well of everybody. I was hoping he'd considered the Milsons as a possible suspect himself, and with a little prompting, he did.'

'You're clever, Adam, but I'm beginning to understand how you work. You plant ideas in the minds of people, then stand back and allow them to flower and bear fruit before harvesting the answers. I can hazard a guess why you want to take me to Dorchester. Can it be that there's something there you hope I'll recognize, since it will strengthen your own belief that I'm Serafina Honeyman.'

She could have eaten the amusement from his eyes with a spoon.

'You're right, Serafina, but I also want to spend the afternoon in your company, so go and get your bonnet and let's put my theory to the test.'

'Damn you, aren't you going to tell me what it is?'

'Of course I'm not. If you thought I would, then you can't read me as well as you imagined.'

She said quietly, 'I sometimes can't deal with the feelings inside me. I want to be the person you say you've discovered—'

He placed a finger over her mouth, and said, 'The person I've discovered is right here in front of me and nothing will change that, not even a name.'

It was a pleasant journey through lanes lined with summer hedgerows that were woven through with honeysuckle and dog roses. The fields were filled with ripening corn and the meadows were a blaze of misty foxgloves and forget-me-nots swaying amongst the golden buttercups. The air was warm, the sky blue with pale wraiths of clouds. The sunshine was dappled with shadows where the leafy branches of the sycamore and elm trees hung.

There were men in the fields, gathering hay. Scythes swished through the stems of long grass while the other field workers casually pitched it up on to the carts.

Serafina felt happy and relaxed. They didn't talk much, but every time her glance met Adam's and they exchanged a smile she could empathize with him in some secret way. She warned herself that it could be due to her imagination.

Dorchester was a small, but pretty town. Today it was bustling with farmers, for the market was in full swing. The smell attracted the flies.

'I'm sorry, I didn't know it was market day,' he said, when she wrinkled her nose and laughed.

They left the horse to rest at the stable and began to walk, following the roman wall, which seemed vaguely familiar to her. A church shortly presented itself – one that seemed even more familiar. Her smile faded and she sucked in a breath. When they went up a small incline, there at the top stood a rambling stone house in an acre of garden. The scene hit her with such force that she could hardly catch a breath. A sense of belonging closed a hand around her midriff and gently squeezed, as if trying to pull her into the garden.

'*Serafina . . .*'

The name on the wind was for her alone. For a moment she saw the old woman seated on a stone bench, with a small child leaning against her knee. The woman looked up and smiled. Then she was gone. Serafina felt comforted by it.

Her breath caught on a sob and she placed her hand on Adam's sleeve. 'There used to be a pond with a stone figure of a fish leaping out of the water, just by that bench. Yellow and purple irises grew around the bank. Now it's a rose bed.'

He took her hand and gazed at her, half quizzical. 'I thought you might remember the house. Do you want to go inside? The owner might allow us entry.'

'There's no need. I know what it's like inside since it gave me shelter, unless the memory I have is a false one. I'm only one of the memories it harbours in its walls, just a small handful of years. But it gave me something to take with me, the knowledge that I was loved once – just a small warm fragment. That was a good start to life, don't you think? I don't want to stay here any longer, Adam. Can we go back to Poole?'

'We'll stop for refreshment somewhere first. There's bound to be a stall that sells lemonade and pies.'

It was early evening when they reached the boarding house, just in time to tidy up for dinner.

Later that night, just before she got into bed, Serafina gazed through the telescope at the harbour. There was a large moon. It scattered a cool glow to dance upon the ripples and left gleaming white patches on the windows of houses. It also painted a slowly moving stripe across her pillow and the wall. Did the same glow touch on her father's face as he paced the deck of his vessel? She placed a kiss in the palm of her hand and folded her fingers over it. Reaching out, so the shadow of her hand was captured in the moonlight, she freed the kiss and sent it winging on its journey across the water to him.

Erasmus Thornton went about his duties in his usual thorough manner. He'd signed on two former employees of the Thornton

Shipping Company in Melbourne. Not that he'd needed them, but both were former employees who'd sailed with Nick on the *Saramand* before she'd foundered. Nick had told him that, without them for companions and the help of the local natives, he probably wouldn't have survived in the wilderness.

Erasmus had decided to keep the cook on, since Red had a good reputation for doctoring as well, something that his daughter-in-law Marianne could attest to. Although the younger man was competent, his heart wasn't in the sea. He was ready to put his youthful adventures behind him now and settle down on shore. He just wanted to get home, and no doubt Nick would find him a job in that emporium of his. The pair had a pouch of gold dust and small nuggets apiece as the result of their foray into the goldfields.

'It's not a fortune, Captain,' Red had said with the humble confidence of a man who knows he finally has some worthy savings behind him. 'But there's enough for Sam here to buy his mother a small house, and if the crew gets wind of it, it might prove to be too much of a temptation. We know you're honest, Captain, which is why we waited for the *Daisy Jane* to arrive in port.'

His reputation as being honest pleased Erasmus. Thievery wasn't the type of trouble he wanted on board, and neither would he tolerate it, though he conceded that gold might incite the greed in men. So he'd made room in his personal strongbox, which was bolted to the deck and had a stout padlock.

The ice shelf in the Southern Ocean had been larger than usual this year. *Daisy Jane*'s sails and deck had been coated in ice, making the ship dangerously top heavy so he'd had to shorten sail, lest they capsize. The water under them had been sluggish.

The man who'd been keeping a watch for icebergs had gone to sleep in the crow's nest, and had never woken up. His body had been frozen stiff when they got him down. The life of a seaman was hazardous on all counts, but Erasmus didn't feel easy when there was a mysterious death on board. He'd said a prayer over the body and they'd buried him in the deep. As soon as the body had disappeared under the water the wind had changed, the air had grown warmer and the ship had regained its former suppleness.

The Southern Ocean had taken its toll, and the atmosphere on board lightened as a result. Not even the Atlantic doing its furious best to blow them in circles could get them down. *Daisy Jane* would have none of it. She was a ship who knew her own mind, and who knew her way home, and as Erasmus set a course that would take them across the short stretch of water from the Isle of Wight into their home port, he could almost smell that home.

So could the crew that morning, and they could obviously smell the delights of shore leave, shouting cheerful insults at each other as they scrubbed the deck, each looking forward to some time ashore. Most had grog and women on their minds, though some had wives and children waiting for them.

He was a family man himself, with Daisy and Nick, Marianne and little Alex. He'd been looking at the moon the night before when he'd thought of the girl he'd possibly fathered. Serafina they called her, and he'd wondered if Adam Chapman had managed to track her down. He wished he hadn't listened to Marianne now, but she had such a way with her . . . and he smiled.

Providing that the detective had tracked her down, and should she prove to be his child, what could he offer a girl of her age? A home? He had none but his ship. A father? Eighteen years was too long for him to claim any authority of kinship. He could offer her a future, perhaps? He had money, and plenty of it. He'd intended to leave it to Nick.

Erasmus sighed. He had the feeling that he may have opened a Pandora's box. Then he remembered – the girl may have been fathered by George Honeyman. He wouldn't feel any responsibility for her if that was the case, so he needn't worry about it until he knew.

'So why do I feel so disappointed at the thought she might belong to George,' he said out loud to a seagull flying overhead, and he found his own answer. The girl would be the result of the love he'd shared with Caroline Honeyman – a gift from beyond the grave that he'd never thought to have.

When Serafina woke she rushed to the window and searched the harbour with the telescope. Nothing! But beyond the harbour on the horizon were two ships in full sail. From here, she couldn't tell if they were coming or going.

She washed with the jug of water a housemaid had brought her earlier. It was lukewarm now, so it raised goosebumps on her flesh. She scrambled into a stiff petticoat, pulled on her stockings followed by some pretty pantalettes and a chemise top. She grinned. The pantalettes were certainly feminine, if a little wicked, but she loved the feel of them against her skin. Over the top went her prettiest skirt and matching day bodice, one of pale-blue taffeta with a lace collar and cuffs.

She hadn't braided her hair yet, and it hung down past her waist.

'Serafina, are you awake?' It was Adam's voice, soft against the door panel.

'Come in.'

He was careful to leave the door open, and smiled at her. 'That's the first time I've seen your hair loose. It's like a length of silk.'

She made a face. 'I'm not very good with hair.'

'Allow me to see if I can do something with it for you.'

Deftly he divided it into three, braiding it neatly. She tried not to shiver as his hands gently handled her hair. He coiled the braid around her head and secured it with pins, then threaded some silk violets behind each ear.

'You should be a lady's maid. How did you learn to do that?'

He laughed. 'Celia sprained her wrist once, and she told me how to do it. She said it was a pretty, no fuss hairstyle that anyone can do. I'm pleased to have been of service.'

'Thank you, Adam.'

He placed a kiss on the top of her head. 'Shall we go down for breakfast?'

But her eyes had been drawn to a ship just coming from behind the largest island. Still shivering from the effect his kiss had on her she swooped in a breath. Forgetting to exhale when she lifted the spyglass and saw the flag fluttering at the mast, she squeaked, 'There's *Daisy Jane*.' Her gaze sought out the small dark figure standing at the wheel. Was that Captain Erasmus Thornton? It was too far away to see him properly.

She had a sudden attack of nerves and turned to Adam. 'Would you mind if I went to see him alone?'

'If that's what you want, though I imagined you'd feel more comfortable being introduced.'

'It would be better if we met each other without anyone looking on waiting to see our reaction to one another. Otherwise I'll feel awkward and I won't know what to say to him. Then I'll probably faint dead away, fall into the harbour and drown.'

He chuckled at her fanciful reasoning. 'You might be run over by a horse, too. Shall we eat breakfast first? There's time before the ship ties up at her berth. Then I'll escort you down to the harbour and let you off the leash.'

As if she was straining at it like a dog needing to chase after a rabbit! All she felt at the moment was that she might run in the other direction. No, that wasn't true. 'Everything is darting madly around inside me, like lightning.'

'I know. Sparks are coming out of your ears and I can hear them crack.'

She laughed. Their table was in the dining room window, and she gazed down the slope to where the roof of the house they were building next door was just visible behind the tops of the trees that marked the boundary. 'That cracking noise is coming from the house they're building next door. It's a man putting slates on the roof. There must be hundreds for a house that size.'

'I daresay.'

'I'm talking about nothing, aren't I?'

'You're filling a space with words because you need to stop yourself from thinking. Calm yourself. If you need me I'll be within shouting distance, and I promise I'll slay all your dragons. Now, eat. Your stomach will gurgle if it's empty, and that will make you laugh at the wrong moment.'

Serafina laughed, just to prove him right. Adam was so confident and sure of himself. She tried to draw on his calmness but couldn't find any inner quietude.

'I'm as jumpy as a bag of fleas.'

Now it was his turn to laugh, an unexpected and slightly muted guffaw that made her giggle. She tried to eat, but couldn't manage much since she was too nervous. But she ate some fruit preserved in juice, and she nibbled at a slice of toast spread with gooseberry jam on, just to please Adam. She washed it down with some tea.

Finally it was time to leave.

'It's a fine day, so we can walk to the harbour,' he said.

Her eyes slid his way. 'Adam Chapman, have you ever been punched by a woman?'

'Not yet. I'd better hold your hand by way of a precaution,' and he did, smiling in that calm way he had. 'Erasmus will have things to supervise first up.'

'I don't give two figs about what Erasmus has to do first. He may have hired you to find me. But that doesn't mean he owns me. Let him put his life on hold for five minutes. I'm scared . . . I'm really scared and shaking all over. Allow me to get this over with . . . please.' She picked up speed, dragging him behind her.

'Slow down, you'll be all hot and bothered when we get there.'

'I don't care.'

There was a cab passing and Adam hailed it. Soon they were deposited on the quay, not far from where *Daisy Jane* was berthed.

The quay itself was all a bustle, the stalls selling eels and cockles doing good business. Ships' provisions, crates of chickens, barrels of water and salted beef were waiting on shore to be loaded. Men stood amongst what seemed a disorganized mess to Serafina, ticking off items on lists with thick stubby pencils.

Daisy Jane was a hive of activity. Great bales of wool were being swung ashore and loaded on to carts.

'I'll wait here, by the Guildhall,' he said, and gazed at his watch. 'You have half an hour before I come on board to rescue you.'

'Now who's nervous.'

He pulled her against him in a brief hug, then turned her to face the ship and gave her a gentle push. 'Go now, and good luck.'

Her knees were shaking as she dodged round the many obstacles in her way. She was crossing the gangplank when somebody cried out, 'Get out of the bloody way, woman!' An arm snaked around her waist and she was lifted off her feet. There was a glimpse of dark water below her as she was swung across the gap and over the side, where she was set firmly on a planked deck. A pair of dark, furious eyes stared into hers as a large crate sailed across the space Serafina had previously occupied.

She knew without telling who this man was. He was taller than she'd expected, slim and muscular with grizzled hair and a weather-beaten face that still possessed a rugged, but well-formed grace. No longer angry, those hard, dark eyes of his were scrutinizing every inch of her face. He must recognize something in her . . . *he must!*

'Captain Erasmus Thornton? I'm Serafina,' she whispered.

'Aye, I know who you are; you should have shouted out that you were boarding.'

'I've never been on a ship; I didn't know I had to. I'm sorry.'

'Aye, you wouldn't have known then.' His smile came easily and warmly, so she wondered why she'd ever imagined that she'd be scared of him. 'I thought you would look like your mother, but you don't . . . rather you resemble mine, I think. My sister Daisy will know. She pays mind to such things.'

With that Serafina knew she'd been claimed, but with reservations. A couple of tears trickled down her face. She was going to cry. Taking out her handkerchief she surreptitiously dabbed at the tears.

He gazed at his crew, each with an ear or an eye directed their way. She'd given no thought to the notion that he might have preferred some privacy for the meeting. 'I'm sorry, I should have thought you wouldn't have wanted to meet this way.'

'I'm not ashamed of you, if that's what you're getting at girl. Let's go aft where we can find a quiet place to talk.'

'You don't mind me coming unannounced then? Adam said you would be busy at this time. I'm sorry I got in the way.'

'You would have been sorry if that crate had clouted you. It nearly parted my hair. And I guess I'm not too busy to meet you, young lady, but you're right, I'd have picked a better place.'

'I was too impatient, I know, but it's been months, and I couldn't bear to wait any longer.'

'Never mind, what's done is done.'

'I was keeping watch, and Adam made me eat breakfast, even though I saw the ship coming in. He's waiting on the quay. He said he'd come to rescue me in half an hour.'

Erasmus laughed at that. 'I guess I do frighten strangers off if they don't know me, since I don't suffer fools gladly. Have you met the rest of the family yet?'

'No . . . Adam said . . . well, I wanted to meet you first . . . it was only right that I should, just in case you didn't like me.'

They sat together on a short flight of steps and looked at each other. A grin appeared on his face. 'I'll be damned.'

Laughter bubbled up inside her. 'I'll be damned too. I thought that this day would never come. What should I call you?'

'What do you want to call me?'

She shrugged. 'I don't know, I've never had a father before . . . that's if you *are* my father.'

'And I've never had a daughter before. Call me Erasmus if you like, like Marianne does.'

Worry filled her eyes. 'You *are* convinced, aren't you? Adam said there's a slight chance that I might be a girl called Mary Fenn.'

'Let's assume you are my daughter . . . what does Adam know?'

'He's clever, and leaves very little to chance. If I had anything to hide I wouldn't like him to be after me.'

'He must be good since he found you, something I wouldn't have thought possible. And he's won your heart in the process by the sound of it.'

She felt her face warm. 'Yes . . . I suppose he has.'

He took her hand in his – a hand that was just as calloused as hers had been, before Celia's salve had begun to help soften them. 'What if I told you that I've missed you?'

'Missed me . . . how could you when you never met me?'

'Even though I thought you'd died at birth, I've always wondered what you looked like and regretted not having my own daughter at my side, or even seeing you as a baby.'

Serafina remembered she needed to tell him of the charge against her. 'There's something you need to know . . .'

There came a shout from the quayside. 'Erasmus, where are you?'

He stood, and with Serafina partly concealed behind him he waved, a wide smile appearing on his face. 'I'm here, Marianne.'

'I found Adam loitering on the quay and looking suspicious. He's told me that Serafina is with you. I'm dying with curiosity. May I come aboard?'

Indeed, Adam was standing by Marianne's side, looking slightly bemused.

'No you may not. I'll be up at the house in a little while and will bring Serafina with me. What are you doing, coming to the quay by yourself? Nick will smack your arse for you when he finds out.'

She laughed at such a notion, then placed her hands on her hips and scolded him. 'Usually you're more hospitable. What are you thinking of, when I ran all the way down the hill and got a pain in my side for my trouble? You can't keep her all to yourself, you know. I'm not going away; I'll just wait here on the quay. Best to let me on board, though, then we won't have to shout our business back and forth.'

'I've already got one woman on board, and she nearly brained her damned fool head on a crate. Two will be double the trouble. You stay there, do you hear me, Marianne?'

Crawling with curiosity, Serafina stepped out from behind him to gaze at the woman Adam had talked so much about. She was lovely, and when their eyes met a beautiful, welcoming smile spread across Marianne's face and she blew her a kiss. Warmth flowed through Serafina and she called out, 'Marianne, thank you so much for the gift.'

'Lor, it was nothing compared to what I was going to send you, but Adam and Nick insisted on taking half of it out. However, I've kept it all for you. Don't let Erasmus frighten you; he's not as fierce as he pretends to be.'

By this time most of the crew were listening, and grinning amongst themselves.

Behind Serafina, Erasmus chortled, 'I most certainly am. However, I can see that you ladies have several matters of national importance to discuss.'

'Of course we have, dearest Uncle, since we'll probably discuss you fine gentlemen when you finally allow us to get together and gossip. Of course, if I'm forced to carry on a conversation here it will end up as common knowledge around the dinner tables by tonight.'

'Aye, there's that, but since when have we allowed it to bother us,' he grumbled, and there was a moment of awkwardness when he gazed at Serafina, seemingly unaware of how he should treat her. Then he leaned forward and gently kissed her forehead.

She gave him a hug in return, a quick one that didn't give him time to react, since he didn't look like a man who hugged strangers.

'Better you go with Marianne, else she'll stay there all day if you don't.'

'But, I wanted to tell you—'

'It can wait, since your sister can't . . . and I do have work to do. Over the next few days we'll find some private moments when we can talk together.'

Her sister! Little coils of excitement sprang about inside her as Erasmus took her to the gangplank. She wondered what everyone would do if she did cartwheels along the quay.

He raised his voice. 'Off you go, then; it's safe to go ashore since the entire crew has turned into a cage of drooling monkeys instead of getting on with their work. Marianne, you look after her, now. Take a cab from the rank, and if you see Nick, tell him that Red and Sam are on board. Adam, join me on board if you would.'

A short time later Adam and Erasmus watched the two women walk off, chatting together as though they'd known each other for years. As they reached the cab rank near the turn off to the High Street, they exchanged a hug before they got inside.

'Now there's a sight,' Erasmus said with some satisfaction as the cab moved off. 'George Honeyman would turn in his grave.'

Adam shrugged. He wasn't interested in the former family rivalry, except as a means to an end. He'd always had a strong feeling that something had been left unsaid by somebody – something that would resolve the whole issue. Still, he was happy that Serafina had been accepted, so far. 'What do you think, Captain? Is she yours?'

Erasmus's mouth curled into a grin. 'I reckon there's some strong similarities to my mother, at that. Anyway, she's got herself a pa as far as I'm concerned.'

'We have to be sure. Between you and me there's some other business concerning Serafina that she doesn't even know about yet. It regards property that has been fraudulently claimed by another. By now the lawyers should have that investigation well in hand, and before it can be settled Serafina's connection must be proved beyond a doubt.'

'Can't the girl remember who she is?'

'She has memories, but because of certain circumstances in her life she is unsure, and you need to be told about those.'

He nodded. 'Come to my cabin. We'll talk over coffee and I'll settle your bill if you like.'

'No charge, except for necessary expenses. You'll receive a detailed account in due course.'

'I always pay my way, mister.'

'Not this time.' Adam grinned at him. 'You could call this a labour of love, since you'll end up being my father-in-law if Serafina will have me. I intend to wait a while though, and allow her to get used to this new set of circumstances. Would you have any objections?'

Erasmus scratched his head. 'I'll be damned . . . what am I supposed to say to that when I've only been a father for ten shakes of a rat's tail? You'd better ask me when the time comes.'

He raised his voice. 'Take over Mister Grimshaw . . . seems I've got some talking to do.'

'Aye, aye, Captain,' came the reply.

Sixteen

Serafina had fallen immediately for Marianne's charm during the short ride up Constitution Hill, though she found her chatter a little overwhelming. The house she was taken to was solid, though it seemed a little cramped after Leighton Manor.

'You must move in with us. Aunt Daisy won't mind. It's her house, you see, only she doesn't live here now she's married. We're only living here ourselves until our new house is built. It's got a view over the harbour. There's a boarding house next door, but it's very respectable so there won't be any undesirables loitering in the district.'

'I believe it might be the boarding house where we're staying, since there's a house being built further down the hill. No wonder Adam laughed when I asked him if we could see your house from there.'

Serafina smiled when Marianne said, 'Adam didn't tell me you were staying there. I was there yesterday afternoon, to see how the building was progressing. He could have introduced us then. He is so infuriating, making me wait until Erasmus arrived. What if the ship had sunk? We'd have waited for ever.'

'Under those circumstances, I doubt it. As it was he hired a vehicle and showed me the . . . countryside around Dorchester. It's very pretty here.'

Marianne shrugged. 'I find that the town can make me feel closed in at times. I grew up on the heath, you see, and my . . . our . . . sister still lives in the family house. Nick says the new house with the view over the water should suit us both. He used to be a sea captain, and was master of the *Samarand*. The ship had a reputation of being unlucky. I fell down a hatch when I first went on board, and I wasn't found for two days. On Nick's very next run to Australia, the ship was overturned by a huge wave, and Nick lost most of his crew. He gave up the sea when he finally got home. That's when he opened the emporium. I didn't see him for nearly a year after he was shipwrecked, and I thought he was dead. I gave birth to our son during that time.'

'That must have been hard on you.'

'Well, you're right of course, Serafina, but though everyone thought he must have drowned, I never gave up hope because, somehow, I knew he was still alive.' She abruptly changed the subject. 'Serafina is such a pretty name. I knew you had that name; I heard it whispered on the wind when I was on the heath. I was with Nick, and he didn't laugh or turn a hair when I told him. We have gypsy blood through our mother's family, though it goes back a long way. Charlotte doesn't believe in such things . . . she doesn't want to really, so she tends to deny it to herself. Adam named your file Serafina after I told him.'

'I've heard my name on the wind too,' Serafina confessed. 'I was with Adam. We both heard it the first time. And I heard it again just yesterday. Adam took me to the house where he thinks I spent my early years. I recognized certain things . . . and I saw a woman who I believe was my aunt.'

'Then the gypsies will know you are here. That must have been Constance Serafina Jarvis you saw, who was my aunt too. Only she didn't get on with my father. He was incensed when she died and left most of her money to charity. He thought it should have gone to him. How wonderful if she's come back to haunt the place! I do love family skeletons, don't you? Everyone tries to cover them up but they always come to the surface.'

'I don't think she was a ghost, because I was with her. It was more the experience that I saw what I wanted to see. And of course, I *am* the family skeleton, so can't really see it the same way as you do,' Serafina said morosely.

'Oh, but of course you are . . . oh, don't worry about it, my dear. I would be gripped with delight if it were me, since it adds an air of mystery, and people notice you. The Honeyman and Thornton families are gossiped about all the time. We have terribly wicked reputations. There's the gypsy blood, though God knows it's well diluted. Then we have the affair between my mother and Erasmus, and her death . . . then you . . . the innocent lamb who was cast out of the family. And Charlotte married a man she'd only just met to spite Nick, who had been in love with her since childhood. As for Charlotte and Erasmus, they hardly talk to each other because of the scandal your birth caused, so Charlotte might not be as welcoming of your return to the family as she should. But she'll come round to it, I promise. Oh yes, I nearly forgot. When Nick and I married we kept it a secret, but there was a dreadful scandal and Charlotte threw me out and didn't speak to me for a whole year.'

Serafina's head buzzed. 'It sounds as though there is a melo-drama a minute.'

'Oh, it seems like it sometimes, but your drama beats all.' Tears flooded Marianne's eyes. 'I can barely comprehend a more cruel act than my father casting an innocent infant from her rightful home. I shall never forgive him, and it's a wonder you want to know us at all.'

Serafina hadn't really wanted to know them, but had allowed Adam to talk her into it. She couldn't be churlish and say so, though she experienced a sudden, crushing need to be back in her little nest at Leighton Manor. But she'd cut herself adrift so couldn't blame anyone else, she reminded herself, and was under suspicion of theft. The thought made her feel sick so she stopped thinking about it.

Serafina found herself taken into a hug that a boa constrictor would have envied. If her sister kept this up she'd end up with cracked ribs, she thought, and she patted Marianne awkwardly on the shoulder. She felt relieved when a knock came at the door and Marianne set her free.

There came an exclamation when Marianne opened the door. 'Aunt Daisy, how wonderful to see you . . . you'll never guess who is here!'

'Of course I can guess, you ninny.' A slim woman in a grey dress appeared and was introduced as Mrs Phipps. Dark-brown eyes that eerily resembled Erasmus Thornton's raked her sharply up and down. 'You're the spitting image . . . yup, you're a Thornton all right, from the female side, anyway,' she said with some satis-faction. 'This is going to cause a good old stir of the stew in church come Sunday.'

Serafina was folded into another bone-crushing hug. She was being given hardly any room to breathe by these people . . . her *family*. She felt trapped, the air in the room seemed dense and she wanted to run, except there seemed to be no way out. To her dismay she began to weep.

'There, there, my dear,' Daisy said. 'It's all been too much for you.' Serafina was led to a chair, where two concerned women with faces just as wet as hers gazed at her.

'Sorry . . . I don't know what's come over me. I'll be all right in a minute.'

But she wasn't all right. She wanted to go home, but realized that she didn't have a home now, and she couldn't stop crying.

'You're just overwrought. It's my fault for insisting on seeing you before you were ready. I'll never forgive myself.' The dark-blue eyes of Marianne were awash with tears now. 'Lord, I'm such a fool.'

She couldn't let Marianne, who'd been so generous and sweet towards her, take the blame. 'You're not . . . it's me that's the fool,' Serafina said, and they hugged each other and started to weep on each other's shoulders again.

'Now we've decided that we're all fools, I'll go and make us some tea and we'll drink to it,' Daisy said over-brightly.

A minute or two later a large, handsome man with black eyes appeared. 'What the hell's going on, Aria? The place is full of weeping women. Aunt Daisy is in tears in the kitchen, and you're bawling like a couple of Irish banshees in here . . . and where's Alex?'

Marianne wiped her eyes with a lace handkerchief. 'He's with the maid, upstairs.'

'Alex is bellowing as well, now he's heard all the noise. He thinks we're having a party and ignoring him. Go and get him, would you, while I sort things out here. It sounds like a wake rather than a reunion.'

A large expanse of clean white handkerchief was placed in Serafina's hand, and the man grinned at her. 'Here, blot your eyes before you drown yourself. I'm your cousin, Nicholas Thornton, Nick for short. I only use Nicholas when I want to appear dignified.'

She gave a faint smile as she gazed at him. He was brimming with confidence. 'You look quite dignified to me. I'm Serafina . . . Sara Finn . . . Fenn.' She sniffed and wailed, 'Oh . . . I'm so mixed up that I don't know who I am any more, and I don't really care.'

'My guess is that Aria hasn't stopped prattling at you. She does that when she's nervous and can spin people like a top without even trying. Where's Adam? Why isn't he with you?'

'He's with Captain Thornton on his ship.'

Nick nodded. 'How did my uncle react to the sight of you? Was he civil?'

She nodded. 'Mostly, though we spent only a few minutes together. He was taken aback at first, I think. I did things all wrong. I wouldn't listen to Adam and insisted on going on board by myself and without introduction.'

His chuckle was like cream. 'That sounds like a Honeyman trait; the womenfolk never do what they're told. Then Aria turned up and took charge of you, I suppose.' He took her chin between his finger and thumb and gazed at her face. 'No wonder my uncle was taken aback. He had some romantic idea in his head that you'd resemble his lost love, Caroline Honeyman, but you don't, and thank goodness, because Aria is the very image of her, and another one in the house would cause mayhem. You greatly resemble Erasmus and Daisy's mother though, which is no bad thing. There's a picture of her in the attic room upstairs. Erasmus will probably show it to you later. If he forgets, ask him if you can see it. It might make you feel as though you belong somewhere definite in the family.'

She liked this man. 'Thank you, Nick, you're very kind. I feel like an idiot for crying.'

He kissed her on both cheeks then released her. 'Of course you do. To be honest, I cried myself when I first met Erasmus, but I was only young then and I thought he looked fearsome. He told me to stop snivelling, said my father was dead and my mother had begged him to take me off her hands because my stepfather and brothers were being cruel to me.'

'Oh, how dreadfully sad,' and she sniffed, though was grateful for the connection that their similar early childhoods provided.

'Hey, don't you start crying all over again. There are only so many tears I can cope with in one day. It was actually the best day of my life. I just didn't realize it at the time. Are you feeling less soggy now?'

She nodded.

'Thank goodness for small mercies,' and his sigh of relief made her laugh.

'Papa!' The young boy who wandered in was the image of his father, and he had a smile as wide as Nick's as he scrambled into his father's lap. Laying his head against Nick's chest he stuck his thumb into his mouth and stared at her, then he gazed up at Nick and whispered, 'Lady.'

'Say hello to your new aunt, Serafina.'

''ello, Fina.' When the boy giggled Serafina's heart melted. He was a handsome boy with dark liquid eyes and curly dark hair like his father.

'Serafina, this is your nephew, Alexander Thornton . . . Alex for short.'

'Hello, Alex.' She gazed from the boy to Nick and smiled. 'He looks like an angel.'

'He's wearing his disguise at the moment. He has a pair of horns hidden under his curls and a long tail with a pitchfork on the end of his spine, haven't you, Alex?'

Alex solemnly nodded. 'Me good.'

When Nick laughed Alex did likewise, and to prove his point the toddler fished Nick's watch out of his pocket by the chain and held it to his ear. 'Tick-tock tick-tock,' he whispered, then put it back where it belonged and began to investigate the other pocket. There, he found what he was looking for, something wrapped in tissue paper. A grin widened his mouth. 'Ahah!' Tearing the wrapping from a piece of rose-coloured Turkish delight, he tossed the scrap of paper on the floor then stuck the sweetmeat in his mouth. One cheek bulging, Alex gazed at his father in triumph.

Serafina laughed. 'He's certainly got charm. Have I got any more nephews?'

'Three, and one niece. They're Charlotte and Seth Hardy's brood.'

Marianne bustled in carrying a tea tray. Daisy trailed behind with a plate of sliced fruit cake.

'Goodness . . . what on earth is Alex eating?'

'A snail,' Nick said.

Apart from a grin, Marianne didn't turn a hair. 'Then let me put a napkin under his chin before he dribbles it all over you. Keep him on your lap till it's all gone, Nicky darling.' Tying the napkin in a knot at the back of the boy's neck, Marianne kissed both of her males, momentarily exchanging an intimate look and a smile with her husband before taking up position behind the tea tray. They seemed happy together.

Daisy Thornton took a seat next to her, she was red-eyed from crying and Serafina imagined she looked the same.

'I suppose you think I'm an idiot, Missy.'

'No, Mrs Phipps, of course I don't. I know this must have come as much a shock to you, as it did to me. I thought I had no relatives left alive until Adam contacted me, and was unaware of the circumstances of my birth. Now my whole life seems to have been taken apart, examined, and put back together differently, so I now feel as though I'm someone else altogether. It's a little uncomfortable.'

Daisy patted her hand. 'We'll soon get used to one another.'

'I expect we will, and I'll try and find employment as a housekeeper, so I won't get underfoot and can pay my way.'

'Find employment as a housekeeper?' Marianne said faintly. 'You don't have to go that far.'

'But I'm used to keeping myself busy.' Her glance travelled to Daisy. 'I understand that you're married to Reverend Phipps. I used to work for a reverend when I was young. He was . . . *horrid* . . . mean, and very strict, and pompous. He acted as though everyone was beneath him. His wife treated me well though. Elizabeth was my friend in the workhouse until she married him. Even after her marriage she was good to me, and she taught me lots of things, for which I'm grateful.'

'Oh, Phipps isn't in the least bit pompous. He makes me laugh, and he encourages me to use my own mind and have my own opinions.'

Nick chuckled. 'He knows better than to try and stop you, Aunt Daisy. I don't know why you waited so long before you accepted him.'

'I had you and Erasmus to make a home for when you were in port.' She gave Marianne a fond look. 'Now Marianne does it.'

'Erasmus will have to come to the new house when it's finished.'

Daisy smiled. 'Not necessarily. If everything goes well and Serafina decides to stay with us she's welcome to make her home here. Erasmus is a creature of habit, and he grew up here.'

Nick said, 'Serafina will need employment under those

circumstances, and I'm sure I can use her in the emporium once she's settled in and decided what she's going to do. There's plenty of accounting work, or if you don't fancy that I could make you the supervisor of the female staff. If you'd prefer not to work for me, then I'm sure I'll know someone who would be willing to employ you. In the meantime, don't worry about anything. There's no rush, and you might meet a nice young man, fall in love and get married.'

All enthusiasm, Marianne said, 'We must entertain then; you know several unattached young men, Nick. We'll invite them all to dinner so they can meet her.'

'All at once?'

'Goodness, no, Nick! Men find safety in numbers and they talk about boring things like the economy and politics instead of paying attention to us women. You have to catch men alone if you want them to notice you, Serafina.' There was only one man Serafina wanted, but he was probably out of her reach when it came to marriage. 'I appreciate the offer of a job, thank you, Nick. As for meeting men, I'll put that on the bottom of my list for a while if you don't mind, Marianne.'

Mischief filled her eyes. 'How disappointing. I was going to ask Adam to join us for dinner tonight, too, though I expect Erasmus will bring him home, anyway.'

'Adam isn't a suitor, of course, our relationship is very professional.'

'Oh, what a shame,' Marianne said smoothly.

She sighed, said, 'Yes, I suppose it is,' then smoothed nervously at her shirt. 'Oh dear, I've got nothing to change into. My luggage is at the boarding house.'

'Didn't I tell you that I kept everything that wouldn't fit into the baskets? The wardrobe is stuffed with clothing that belongs to you. Heavens, we must do something about that hairstyle.'

'Adam fashioned it for me.'

'Adam did?'

Three pairs of eyes gazed with interest at her.

'I never learned how to dress hair.' Serafina felt the colour creeping under her skin and hoped nobody noticed. 'He's a friend, and nothing else,' she said, much too emphatically. 'He learned to do this style for his sister, Celia, when she sprained her wrist.'

When Nick winked at Marianne and the pair exchanged a grin, she coloured even more.

Standing, Nick handed Alex over to his wife. 'I've got to get on now; I want to see my uncle before I go back to the emporium.'

Marianne exclaimed, 'Oh, I forgot to tell you. Erasmus gave me a message to pass on to you if I saw you. Red and Sam are on board.'

'I'll be damned,' he said with a smile. 'That's good news. I'll see you all a little later, then.' And he was gone.

Marianne asked, 'Is Reverend Phipps coming to dinner, Aunt Daisy?'

'If he doesn't, he can go without.'

Marianne began to panic. 'Oh, lor . . . I hope I've got enough food for us all,' she said despairingly. 'I'm not used to cooking for a lot of people. The silver needs cleaning and the best table-cloth needs ironing. I was going to take Alex out for his usual walk to get some fresh air. He gets fractious if he misses it, and sleeps badly. Then there's the leek and potato soup. I forgot about it when I saw *Daisy Jane* at the berth, and realized that Serafina must have arrived as well.'

Daisy smiled at her panic. 'I'll go to the butcher and buy a double shoulder of lamb. The butcher's boy can deliver it straight away. He can also deliver some apple pies from the pie shop next door. I'll make some custard and bring it back with me. You've got plenty of vegetables in the larder, and more in the garden. Tell the maid to prepare some of those, and ask her to stay on and help serve the dinner and wash the dishes afterwards. She'll be glad to earn some extra money. Serafina, what can we find for you to do?'

Managing a house was something Serafina was more than capable of doing, and she had picked up many cooking tips from Maggie at Leighton Manor. Her sister was as lovely and generous as she'd been led to believe, but she didn't seem to have the skill to organize a dinner for unexpected guests.

Calmly, Serafina said, 'Take Alex out for his walk if you like, Marianne. I'll make the soup and some mint sauce to start with. You have mint in the garden, I imagine? Then I'll clean the silver, do the ironing and see to the table. After that I'll see what else needs doing. With your permission I'll soon discover where everything is. We'll get it all done, and with time to spare, you'll see.'

Galvanized into action, she soon had everything under control, and by the time Marianne returned the table looked pretty with candles, shining silver, crystal glasses and arrangements of white rambling roses picked from the garden.

Alex was fed and bedded down for the night. He'd gone to sleep in an instant, sucking his thumb.

Gently kissing his flushed cheek, Marianne said, 'He's such a love; I adore him.'

Serafina was inclined to agree with her.

The two women stripped down and washed, then dressed. Marianne picked a blue gown to match her eyes, and insisted that Serafina wear a creamy gown the colour of roasted almonds. It was decorated with embroidered yellow roses and trimmed with a deep lace collar. Her hair was parted in the middle and Marianne used the tongs to curl pretty ringlets at either side, securing them with white silk flowers.

'Do you have any jewels?' Marianne asked.

The thought of jewels brought the worry to Serafina's mind, of that awful moment when the ring had dropped from the handkerchiefs on to the desk.

'You can wear my pearls if you'd like to.'

Serafina experienced a rush of warmth at Marianne's generosity of spirit. She kissed her cheek. 'Thank you, Marianne, but I can go without. I'm not used to wearing jewellery, and the gown is so very lovely. Will I be meeting Charlotte before too long?'

'Charlotte hasn't been well since the birth of her son, James. Doctor Beresford said she's suffering from melancholy, which is quite common apparently.'

'Oh . . . I'm sorry.'

'Be patient with Charlotte, I beg you. When we lost our mother, Char became everything to me. She takes her responsibilities too much to heart, but I love her dearly, and so will you when you get to know her.'

'I'm sure I shall.'

★   ★   ★

Daisy and the reverend arrived early to help out, and the reverend made himself busy, choosing two bottles of red Bordeaux from the wine cupboard, and resting and decanting them.

Half an hour later the three men arrived, carrying Serafina's wicker baskets between them. They were laughing and jostling each other in the relaxed and uninhibited manner men assumed when they've indulged in one glass of wine too many.

But they were steady on their feet, and definitely not inebriated. They took the baskets upstairs to the room Serafina had been allocated. She was glad she'd thought to tidy up the mess Marianne had made, scattering clothes and accessories about the place.

Adam's eyes widened at the sight of her when he came down, and when he kissed her cheek she was hard put not to turn her mouth to his and taste the brandy on his breath. Tension between them was activated by their closeness, a thrill of attraction that tugged gently and implacably at her. What would happen if she moved across the small gap between them, she didn't know, but there was a longing to do so inside her that was hard to control.

'How lovely you look,' he said.

Marianne told him, 'She would have looked lovelier if she'd had some jewels to wear, but she refused to borrow my pearls.'

Serafina's eyes met Adam's, and they exchanged a rueful smile. 'Serafina is already a pearl, and so are you, Marianne,' he said.

Nick elbowed Adam gently out of the way. 'My turn, I think.' He kissed her on both cheeks.

Adam moved on to Marianne, then to Daisy.

Erasmus was at the end of the line. She gazed at him, and he smiled and held out his hand to her. Pulling her against his side he kissed the top of her head.

When they were settled around the table, he filled their glasses and said simply. 'A toast. Ladies and gentlemen, please welcome to our family, my daughter. Serafina Thornton.'

Serafina closed her eyes for a moment, basking in the feeling of belonging, then a little chill of doubt moved in once again.

Seventeen

London

Finch Leighton was annoyed that he'd missed Frederick and Jane. Blanche Milson said carelessly, 'Oh, they've gone to Kent to stay with friends, and intended to drop in on you at Leighton Manor. They'll be back at the weekend.'

He'd sent his new housekeeper down to Leighton Manor, and with her a strong young man of all work to help the ageing Joseph, since the house needed some maintenance repairs. He'd also sent instructions that the Milson pair was to be refused admittance to his home there. Finch hoped that the staff didn't mention the stolen jewellery to them . . . though they might now guess that he was on to them with the ban in place – or discovered his impending marriage to Celia, come to that.

Finch didn't let his anger show as he informed Blanche, 'Frederick is supposed to be training for a position with the East India company at my expense.'

'Freddie said that the man he was training under was terribly rude to him. He decided he didn't want to go abroad to live in a hot climate and be pushed around by an inferior little clerk. Besides, he learned all he needed to do, since he's always been good with money.'

Good at spending it, especially if it belonged to other people. Drily, he murmured, 'So I've noticed.'

'Besides, now Freddie's trained he'll have other prospects. As for Jane . . . I might as well tell you that she has an offer of marriage, and will be celebrating her engagement this weekend.' A trifle reluctantly, she offered, 'You'll join us, of course.'

'Who's the man?'

'Oh, you don't have to worry that she's marrying somebody unsuitable. He's a businessman called Bartholomew Craven. And Bart has promised Freddie a job, in one of his warehouses.

No doubt he'll be trained in management, so it will all be kept in the family.'

'Bart Craven is in his fifties,' and he was much too old for Jane. But that was her problem. He also had a reputation of being cold-blooded, and if Frederick thought he'd be put in a management position, he'd soon find out different. Bart was a businessman through and through, and his managers were hard-worked and astute, though Finch had heard that he paid them well. He doubted if Frederick would last five minutes in that environment. 'Wasn't Bart a particular friend of yours at one time, Blanche?'

'My dear Finch, Bart still is a friend, but he needs a wife who is young enough to provide him with an heir, and who is able to host his parties. I introduced them myself, with the desired outcome clearly spelled out. He was very generous to me when Jane accepted him. Just as well, since the lease was due on this house.'

He gazed around the room. 'This house is larger than you need, and way beyond your means now, Blanche. It was a pity you took out a loan against it. You must look for something cheaper to lease.'

'Oh, this house is so convenient, and I'm sure Bart will help me out when Jane is his wife.'

'So, Blanche . . . you sold your daughter to the highest bidder. How very callous of you.'

'Oh, don't be so stuffy, Finch.' Blanche gave a short laugh. 'Jane isn't an innocent, hasn't been since she was sixteen when I caught her with Freddie's best friend. It's you who set the terms by disinheriting them.'

'They were never my heirs in the first place, and under the circumstances I've been very generous to them.'

'But they had expectations that you didn't discourage. You'll never marry and produce children now. You were too enamoured with Diana. How foolish, when she was constantly unfaithful to you . . . we used to laugh about it together.'

Finch could imagine it, but he was well and truly over Diana now, and Blanche's cruel jibe about her infidelity washed over him. He'd left instructions that his late wife's room must be emptied of everything, and the clothing and furnishings burned.

'Jane has told me about the room, about the jewellery scattered about, the unmade bed and Diana's clothes thrown over the chair. I understand that your housekeeper stole most of her jewellery . . . or is she more than a housekeeper? Freddie says she is. I suppose that even a blind man has his needs. You should have given the jewels to Jane, after all, Diana did say she could have them if she died. Well, it's gone for good now. *Pawned* by that snippet from the workhouse. And it serves you right. I wager that the girl doesn't seem so attractive to you now.'

Right now Finch's most urgent need was to take Blanche's yapping neck in his hands and squeeze the life from it. With a great deal of effort he resisted his homicidal urge. He'd learned from Adam Chapman that being a good listener brought its own rewards – and just at this moment he was learning a lot. If Jane and Freddie knew the contents of Diana's room, then they'd been inside it. That meant that they had stolen a key. He imagined it was the one he'd mislaid in London – found later at Leighton Manor. And Blanche had put a lot of emphasis on the word: Pawned.

'Freddie tells me the girl is an opportunist, and that she made advances to him. Not that he was interested, of course. He said she was a plain creature who was looking for a wealthy husband. How would anyone with self-respect want a blind man as a husband, anyway?'

His wonderful Celia, for one, Finch thought.

'Jane understands what's required of her, and once she's satisfied the condition of giving him an heir he'll settle an amount of money on her and she'll be free to do as she wishes.'

'If you think that, then the pair of you are more naïve than I imagined.' What Bart Craven bought he possessed, and he'd want more than one heir for his money.

'Bart has promised that if he dies without issue, then Jane will inherit everything. She will also have the settlement you promised her. And so will Freddie when he marries.'

'Frederick has been given his last opportunity to make something better of himself. He's wasted it. I will not allow him to spend the rest of his life being a wastrel on my money so I intend to withdraw his allowance along with my help. I also intend to withdraw Jane's since she now has her hand in another man's pocket.'

Blanche looked alarmed. 'Don't be silly, she's done exactly as you asked, found herself a husband. Speak to Freddie on Saturday, Finch. You can turn him to your way of thinking if you've a mind. He'll listen to you, as he always does.'

'Only when he needs money.' He was finished with Frederick, except for one thing, but that could wait until Saturday. Looking forward to escaping from the stuffy red atmosphere of Blanche's drawing room, Finch placed his hand on the shoulder of the waiting Oscar.

When they were outside he took a breath of fresh air. 'Take me to Adam Chapman's office, Oscar. And if we pass a flower seller on the way buy a dozen roses . . . red ones, and a vase to put them in.'

'Yes, sir.'

Adam's establishment was just a few steps from the florist shop. 'Finch, what a surprise, and how lovely to see you,' Celia said, and the genuine pleasure in her voice filled him with joy. 'Adam's not here, but I'm expecting him any day.'

'It was you I came to see, not Adam. Can you take time to walk with me? There's something I want to talk to you about.'

It didn't take long to bring her up to date on events, and for them to come up with a plan.

'Let me know later how everything went,' she said when they got back, and taking his face in her hands she kissed him on the mouth.

He replied in kind, then said, 'I love you,' and he laughed when Oscar gave a discreet cough, reminding them they were standing in a doorway in London.

There were several jewellers and pawnshops in the area, but not too many to cover in one day. Finch enlisted Oscar for the task of visiting each one. By the time his servant had returned he'd recovered most of the jewellery. It had cost Finch a fortune, but it was worth it. Still missing though, was the sapphire set.

Oscar said, 'Most of the shops named the seller as being someone called Sara Finn. I also have two bills of sale signed by the seller, who named herself as Sara Finn. But the description given to me of the woman was that of Miss Milson, and I'm almost certain that it's not Miss Finn's signature.'

'Well done, Oscar.'

'You should have her charged with theft, sir.'

'I know I should, but I have a much better punishment in mind. If my late wife promised the girl her jewels, then Jane shall have them. I shall insist. Did I bring that diamond ring with me?'

'Yes, sir, it's in your waistcoat pocket.'

'Oh yes, so it is . . . and make me an appointment with the doctor.'

'Are you ill, sir?'

'Mind your own bloody business, Oscar.'

'If you insist, sir,' and Oscar laughed.

Come Saturday, Finch picked Celia up from Edgar Wyvern's house. In the darkness of the cab he took her in his arms and kissed her. 'You're wearing your lavender gown.'

She laughed. 'What makes you think that?'

'It rustles when you walk, and you told me that you only had one best gown, and that was lavender.'

'You have a good memory, but Edgar Wyvern has bought me several new gowns of late. I have gowns in yellow, blue, rose pink and rose red as well. In fact, I'm quite the lady now.'

'You've always been a lady, Celia, my love. I do adore you, you know.'

'And you know I love you. I felt comfortable with you from the first moment we met, as though we were always meant to be.'

'So what colour is your gown?'

'It's the lavender one. I chose it because I knew you'd hear the taffeta fabric rustle and remember the colour. And I knew you'd comment on it to prove how clever you are.'

'That's cheating.'

He laughed when she chuckled, and she kissed him again, awakening all sorts of feelings inside him – feelings he'd never thought to have for a woman again.

'I'll have to go to Poole and apologize to Serafina after this.'

'She won't expect it, but yes, you must. It will be good for her to know there is no longer any suspicion attached to her. Her feelings would have been dreadfully hurt by what happened. She was very attached to you.'

'I was a father figure to her, and by now she should have

someone more suitable to replace me, if the man will accept her. Serafina has a good heart, and she'll forgive me.' He hesitated for a few moments, then said, 'I shouldn't have presumed to involve you in what's about to happen, Celia, and it will probably reveal a side of me that you might not like. Would you like to return home?'

'Certainly not. To commit a crime then deliberately lay the blame on someone completely innocent is despicable behaviour. You're letting Jane Milson off lightly, and she's lucky she's not being arrested. She does deserve to be exposed though, if only to herself.'

The room was warm, and lit by hissing gaslights, despite the fact that the daylight hadn't faded yet. The cigar smoke made Celia's throat tickle. Frederick had a wary look on his face when he saw Finch. 'Good evening, sir.'

'Frederick, this is Miss Chapman. You might have heard of her brother, Adam Chapman, he's a private detecting agent.'

Celia noted that Frederick's face drained of colour. 'No, I can't say I have. How do you do, Miss Chapman.'

'I'm well, Mr Milson.'

'We won't stay for long,' Finch told him.' We have a previous engagement.'

'I'm sorry I missed you at Leighton Manor, Uncle. You have a new housekeeper, I see . . . and a different groundsman. They refused to accommodate us.'

'I left instructions to that end. Surely that didn't surprise you, Frederick.' Finch's smile had a sharp edge to it.

'May I ask why, Uncle?'

Finch didn't feel a need to enlighten Frederick since he knew the answer. An awkward silence developed, then he said, 'Where's Jane, I have a gift for her?'

'She's over there, talking to Bart. He has promised me employment, thanks to you for arranging for my training. That was awfully good of you, Uncle. I shall have to start as a tally clerk of course, but it won't take me long to work my way up.'

'It *was* good of me, wasn't it, Frederick? By the way, do you have the fifteen pounds you borrowed from my housekeeper?'

'Fifteen pounds . . . I *borrowed*?' Frederick said, his voice strangling in his throat. 'I can't remember . . . I say, Uncle, I'm a little pinched for cash at the moment, but I was going to repay it.'

'It's better to be pinched for cash than pinched by the constabulary, young man. Too bad for you, Frederick, but the money represented three years' work for that young woman, and she needs it more than you do. Perhaps you should ask Bart Craven to lend it to you, though he doesn't part with his cash easily, and I daresay he'd be interested in what you wanted it for.'

Quickly, Frederick said, 'I daresay I've got enough cash in my room . . . about my allowance . . . ?'

'What allowance is that, Frederick? Oscar, go with Frederick and make sure he pays his debt. If he tries to make a run for it, break his arm.'

Oscar cracked his knuckles. 'Now you're getting into the swing of it, sir.' He grinned when Celia's eyes widened and he winked.

'Now, where did you say Jane was? Over by the window . . . come, my dearest Celia, be my eyes.'

She whispered, 'Did you say there was a sapphire set missing? Miss Milson is wearing a blue necklace with a matching butterfly brooch and earrings.'

'Thank you, Celia, that sounds like it. Is she with anyone?'

'An older woman. They look alike. The man has just left; he's going through to the other room where men seem to be gathering to play cards.'

'I imagine she's with her mother Blanche. I'm glad she's there, since she will now get a first-hand account of what her daughter and son have been up to.'

Jane Milson was dressed in a blue gown. She was pretty but her face was discontented, and her smile tight as she turned towards them. She faltered, then recovered. 'How lovely to see you, Uncle.'

'Is it, Jane?'

'Why, of course it is.'

Jane's eyes raked Celia up and down. 'Aren't you going to introduce us to your *companion*, Uncle?'

'Let me get two things clear, Jane. First, I am not your uncle. Second, this lady is Miss Celia Chapman. We are engaged, and she will shortly become my wife.'

Jane's face registered her shock. 'Married . . . why didn't you tell us? I thought . . . we all thought.'

'My private life is actually none of your business.' He held out a bag. 'This is for you, Jane, a gift. After all, Diana did promise them to you, did she not?'

Opening the bag, Jane gazed inside. She appeared stunned by what she saw, but gathered her wits about her fast. 'Freddie and I understood that your housekeeper was under suspicion of stealing these.'

'How did you know they were missing?'

'How do I know? Gossip, I suppose.'

'It wasn't gossip, since it was kept quiet. You are also aware that it wasn't my housekeeper since it was you and your brother who stole it, though you tried to blame it on her, you pair of nasty little vipers.'

Jane and her mother gasped, but said nothing.

'With the evidence I've got I could have both you and Frederick arrested and charged. You even signed Miss Finn's name on the sales receipts. And you have the effrontery to wear Diana's sapphires tonight, knowing I would be here. Did you think you'd be safe because I'm unable to see clearly?'

There was a tremor in Jane's voice now. 'I only borrowed them. I intended to put them back . . . and if you recall, I did ask you if I could.'

'I know you did, and I refused, *if you recall*. And to put that ring in my housekeeper's purse and steal her savings at the same time, is the lowest of any low act I can think of. What type of person would do such a thing out of spite, with the likelihood of an innocent girl being arrested and imprisoned? Did you think that because Miss Finn was without family and obliged to support herself, that nobody would believe she was innocent.'

Jane whined, 'I didn't want to do it. It was Freddie's idea, he made me, and it was him who took the money. It wasn't much.'

'It was all Miss Finn had, and she'd earned it through honest toil . . . something you've never heard of. Now, thanks to you she has no employment and no savings.'

'Lower your voice, I beg you,' Blanche begged. 'People are looking. I had no idea they'd done something against the law. What are you going to do about it, Finch?'

'To my shame, absolutely nothing. I'm going to let them get away with it. But from now on, unless it's unavoidable I never want to see or hear from any of you again. Is that clear?'

Celia received a look of such scorn and malice that she nearly took a step backwards. 'I suppose this dowdy *creature* will suck you dry.'

Beside her, Finch sucked in a breath. 'No, Jane, it's women like you and your mother who think they can flatter a man and empty his pockets at the same time. I was a fool, but I feel you're about to learn the hard way that not all men are as easy-going as myself.'

'I don't know what you mean.'

'I daresay you will find out when you are married.'

Celia gently squeezed his hand.

Blanche cried out, 'But what about their settlements, Finch? You promised, and we are in debt on the strength of that promise.'

'Haven't you yet learned not to spend money that you don't possess?' The laugh he gave had a note of disbelief in it. 'Do you imagine I'm going to settle anything on your children after what they've done, Blanche? The jewellery is all Jane will get, and that because I want nothing in my home to remind me of your sister. Enjoy it, Jane, and every time you wear it be reminded of what a conniving little brat you are. And that's all I have to say to you.'

Feeling Finch begin to tremble, Celia placed her hand on his sleeve. 'Oscar is waiting at the door, Finch. Shall we go?'

He allowed himself to be led away.

'Remind me not to get on your fierce side,' she said calmly when they were outside. 'How do you feel?'

'Relieved . . . but angry that she dared to insult you so.'

'Don't allow it to trouble you, since it was only temper. Besides, have you thought that there might be some truth in the rumour that I'm a creature? I do have six legs and a set of antennae.'

'The last beetle I set eyes on was quite beautiful.' Finch gave a bit of a laugh. 'Oscar? How did you manage with Frederick?'

Oscar doffed his hat to a young woman going past them, who offered him a cheeky smile. Head to one side he watched her walk away, grinning to himself. 'It was like taking a bottle from a baby, sir, only my hand slipped and Mr Milson got a bloody nose out of it for his trouble. The money fell out of his pocket while I was looking for his handkerchief. Not quite fifteen pounds, but near enough.'

'Well done . . . now, my dear, how shall I entertain you? Shall we all go and have supper, then go on to the theatre – unless there's something else you'd rather do, Celia.'

The girl was lingering on the corner, and Oscar was still looking at her.

'I've had enough entertainment for one night, Finch,' and she kissed his cheek. 'Why don't we go back to your home? I'm certain that your cook can provide us with a cold supper and we'll spend the evening together. After I've beaten you at chess we can relax and talk about this and that until it's time for me to go home. I'm sure Oscar won't mind taking the evening off, will you Oscar?'

'That would be most appreciated, Miss,' Oscar said.

'There you are, then, we're agreed, Finch.'

'Except for one thing, Celia, my love. What makes you think that you'll beat me at chess?'

'I always do.'

'Only because I've allowed you to. You play a defending game. Tonight the gloves have come off and I'm in an attacking mood.'

'We shall see, Finch. I'm a very good defender, and I cheat if I feel threatened. Your chess men could end up anywhere.'

'I'll put a shilling on Miss Chapman's game,' Oscar said with a laugh.

Finch gazed towards his manservant. 'Are you still there, Oscar? Miss Chapman will look after me, so off you go. I'll order a cab to take her home later, and will escort her there myself.'

'Goodnight then, sir. Goodnight, Miss Chapman,' and he was gone.

'What's the evening like, Celia?'

'Soft and faintly hazy. The sky is clear though and there will be a moon later on. It's still early and there are plenty of people abroad, so we have time to walk safely across Hyde Park to Victoria Gate if you'd like to. I'll describe it to you.'

'I'd like that.'

'Now, I'm going to ask you something, and I'll need a truthful answer.'

'Go on.'

'When you were giving Jane that dressing down you asked her if she thought she was safe because you couldn't see her clearly.'

'What of it?'

'Explain to me what you meant by *clearly*.'

The silence in which they strolled was comfortable as well as contemplative. Eventually, Finch shrugged. 'You don't miss much, do you, not even a slip of the tongue? I've been seeing moving shadows and light of late, but not definite forms. And sometimes there is colour, but it comes and goes. That's all I can say.'

'Did you intend to tell me?'

'Eventually, but only if there was any encouraging news, otherwise there was no point. I've yet to consult with my doctor. I imagine he'll send me to someone who has made a study of eyes a speciality.'

They walked a bit more, then Celia said, 'I'll pray that something good comes from it then, Finch. I wonder how Serafina is getting on. When are you going down to Poole?'

'Next week perhaps.'

'Would you mind taking her a note from me, even though I'll probably mention you a hundred times in it?'

'As long as it's all complimentary, of course I wouldn't mind.'

Dearest Serafina,

I do hope everything is proceeding satisfactorily with your reunion. I think of you often. Though Finch will tell you the main news, I must tell you how magnificent he was at routing Frederick and Jane Milson . . . and Oscar punched Frederick on the nose and collected your fifteen pounds from him. As for their mother . . . honestly, she is the most awful woman, and so greedy.

You will forgive Finch, won't you? He never believed that you took the jewellery . . . and he found it where Jane had sold it. She had used your name, so you would be blamed if it were discovered. But of course, the receipts were dated, which unravelled their little scheme completely. Finch intended to give you that rather vulgar ring that was planted in your purse, but changed his mind because he felt it would only hold unpleasant memories for you now. Instead, we have bought you one of your own, a rather sweet ring, which I chose myself. I do hope you like it.

She loved it! Serafina held out her hand and admired the ring. The creamy pearl in the centre was surrounded by small diamonds and the message *friends forever* was inscribed inside it. She decided to read the rest of the letter later, pleased that the matter had been dealt with and she wouldn't have to tell her father that she was under suspicion.

Mr Leighton had called on her at Marianne's house, just after Marianne had left to visit her sister.

'Alex loves playing with his cousins, and I am hoping to cheer Charlotte up. I do hate it when she mopes,' Marianne had said, 'and some gossip will be just the thing. Will you be all right, alone?'

The thought of being alone with her thoughts for company had been entirely welcome. But it hadn't been long before Oscar and Finch Leighton had turned up. Over tea she was informed of the outcome of the investigation, and assured of her own innocence.

'You shouldn't have come all this way, Mr Leighton. And thank you for this beautiful gift. It wasn't necessary.'

'I wanted to come, Serafina. I wanted to apologize to you personally, and most of all I wanted to apologize for all I had put you through. You must have felt insulted by losing your position, as well. That was insensitive of me.'

Any hurt she'd experienced in the past melted away at the sight of him looking so contrite. 'I do understand. Besides, it would have been impossible for me to remain friends with Celia if I'd stayed.'

'Not impossible, but slightly awkward.' He took her hands in his. 'You know, Serafina, no matter how expertly you scrubbed and polished, in your heart you never quite mastered the attitude required by a servant.'

'You should have said; I would have tried harder.'

'I know . . . but I liked your funny, bossy little ways, and didn't think it mattered at Leighton Manor, since I no longer entertained there. But from now on I will. Tell me . . . are you happy?'

'Oh, of course . . . I've been made welcome by the Thornton family, and my father has claimed me. But they overwhelm me a little, since they are all so confident. They have a past together, you see. I have yet to meet Charlotte Hardy, who has not yet recovered from the birth of her youngest son, by all accounts.'

'You sound doubtful.'

'I've been warned that she can be difficult, and cannot be convinced that I'm her sister. Because she doubts it with so much conviction, then so do I.'

'Do you think she might be avoiding you?'

'It's possible, since she disapproved of the quest that might find me, and she had always been at odds with my father, Erasmus Thornton. Indeed, I might even be the cause of her indisposition. I've been introduced to her husband, Seth, who is extremely pleasant. Marianne says that if Charlotte can be brought round to accept that there's Honeyman blood in me, then she'll have to accept that the other half is Thornton and come to terms with it. I've seen a portrait of my Thornton grandmother, and although she looks stern in it, I'm very much like her.'

'But you have reservations?'

She sighed. 'I've become aware of the fact that I'm not the cause of a family feud that started nineteen years ago, but I'm actually the consequence of it. I don't know how to cope with the pressure of being what they expect Serafina to be.'

'Which is?'

'Different things to different people. Thornton or Honeyman? Daughter, sister, cousin, aunt . . . cuckoo in the nest . . . imposter . . . ? In other words, I'm totally confused.'

'I imagine they are too. Can you cope?'

'I hope so. I shouldn't have bothered you with it when it was Erasmus Thornton who instigated the whole thing. With her husband's permission, Adam has made an appointment to call on Charlotte Hardy in the morning, to discover why she's so reluctant to see me. He intends to take the train back to London the following morning, since he must get back to his business. I won't feel quite so strong without him to lean on.'

'We'll be on the same train, then. Adam wouldn't leave you if he didn't think you could cope, you know.'

'I suppose not, and I'm being selfish, when he's done so much to help me. Oh dear, my presence seems to have caused so much running around for everybody. Would you like to join us for dinner tonight, Mr Leighton? I'm sure Marianne wouldn't mind, in fact, she'll be peeved at the thought of being absent when you called.'

'I was hoping you'd join me for supper at my hotel . . . Adam as well, and your father. I'd like to meet him while I'm here. And of course, your hosts, Mr and Mrs Thornton.'

'I'd like that, thank you, Mr Leighton. What will happen to Jane and Freddie?'

'Nothing, though you can press charges if you wish, Serafina, since it was a deliberately malicious act against your good name. I'm hoping they'll learn a lesson from being found out, since they've lost more than they gained from the crime.'

'I can rise above the spite, and I wouldn't want them to go to prison for the loss of a few miserable pounds. Also, you've always been kind to me and I wouldn't want you to be embarrassed. I'd live the rest of my life with that on my conscience.'

'That's kind of you, Serafina, better than they deserve, but who said your money was lost? Now . . . let's move on to something more pleasant. Celia has requested that you come a week early to attend her at the wedding.'

'I'd love to.'

'I'll send Oscar down to escort you back to Leighton Manor when the time comes, then.' Sliding a hand into his pocket he brought out an envelope. 'Here's the cash that was stolen from you, and don't throw it back at me this time. Frederick admitted he'd borrowed it, and he found himself in the happy position of having just enough cash in his pocket to reimburse you – albeit, a little reluctantly.'

To which information Serafina burst into laughter, and Finch chuckled as he said, 'Ah . . . from your response I imagine Celia must have informed you of Oscar's heroic role in her letter.'

Looking pleased with himself, Oscar cracked his knuckles.

Eighteen

Charlotte was in bed when Marianne arrived at Harbour House. She gave her sister a hug. 'I was so worried when Seth told me that you were ailing.'

'Seth worries needlessly. I just feel sad. I can't be bothered about things, and I cry for no reason. It's nothing serious, or so Dr Beresford tells me. He said that many mothers feel like it after giving birth to an infant.'

'I've brought Alex to cheer you up, and he's promised to be on his best behaviour.' She gave her son a kiss. 'Be polite and say hello to your Aunt Charlotte.'

Alex offered her a replica of Nick's smile. 'ello anty calot.'

'As if I needed another child in the house,' Charlotte murmured, but managed a smile for him. 'Hello, Alex, my love. I've got to admit, he's irresistible, Marianne. He's got all of Nick's charm and good looks. Isn't it about time you produced another one?'

'Lor, I'd love another one and so would Nick. It's not through lack of trying, though that's not a chore . . .' She blushed. 'Well, never mind.'

Charlotte rang a bell and the nursery maid came through. 'Take my nephew to play with the twins, Mrs Stevenson. Is James awake?'

'Yes, Ma'am.'

'Then bring him in and I'll feed him.'

'I'll get him. I want to greet Jessica and Major Mitchell, anyway.'

The twins fell on them both with excited cries of delight, and soon the cousins were rolling around the floor together and being generally noisy.

Covered in kisses, her bonnet knocked awry, and having stirred them all up, Marianne picked up James and carried him through to Charlotte to be nursed. 'I swear that Jessica's ringlets get brighter each time I see her . . . and have you ever seen a boy more like his father than Major Mitchell?'

'Apart from Alex, you mean.'

Marianne gently twisted a curl of James's baby hair around her finger, and she experienced a yearning inside her for another infant at her breast. 'James is a handsome child. He looks so serious. I think he takes after our father for looks, and his eyes are more green than grey.'

Charlotte shuddered. 'I hope he doesn't turn out to have his nasty nature.'

'Oh, Charlotte, James is so placid, but he has Seth's strong and dependable look to him, as well. Our father can have no influence on his mind since he is dead and gone. Why can't you let the past go?'

'What's the use of doing that when it comes back to haunt us.'

'When are you going to see our sister?'

'Don't nag me about it, Marianne. I just don't feel like seeing her at the moment. I haven't recovered from James's birth.'

'James is seven weeks old now, and you're using him as an excuse. Serafina has already been rejected by us once, she must feel absolutely low at being scorned all over again.'

'Why should she feel scorned? I didn't ask her to come here, and I'm not convinced she's who she says she is. I just don't feel that I'm up to the strain of meeting her yet.'

'I find your reluctance to meet her strange, since I have told you that she's a dear girl, who is slightly overwhelmed by us, but grateful all the same. And she has asked for nothing . . . in fact she said she must find work to support herself, as she's always had to.'

'It's probably a ploy to gain our sympathy. You have always been too trusting, and your good nature is easy to take advantage of.'

'Adam has investigated her background thoroughly. Although there's some doubt, it's so slight that it isn't worth bothering about. She's the image of grandmother Thornton, but not so grim-looking thank goodness. Erasmus wants Serafina to take the surname of Thornton, that's how sure he is.'

'She's welcome to it, and to him.'

'You don't mean that Char . . .'

'Yes, I do mean it.' She began to cry. 'Oh, I know you think I'm horrid. I hate feeling like this, as though I have no control over anything . . . And poor James. Just because he looks like our despised father and is always so solemn, I feel as though I mustn't love him as much as the others. My sadness and guilt is being fed to him through my milk.'

'Oh, my God, you mustn't think that way about him when he's so small and innocent else it will become a habit. He loves you dearly and relies on you for his very life. He will smile when he's learned to from you, and he'll be an absolute charmer.'

'But Marianne, don't you see . . . if I think all these awful thoughts I shouldn't be a mother at all, because I don't deserve to have such beautiful children.'

'Don't deserve to have them? Of course you do. Get a hold on yourself, Charlotte. These children are Seth's as well as yours. He loves them and he loves you. They need you.'

'I know they do,' she said miserably. 'I just feel unworthy.'

'It's because we were made to feel that way when we were children. We mustn't pass that on to our own children, Char. We must give them all the love we can, so they will feel worthy. That's what Serafina missed in life. Through no fault of her own she grew up without us as sisters, and she lacked the love we would have shared with her. Now we owe her that.'

'You always do this to try and soften me.'

'You are soft, you're just too stubborn to admit it.' Marianne managed to get her arms around the pair of them. James had green eyes with grey flecks and seemed oblivious to his mother's distress as he gulped down his breakfast in the first frenzy of feeding. 'You need to get out and get some fresh air. When James is finished, get dressed and we'll walk out on the heath. The heather will be in bloom and we can go up to the copse to see if the gypsies have arrived. Perhaps one of them can give you a herbal tonic.'

Charlotte turned her face away. 'I'm too tired.'

Time to get tough with her, Marianne thought. 'You stop this nonsense at once, Charlotte Hardy. Do you realize you were thinking and talking about your son in the same way our father must have thought about Serafina? Would you give him away to strangers?'

Charlotte gazed at her in horror. 'Of course not, and it's a different thing altogether, since that didn't happen. Pa didn't give her away . . . Oh, stop twisting things, do! I'm not well.'

'And father was unwell – he was sick with grief and anger. It made him abandon a newborn infant, one that could have been his own flesh and blood. No wonder Seth is worried about you. And if you talk this way in front of Lucian Beresford, be careful you don't end up in an institution. He has turned out to be so pompous, and to think I thought I was in love with him, once. I pity his wife.'

'He takes his doctoring too seriously, and his wife is pompous too. You don't think I'm mad, do you? I've heard that mad people have staring eyes and that they froth at the mouth, and scream and shout and gibber nonsense.'

'Lor, of course you're not mad, the very idea! I refuse to have a mad sister, it would be mortifying. The Stanhope sisters would throw stones at you.'

Charlotte's laughter had a modicum of spontaneity to it.

'Come on, dearest Charlotte. Make an effort. Remember how you stood by Seth when your stepson was abducted by his own grandfather. You took John under your wing and treated him like one of your own, and he's growing up such a lovely, polite little boy. You're a good mother, Charlotte. You'll come to love James as much as you love your other children, just you wait and see. You must try and convince yourself to do the same for Serafina.'

Charlotte sighed. 'I hate feeling like this, and Serafina has nothing to do with it, because she doesn't exist. If you mention her again I'll shake you until your teeth rattle and drop out of your head.'

'I'll stay for a few days and look after you if you like. I'll cheer you up with all the gossip, and you'll soon begin to think sensibly again.'

Charlotte clutched her arm. 'Would you stay? What about Nick, will he allow it?'

'He'll grumble like a bear, since he thinks it's expected of him. A short absence will allow him to contemplate my finer qualities, and I shall tell him so.' She grinned at the thought. 'Besides, he and Erasmus will have Serafina to look after them. She's wonderful, and helps me a lot about the house. She's ferociously efficient.'

'Oh, change the subject, do, Marianne. I'm sick of hearing her name.'

Marianne grinned to herself as she walked to the window and

threw it open. There was nothing like a good argument to light a flame under Charlotte. 'Just smell that air, Charlotte, there's nothing like it anywhere else in the world.'

'The tide's out and the mud stinks, that's why.'

'When we move into our new home Nick is going to buy a telescope, and we'll be able to see you across the water from the lookout. You must get one too, so the children will be able to wave to each other.'

'They'll probably fall out of the window, especially Jessica. She's like you, in that she doesn't sit still for five minutes.'

'You have no romance in your soul.'

Charlotte managed a grin. 'You're wrong. I can conjure up plenty of romance at the appropriate moments. That's how I got James. Despite what I said, I do love him dearly, you know.'

'I know. When Seth goes to fetch John from school I'll ask him to collect some things for Alex, and he can tell someone what's going on. I can always borrow your clothes.'

'Adam is visiting tomorrow. Seth told me that he has something that he'd like me to look at. He said it might convince me that Serafina is related, but I think he'll be disappointed.'

Marianne was curious as to what it could be, but the fact that Charlotte was allowing Adam to present that evidence convinced Marianne that her sister was trying to overcome the stubborn stance that she'd taken towards the issue. She just wished Charlotte would believe in her instinct more. 'There you are, then.'

'What's that supposed to mean. Honestly, Marianne. I can't imagine what evidence he has that would be conclusive enough to convince me. I know she is dead.'

'How?'

Shrugging, Charlotte detached James from her breast and gently patted his back until he gave a loud belch. She settled him on the other breast, sighing contentedly when the sleepy-eyed infant began to suck.

'Adam might surprise you. How exciting; I can't wait to see what the evidence is. I think Adam's in love with Serafina, by the way. The looks they exchange . . . so poignant, like long, languishing sighs. I have a feeling Serafina won't be with us for long.'

Laughter trickled coolly from Charlotte. 'Adam is such an

elegant man. I can't imagine him married to someone who has grown up in a workhouse and held a position as a household servant. I do hope he doesn't intend to bring the girl with him as well. If he does I shall refuse to see either of them.'

'How very mean of you, Charlotte, especially after all Adam did for you in the past. And if you hadn't married Seth we might have ended up in a workhouse, ourselves. But no . . . because whatever you think of Erasmus Thornton, he wouldn't have thrown us out to fend for ourselves. And however cruelly you treated Nick in the beginning, he's never held it against you.'

Charlotte looked ashamed. 'It might have been cruel of me, but it was the right thing to do at the time. He knows it, and so do you. The pair of you are perfect together. Now, don't lecture me when I feel so wretched and useless. I'm surprised that Seth is so patient with me.'

'So am I.' Marianne sighed. 'Oh, I suppose you'll get over it.'

She couldn't understand why her elder sister didn't want to meet Serafina, though. She was so adamant that Serafina was dead that she couldn't see past it. Apart from the unfortunate circumstance of her birth, Serafina had done nothing to deserve being snubbed like this. Marianne hoped Charlotte would cheer up in the next day or two. Much as she loved her sister, she also loved her husband, and she had no intention of neglecting him for long.

Adam called on Erasmus and Serafina before he left for Harbour House the next morning.

'I've come to collect that doll of yours, Serafina.'

'It's in one of the wicker baskets under my bed. It won't take me a minute to fetch it. Why do you want it?'

'Oh, just in case Charlotte's seen it before.'

'It's one of your straws blowing in the wind, then?' Erasmus said with a grin.

'Exactly, you never know when they come in handy. I'll wait here in the hall, Serafina.' When she'd gone he said, 'When do you leave for Boston, Captain Thornton?'

'I'm giving temporary command of *Daisy Jane* to my first officer, Thomas Grimshaw for a while. It's not much use having a daughter unless I can get to know her. I'm not taking Serafina sailing with me that's for certain. It's too dangerous an occupation, and she's far too precious.'

'She is that,' Adam said softly. 'You've heard of the saying that finders is keepers? Remember that I found Serafina. I'm giving you a year while I get my business in order, which is more than you deserve.'

'I know.' Erasmus grinned. 'That's a fine thing you've done, bringing her home to me, Adam. She's got a bit of ginger to her when she gets her dander up, though . . . same as my sister, Daisy, I reckon.'

'Or yourself, Erasmus. You and your sister are alike in your ways.'

Erasmus held out his hand. 'Could be, I suppose.'

Serafina dashed down the stairs, a smile on her face. 'I've wrapped it in a piece of cloth, since I can't picture you walking along with a doll cradled in your arms. I can't imagine what use it will be.'

'You never know,' he said vaguely. 'I'll see you both at dinner tonight.'

'If you see Mr Leighton, would you tell him that it will just be myself and . . .' she offered Erasmus a tentative smile, '*my father*. Marianne is at Charlotte's for a few days, and Nick has a previous engagement.

'Can I come with you to Harbour House, Adam? Charlotte might want to see me.'

'She doesn't, and I promised I'd go alone this time. Be patient and wait until you're invited.'

He hadn't meant to sound so brusque, and her eyes mirrored the chagrin she felt. 'Why is it me who has to be patient?'

'Because I'm fast running out of ideas, and I'm asking you to be. That should be enough.'

'Hah! I didn't ask you to look for me,' she threw at him, all challenge.

Adam glanced at Erasmus, who grinned and made himself scarce. He then took Serafina in his arms and kissed her softly defiant mouth until she relaxed in his arms. Then he looked into her eyes and saw the laughter in them.

'Hah, yourself,' he said softly, and she grinned.

*   *   *

The heath was alive with birdsong and the smell of the heath gorses tickled at Adam's nose. Fronds of bracken unfurled and stretched fingers of green towards a blue sky stippled with cloudy white stripes. The tide was coming in. Mud creaked and bubbled as water crept and seeped into all the nooks and crannies.

Up towards the copse Adam could see a thread of smoke filtering through the pines from the gyspy campfires. Some of the travellers were heading for Poole, baskets and sacks of goods over their arms. They stood to one side as he passed, their faces closed and secretive. Some touched their caps, as if in respect.

A hand tugged gently at his sleeve and he gazed into a face that was old and wise, and somehow familiar.

Head to one side, he contemplated her with a smile. 'Have we met before?'

'We've heard her name on the wind and my blood will become part of your blood. Buy a sprig of my heather for your sweetheart; in return she'll give you everlasting love and many children.'

'How many children,' he said with a chuckle, intrigued by this gypsy woman.

She turned his hand over and gazed at the palm. 'There will be two strong sons and a daughter called after her mother. Her name will be . . .'

'. . . Serafina,' he said, because he would have no other.

For a moment the wind swirled around their ankles in a circle of leaves and her name was borne away.

The woman laughed and pinned a sprig of white heather to his lapel, murmuring, 'True love is bound to follow.'

For a moment his eyes met hers, and before the gypsy went on her way he could see the eyes of Serafina gazing back at him.

He must have been bewitched, Adam thought, looking back when he reached Harbour House. He could only see two figures on the heath path, two women who stood together. Both looked like Serafina from where he stood.

Still slightly bemused, he knocked at the door at Harbour House.

Seth Hardy greeted him with a smile of welcome. The successful clay and gravel miner had once been an army colonel. His missing stepson had been the catalyst that had started Adam's association with the Hardy, Honeyman and Thornton families – one that had led him to Serafina. Seth had several men working for him now. Tall, upright with his soldierly bearing, and with a direct and honest manner, he was well on his way to being wealthy, and he commanded respect without even trying.

They shook hands. 'Charlotte is a little fragile and has asked me to stay with her for support, Adam. And Marianne will be there. I hope you won't mind.'

'Of course not. I haven't much to offer them as regard to new evidence, just something that might, or might not be of significance to Charlotte. Erasmus has accepted Serafina as his own, and has offered her the legal protection of his name. His lawyer is preparing the papers.'

Charlotte came up behind her husband and her chin went up. 'Tell Erasmus Thornton that since he wasn't married to our mother, if that girl happens to be our sister – though she can't be, since she's alive and our sister is dead – then she would be a Honeyman not a Thornton.'

Adam tried not to grin at her skewed logic, though Seth did. 'Although most of my evidence is circumstantial, I imagine there's enough of that to convince the authorities of the integrity of her background, should the need arrive. I imagine Marianne has related most of the details to you both.'

'With great enthusiasm.' Seth gave a wry smile. 'To be honest, I don't know why Charlotte won't allow herself to be convinced. I certainly am. But at least Charlotte is up and dressed today, for which I'm thankful. Marianne tends to stir her sister up like a stick in an ants' nest.'

'She certainly does not,' Charlotte stated.

Marianne was in the drawing room. Charlotte took a seat beside her, looking graceful and lovely, if a little pale. Marianne was, as always, an exquisite creature. He imagined Serafina next to them. There was a subtle, but elusive likeness about her, but Serafina's elfin looks and her haunting brown eyes registered everything she'd ever suffered or felt. The similarity of the sisters, because there was no doubt in his mind now, lay in their intuitiveness, their passion and their need to be loved.

From upstairs came shrieks of laughter and the whoops of

their children, and Adam remembered the gypsy portent. He'd have three of his own making the same noise if she was correct.

A terrier dog came to sniff at his ankle as he went in. It gave a short bark of greeting as if it remembered his smell, then retired to its basket, content that he'd do no harm to the occupants of the house.

'Marianne, we meet again, how lovely to see you. Charlotte, how are you, my dear, and the baby? It's James, isn't it?'

'Oh, I'm well enough, and James is thriving.' She gave her sister a quick glance and what seemed to be a reassuring smile. 'It seems ages since you were last here. Would you like some coffee?'

Her reluctance was like a wall between them. She was delaying the moment, and he wanted to know why . . . wondered even if Charlotte knew why, or was it instinct nudging at her? Adam didn't intend to be diverted. Charlotte had strength of mind, but he sensed that he held in his hands the one thing that could find the chink in her armour . . . and so did she, because her glance kept going to the parcel he carried. He was glad that Marianne was there beside Charlotte.

'Thank you, but it's not long since I had a cup of coffee. I want to show you something.'

'So I understand.' Her eyes went to the parcel. 'Is that it?'

He placed it in her lap. She began to unwrap it, then stopped to gaze at him, introducing a little humour into the situation by enquiring, 'It won't bite, will it?'

'It's not alive, but I can't guarantee it won't bite, Charlotte.'

'Oh, dear . . . why do I get the feeling that I'm not going to like this.'

'How can you not like it when you don't know what it is?' Marianne said. 'Open the damn thing. I'm dying from curiosity, and I promise I'll save you from whatever's in there.'

'It's a doll,' Charlotte said, throwing the cloth aside. She looked puzzled. 'Am I supposed to recognize it? If I am, I'm going to disappoint you since I've never seen it before. She unwrapped the scrap of shawl from the object, gazed at it, then put it to one side and began to examine the doll's clothing.

He saw her hesitate, then she picked the scrap of shawl up again and scrutinized it. Suddenly her breath hissed between her teeth and the colour drained from her cheeks. Harshly, she asked, 'Where did she get this from?'

'The doll was given to Serafina by Constance Jarvis when she was six or seven. That piece of shawl was wrapped round it, but Serafina has always had it. She called the doll Charlotte because of the name embroidered on it. Do you recognize it?'

'Of course I recognize it. It's mine. I embroidered it for the new baby. It was a gift, and it took me ages because I was only just learning to sew.'

'Oh, Char . . .' Marianne breathed. 'What more proof do you need?'

'She was dead, I swear,' Charlotte cried out. 'I saw it with my own eyes. The baby was lying on the bed, and she was cold . . . so I wrapped her in the shawl and put her in the crib. Then I heard pa coming, he was ranting and raging . . . I hid under the bed. Our mother's blood was coming through the mattress, just slowly, so each drip congealed before the next.' She began to tremble. 'I remember that Pa hit the crib with his fist and the baby began to cry, so I moved into a dark corner between the wall and the wardrobe, where the light couldn't reach.'

Charlotte placed her hands over her eyes and Marianne slid an arm around her. 'Oh Charlotte, how awful for you. You must tell us what you saw, for everybody's sake.'

Voice muffled by her hands Charlotte said tremulously, 'Oh, My God . . . I remember it all now. Pa picked up a pillow and pushed it over the baby's face. He said . . . he said . . . *I'll see you in hell, you Thornton bastard!*'

Seth went to her. 'That's enough, Adam.'

'No . . . it's not, I haven't finished,' Charlotte cried out. 'Let's get it settled once and for all. God knows I've tried to forget it, but I can't, Seth. It comes and goes in little snatches, so I have to push it away to stay sane. I knew I'd have to tell someone one day. I want Adam to know . . . I want Marianne to know, and most of all I want you to know, too, even if you despise me afterwards.'

'I'll never despise you.'

'I tried to run, you see, but pa caught me. He bunched my nightdress in his fist, lifted me off my feet, and he looked at me. His face was dazed and his eyes staring. There was spittle at the side of his mouth. He said, *the bastard girl is dead, and she'll be buried on the heath. If you tell anyone what happened, I'll kill you and your sister. Marianne will go first, because she looks like the whore I married.'*

Marianne gasped.

'He made me promise on my mother's blood, saying the devil would take her soul if I told what I saw. When I promised, his eyes cleared and he sent me back to bed.'

'Oh, my poor Charlotte,' Marianne whispered.

'I locked the door and got back into bed with my sister, but I couldn't sleep. After a while I heard pa leave on his horse. I crept back to my mother's room, in case he'd made a mistake and she was still alive. But there was a sheet over her face, and although I watched for the sheet to rise and fall as she breathed, it didn't. The crib was empty, and I knew he'd taken the baby to bury her on the heath, like he said he was going to. She's dead, I tell you. Pa smothered her. I saw him do it.'

Marianne promptly burst into tears. 'Poor Charlotte, what a burden you've been carrying all these years. Why didn't you tell me all this before?'

'Because I couldn't remember it all, just bits of it. Seeing that shawl brought it all rushing back.' Through her tears she gazed ruefully at him. 'I'm sorry, Adam, but she can't be our sister, though it would be wonderful if she were . . . you see, our sister is dead.'

Adam moved to where she sat, and took her hands in his. He thought fast, knowing he must use all his powers of persuasion to make his words credible. He gazed at Seth, who nodded, then he said, 'Listen to me, now, Charlotte, and I want you to use your reason, not look at this through the eyes and emotions of a terrified child. You as well, Marianne.'

The two pairs of tear-sodden blue eyes turned his way were hard to ignore. He wanted to grin. The Honeyman women were female with a vengeance. Seth and Nick must consider themselves to be the luckiest men alive.

'No, your father didn't kill that infant, you just *thought* he did, Charlotte. On the contrary, you saved your young sister's life.'

'How?'

'First by wrapping Serafina in that shawl to warm her. Then, when you tried to run from the room you interrupted your father in his moment of murderous passion, and brought him back to his senses.'

'Charlotte always did have a strong mothering instinct,' Marianne interjected, and taking her sister's hand into her lap, gently patted it.

'Your father came to his senses because of your intervention. When he rode off it was not to bury the baby's body. He took the infant to the orphanage at Dorchester and left her there. Constance Jarvis knew where the baby had come from because of the shawl you wrapped her in – the gift you gave your unfortunate infant sister – one embroidered with your name. He may have even handed her directly over to Constance Jarvis.'

Charlotte made a soft, mewing sound of assent.

'How else would the shawl have come into her possession? Mrs Jarvis intended to bring Serafina up as her own, but she was taken ill when Serafina was quite young. Even so, Serafina has memories of her, and she recognized the house they lived in. Knowing she didn't have long to live, Mrs Jarvis arranged for Serafina to be raised by loyal servants. Renamed Sara Fenn, she settled happily with them, but when the family perished from a cholera outbreak she was dumped outside a workhouse by a relative. Are you following what I'm saying?'

Two heads nodded in unison.

'There, her name was misspelled in the register and she became Sara Finn. Somehow she remembered that her first name was Serafina. From the workhouse she went to work as a housemaid to a reverend, then she was offered a position as housekeeper to Mr Leighton. That's where I discovered her.'

Charlotte and Marianne gazed at him, then at each other. They exchanged a smile.

When a knock came at the door Seth opened it a chink. 'What is it, Annie?'

'Miss Serafina Thornton is here and wants to see Mrs Hardy. She says she won't take no for an answer.'

'*Serafina?*' Adam felt like laughing. Lord, there was certainly a strong streak of Honeyman determination in her. She must have followed him. 'Of all the times for Serafina to turn up, when I told her to stay at home.'

Marianne leapt to her defence. 'Obviously Serafina preferred not to wait any longer, and why should she when she has every right to be here in the house where she was born?'

'Of course she has, but I can't see her looking like this,' Charlotte said, drying her eyes on the shawl the doll had been wearing.

'You look wonderful with red eyes,' Seth said, and along with a grimace, Charlotte hurled a cushion at him.

Marianne gazed in the mirror and patted the curly tendrils of hair escaping from her bun. 'You're not the only one who looks wrecked. Actually, considering all that you've been through, Charlotte, it's a wonder you look so calm and serene. How horrible to have all that on your mind. Why didn't you tell me? Though come to think of it I'm glad you didn't, else it would have been on my mind, as well. No wonder you always looked so long-faced and miserable.'

This time it was Marianne who collected a cushion, and on the bun that she'd just straightened. A lock of dark curly hair fell over her shoulder.

She turned and winked at him. 'Adam, dear, you've been magnificent. It was so clever of you to work everything out. As for you, Seth, my darling brother-in-law, you are always so solid, and have been a pillar of support, as always. But neither of you are needed now. This moment is for us alone, so . . . shoo!'

Marianne went to the door and threw it wide. 'Come in, Serafina . . . welcome home. As soon as you've made Charlotte's acquaintance we'll go upstairs and you can meet your nieces and nephews and admire them.'

Adam's heart went out to Serafina when he saw her, and his eyes were drawn to the white heather pinned to her shawl. She looked so young and anxious as she said, 'As soon as I realized why you wanted the doll and connected the name on the shawl to Charlotte, I had to come. I was worried for . . . *her*, and I couldn't wait any longer,' Serafina said in her defence as she gazed at him in the doorway. 'You *will* forgive me, won't you, Adam?'

Giving a faintly exasperated smile, he nodded, then tipped up her chin and gently kissed her before whispering in her ear, 'I love you.'

Her smile emerged like a mouse from a hole, cautious at first, then growing in confidence until its luminous beam matched the shine in her eyes. Kissing the tip of her finger she placed it against his lips, a gesture he took as assent as he watched colour wash gently into her cheeks. Her mixture of innocence and mischief was totally mesmerising, her eyes were as wide and as limpid as ancient amber.

From the corner of his eye Adam saw Marianne and Charlotte gaze at each other and grin, well aware of the effect Serafina had on him. Then the two elder sisters moved close to the third. When they drew Serafina into their arms and hugged her tight, tears pricked at his eyes. Gently closing the door he turned to Seth. 'I think I just declared myself to Serafina. Do you think anyone noticed?'

'I certainly did, and as for Honeyman women they don't miss a damned thing. Congratulations, Adam, that was a job well done. I think a cup of coffee strengthened by a dash of whisky might be in order now.' He nodded to Annie. 'We'll be in the study if we're needed.'

But they weren't needed for quite a while.

Nineteen

Poole — a year later

Adam had waited until he could wait no longer.
Serafina had just turned twenty, and there had been subtle changes in her under the influence of her sisters. She was more graceful, more confident in a social situation, and a little more sure of herself. Her father's permission had been sought and the best-kept secret in the combined families was about to be revealed in public.

Having fulfilled the residency requirement, and the bans having been read for three consecutive weeks, Adam now fingered his collar nervously.

The three men were in the lookout in Nick and Marianne's spacious new home. Nick was gazing through a telescope at the heath.

'Have they left yet?' Adam asked him.

'No, but the carriages are outside.' He moved the telescope down. 'You'll never believe this, but there's a small crowd of people outside the house, gypsies by the look of them.'

Seth took the telescope from him. 'Charlotte and Marianne have just left the house, looking like princesses. They certainly know how to put on a show.'

'No wonder . . . Aria hired the best, and most expensive dress-maker in town,' Nick said gloomily. 'And she insisted on matching white horses to pull the carriages. It cost Erasmus a fortune, but he didn't turn a hair.'

Seth glanced at Nick. 'I understand that you're shortly to become a father again.'

Nick chuckled. 'Aye. George Honeyman would turn in his grave like a rat on a spit if he knew how well his daughters were managing without him.'

'Here comes Erasmus with Serafina, we'd better get going.' He handed the telescope to Nick. 'Now there's a virginal beauty.'

'Not for much longer. You know, you're a lucky man, Adam. I wonder if Serafina is wearing those fancy pantalettes that Aria sent her.'

'She won't be, Nick. Charlotte bought her an outfit to wear on her wedding night. It beats me that you have to pay so much for a few scraps of white satin and lace. I hope you can handle the strings on a corselette, Adam. Let us know if you need a hand.'

Adam grinned at the thought. 'You shouldn't be thinking that way about my bride.'

'Don't tell us that your manly tongue has never drooled over the thought of our women in flimsy underwear.'

Adam grinned even more. 'There might have been a couple of thoughts heading in that direction, but I kept my manly tongue and drool under strict control.'

'Saving it for Serafina, were you?'

'Can I see her?'

'No, it's unlucky for the groom to see the bride. Erasmus is looking quite the dandy in his new suit. He didn't hand Serafina over without a struggle, did he?'

'He said we hadn't known each other long enough, and insisted on a proper courtship. I've been back and forth on the London train so often that the train seat is moulded to my backside. How is Erasmus getting on with Charlotte now?'

'They managed to get the name issue sorted out between them without coming to blows. Look, the carriages have just started off.'

'Come on then, we must get there before them,' Adam said anxiously.

'We will. Seth and I have timed it to the last second.'

But Adam was already out of the door.

'He's eager to get himself shackled,' Nick said, 'and who am I to argue. It's not a bad state to be in.'

'I agree.'

The pair soon caught up with Adam, and the three men strode rapidly towards the church. Marianne had insisted on pale-blue jackets with velvet collars over white waistcoats, and with pale-grey trousers and top hats to match.

Tall and handsome they drew the eyes of women, but the Honeyman sisters had chosen their mates well, and not one of them had a roving eye.

It was a fine day for a wedding. The gypsies had seen them off with shouts of good luck and best wishes, and a horseshoe was tied with bunches of heather and ribbons to the back of the carriage.

Serafina's happiness was threaded through with nerves. Not about her wedding night, because her sisters had taken on the role of mentors, and had dispelled her fears. She understood exactly why she felt like she did when Adam was around her, and she was looking forward to her wedding night with some eagerness. She was nervous about being the centre of attention, though.

'You look like an angel,' her father had said before she left the house.

Her gown was made of chiffon over cream silk. The sleeves and trim were of delicate lace, as was her veil, which was kept in place with a garland of creamy roses. She wore the skirt over stiffened petticoats.

Erasmus in the seat opposite was humming to himself, but his eyes were on the sea, and she knew that he'd missed it in the past year.

'Are you looking for *Daisy Jane*?'

'Aye, lass.'

Leaning forward, Serafina placed her hand over his. 'I'll miss you, Pa. We will see each other again, won't we?'

'Try and keep me away. But neither myself nor the *Daisy Jane* is ready to retire from the sea yet. Your man will keep you busy, I reckon, and that's how it should be. I come to London from time to time with cargo, so I can call on you.'

'Thank you for believing in me and accepting me. I'm glad you're my father.'

'I'm not very fancy, and I'm not one for pretty speeches, lass. I've only known you a short time, but I do want you to know that the time we shared together was an unexpected gift. I kept your man waiting as long as possible even though I knew I'd have to part with you eventually. He threatened to throttle me in the end.'

He grinned when she giggled. 'If I go tomorrow I'll die a happy man.'

'Don't you dare say such a thing, Pa. You want to live to see your grandchildren grow up, don't you?'

'Aye, I do, and I shall. But today I must give you away, and I'm going to miss you. But Adam is a good man, who has fought strong and hard for you.' He leaned forward and kissed her cheek, saying gruffly, 'I love you, Serafina, my girl, and I loved your mother too. I reckon she'd be right proud of the way you've turned out. Now, I'm not saying another word else we'll both be bawling by the time we get to the church, and Charlotte and Marianne will never forgive me if you arrive with red eyes.'

The church bells began to ring as they neared St James.

Her sisters were waiting for her, all smiles, and wearing lace that matched the lace on her wedding dress. They carried pink roses.

Serafina could see Adam standing with Nick and Seth, and the love she felt for him reached out from her.

The Reverend Peter William Jolliffe, who had counselled them on the obligations of marriage, and the significance of the vows they were about to exchange, waited patiently for her to finish her traverse of the long, wide aisle. Behind him, the coloured glass window shone in all its glory.

The church was crowded. There were several faces she knew, women she'd met helping Aunt Daisy in her husband's small parish in nearby Parkstone.

The gossipy Stanhope sisters were craning their necks, looking around them and making comments. It was a letter from Lucy Stanhope which had given Adam the first clue to her identity. He had paid them a handsome reward.

The bells stopped ringing and her sisters, having straightened her train and gown, began to walk down the aisle.

'Be happy, Serafina, my dear,' Erasmus said, and she took his arm as they began to follow.

There was Reverend Pawley and with him, his wife . . . her dear friend Elizabeth, who'd helped her when she'd needed it most. Elizabeth blew her a kiss. Serafina hadn't expected them to come, and although she was proud of her background, and of the man she was about to marry, at the same time she felt humble.

In one of the front pews sat the Leightons, behind them, Maggie, Fanny and Joseph Tunney, dressed in their best and smiling at her. She exchanged a smile with Celia, who looked wonderfully happy, because she was expecting a child in five months' time. She stooped to kiss Finch Leighton on the cheek. His sight was beginning to return, and although he still couldn't see clearly, he was making progress. He'd been gazing at the church window with a smile on his face, as if enraptured by the colours.

According to Celia, the specialist doctor had told him that nerves had been damaged by the blow to his head. The fact that he could make out shapes and colours showed that they were beginning to heal. How well they would heal was unpredictable. Since that first diagnosis, he'd regained a little more sight, enough to read large letters, though they were still blurred. They were optimistic.

Adam's mother, Florence Wyvern sat next to them with her husband Edgar. She was very grand, so Serafina was a little in awe of her. Her husband was a lawyer, and had been kind enough to sort out the estate left to her by her aunt, Mrs Jarvis – which had been fraudulently acquired by Tyler Fenn, who was now in prison.

Serafina didn't want to go back to the farm at Gloucester; she wanted to put her past behind her and move into the future with Adam. Rather than sell it, because property always appreciated in price, Adam had suggested that she put tenants in it, so it would bring her in an income from the rent while the property appreciated in value. She was now looking forward to living in London with the man she loved.

To most of the guests she was known as Serafina Thornton, and nobody had questioned that she was anything but a distant relative, since she had the Thornton look.

In the front pews sat Daisy with her husband, who wore a jolly smile. Nick stood a little behind and to the side of Adam, ready to hand over the wedding ring. Her sisters stood at the other side. Erasmus handed her over to Adam, then stood proud and tall with the men.

Adam smiled at her as he took her hand in his. 'I love you,' he whispered.

Reverend Jolliffe stepped forward, his face reflecting the gravity of the ceremony he was about to perform. The ceremony began.

'Dearly beloved, we are gathered together here in the sight of God, and in the face of this congregation, to join together this man and this woman in holy matrimony . . .'

'*Adam Christopher Chapman, wilt thou have this woman to thy wedded wife . . .*'

Adam sent her a smile. 'I will.'

'*Serafina Honeyman Thornton, wilt thou have this man to be thy wedded husband . . .*'

A buzz went through the church when Erasmus exchanged an amused smile with Charlotte, who smiled back. Neither had won the argument about Serafina's name, and in the end they'd compromised on the suggestion made by Serafina. Not that it had mattered, she thought, because today she'd become Serafina Chapman.

'*Who giveth this woman to be married to this man?*'

'I do,' Erasmus said, and looking round at the congregation he informed them rather smugly, 'On account of the fact that I'm her father.'

Serafina exchanged a glance with Adam and they smiled at one another when Marianne giggled and Nick chuckled.

A little while later they joined their right hands and the reverend smiled benevolently on them as he said:

'I pronounce that they be husband and wife together.'